Clouds Over Bishop Hill ╫

Have a good read!

Mary R. Davidsaver

Mary R. Davidsaver

MWC Press · Davenport, IA

MWC Press
An imprint of the Midwest Writing Center
225 E. 2nd Street
Suite 303
Davenport, Iowa 52801
www.mwcqc.org

First edition: August 2016

Cover design: Kenneth Small

Cover photograph: Mary R. Davidsaver

ISBN-13: 978-0-9906190-3-1

For our mothers
Pearl Mabel Poggenpohl Bollinger
Essie Pearl Bollinger Raker Underwood
Christiana Elizabeth Johnson Davidsaver

AUTHOR'S NOTE

This is a work of fiction. Bishop Hill, Illinois, is a state historic site and a national historic landmark with innumerable real-life stories to tell. I chose the avenue of fiction to tell mine. I used my imagination to create names, characters, businesses, organizations, and institutions wherever I could, or otherwise used them fictitiously. Historical figures, events past and present, and geography were likewise subjected to my imagination and altered for this work of fiction. Any resemblance to real life is wholly coincidental.

A young Olof Krans did join the Bishop Hill Colony and later used his self-taught painting skills to document the Colony's early prairie years. Those who want to learn more are encouraged to continue their journey by reading further or visiting the real Bishop Hill in Henry County, Illinois. There's a wealth of information out there and many knowledgeable people to help you on your way.

╫ PEARL ╫

Summer 1915

She hoped he would forget about her and stay focused on making the new portrait come to life. Pearl Essie Anderson shifted her position just a bit, making sure to stand well out of the way of Olof Krans.

"Those were our best days," the gray-haired, bewhiskered old man mumbled. He turned, looked down, and with a weary sigh patted her head.

I'm too old for this, thought ten-year-old Pearl. She endured the condescending touch without complaint because she wanted to see more of the portrait's mesmerizing eyes.

Krans wore a paint-splattered old smock as he stood at his makeshift easel. He returned to his work and droned on about the bygone days of his youth. How the demanding work of building the Prophet's dream of perfection, a colony, a New Jerusalem, on the banks of the Edwards River in Illinois had made him physically strong. The sermons from his Swedish elders had given him spiritual strength. In those days, despite the daily demands of staying alive, the possibilities seemed limitless. Earthly burdens hadn't rested on his shoulders alone. Many willing hands helped lighten the load within the communal society.

Those days had presented challenges. These days brought complaints about getting his recalcitrant body out of bed and moving in the mornings. He said the aches and pains were a constant reminder of the mission, his final goal.

"'Slow down,' they tell me over and over." He scoffed at the thought.

With weathered hands, he picked up a small camel-hair brush to gently add more paint and smooth over a ridge near the left eye. It deepened the shadow and enhanced the brooding effect of the portrait's earnest countenance.

He stepped back to inspect his work. "Perfect," he whispered. "As perfect as an old man can do."

Pearl didn't think it mattered if she were there or not. He spoke to himself more and more, with it seeming to bother him less and less. "I will never do that if I ever get that old," she vowed.

CHAPTER 1

Friday, May 30, 2008

M y grip on the steering wheel tightened as I told off the dark SUV tailgating me. "Come on, moron. Get on with it. Pass." We were coming up on the last big curve before Highway 34 straightened out on its way to Galva, Illinois. I eased up on the gas. I wanted to be alone.

I checked the rearview mirror again, scanning past the freestyle mess of loose brownish curls, and watched as the SUV swung out and accelerated. As it passed, I caught the silver letters on the side spelling out JIMMY and wondered if that might be the driver's name, too.

By myself at last, I could now play the old game, "Who sees the Bishop Hill water tower first?"

Our adoptive parents, Uncle Roy and Christina, used to

issue the challenge when the distant wooden structure hid behind a rectangular highway sign. My twin brother John and I competed for years to be the first to call out, "I do! I do!" Over time, we grew too wise, too sophisticated to be taken in by the simple ploy intended to keep us from poking at each other until someone started crying— usually me.

I thought of John, the firstborn by half an hour, who never let me forget it. The one who got the blond hair and blue eyes, leaving me with the mousy brown hair and brown eyes. The normal-sized human compared to my halfling shortness, as he liked to put it. He, who had the pleasant disposition, could talk to anyone, could easily fit in everywhere. Again, just the opposite of me. His academic life was on hold while here I was graduating from Knox College and making plans for grad school. He was in the Air Force awaiting deployment to the Middle East. I felt a soul-numbing dread if I thought about it for too long.

I muttered under my breath, "This has to be my last summer job. My last trip back." I didn't want to be reminded how much I look like my long-lost mother or how precious my brother was to me. I wanted a new start somewhere else.

I gave my shoulder muscles a quick stretch, trying to relax, and took a minute to scan the fields on either side of the highway. The corn crop for this part of west-central Illinois looked good enough. The young plants had enough height in most places to begin obscuring the furrows, giving the land a fuzzy, verdant hue. One shade of green among many. My high school art teacher often said that one must move out of the Midwest at some point in life in order to realize that the world consists of more than thirty-four shades of green. Or had she said one hundred and thirty-four. No matter. I'd gotten the message.

There in the distance, I made out the dark silhouette of the water tower standing tall above the trees. It still had the look of a derelict missile. I smiled. Maybe some things needn't change.

The water tower disappeared behind a white farm house surrounded by red barns and outbuildings. Instead of turning north onto Smoketree Road and heading home by the most direct route, I made a spur-of-the-moment decision to drive past the Varnishtree Antique Market. It stood like a gatekeeper on the northwest corner where Bishop Hill Road crossed Highway 34.

I'd learned a lot about preservation from Herb Anderson, owner of the Varnishtree. He repeated his favorite saying often enough for me to automatically remember his words: "This too can be saved."

On his corner he created a textbook example of how restoration and repurposing could save an old barn. In the not-so-distant past, it might have been torn down, burned, and replaced by a shiny new metal building. Herb never entertained such thoughts. He referred to himself as an "old-school Swede" and refused to waste perfectly good lumber in a still-salvageable structure.

He worked patiently to resuscitate the Varnishtree barn, leaving the outside essentially intact while making improvements and installing modern features within. After he had it in acceptable condition, he located another old building, smaller, but also in need of saving, and attached it to the back. The addition housed a state-of-the-art woodworking shop where he also displayed his impressive collection of vintage hand tools.

I pictured the walls lined top to bottom with shelves packed with hundreds of wood-shaping tools, each designed for a specific job. He had them meticulously arranged by specialty and use. Some were sculpted brass works of art in their own right. He loved demonstrating how to use those tools to make any piece imaginable.

Herb fixed anything and everything that came his way. He proclaimed that he had taken apart and reassembled thousands of chairs. "Kept them off the scrap heap," he said, "by using modern glue. The old kind just turned to white powder." High-end customers from Chicago came knocking on his door on a regular basis.

He was a consummate professional, and I used his success story for a college paper. I even found an amusing way to explain how he wasn't related to me. Normally, I hated explaining the kinship patterns of all the Anderson clans in the area. Anderson, the Swedish equivalent of Smith, could refer to two separate families that stayed on after the dissolution of the Bishop Hill Colony, or to another one that moved in later. In my experience, you established if a new acquaintance might be a cousin or not soon after the first meeting. Shirttail kin related by marriage, or non-marriage, were harder to parse out. At any rate, everyone learned and remembered as best they could. I considered it a rite of passage. Outsiders rarely caught on to the subtleties of these family trees.

I caught myself smiling again. The smile faded when I came upon the blue tourism sign that directed visitors to Bishop Hill's more out-of-the-way shops. One of its support posts flashed slashes of purple spray paint that looked like the capital letter I, the heart symbol, and the capital letter U.

"Senseless vandalism. And not even done all that well." I felt a little flustered when I realized I'd spoken my thoughts out loud. Refusing to give in to embarrassment in the privacy of my own car, I added, "Well, no matter. Why should I care? It's someone else's problem. Not mine. I'm on my way outta here."

I sped up after completing the turn north onto Bishop Hill Road. My sulking ruminations made me slow to react as a minivan crested the hill, drifted out of its lane, and came straight at me. No visible driver, just a pair of small, white hands gripping the steering wheel.

With a few choice, unladylike words and a sharp swerve to the right, I missed the accident by inches. As the minivan flew past, I caught a glimpse of a white top-knot bun. I knew that hair.

"Pearl," I gasped. "Driving?"

I tried to stop on a shoulder made soft by the last few nights of thunderstorms. The tires of my Chevy Prizm

7

gouged up gravel and shot it into the undercarriage, creating a deafening racket. I stood on the brake. The car slid forward, then sideways into the ditch. The level plane of the familiar country road pitched askew as grass, weeds, and spindly brush scraped the car's passenger side. I flashed on the driveway and culvert closing in on me. I screamed. Suddenly the car's forward momentum ceased without hitting anything major. I sat tilted at a weird angle. My whole body shook violently. I gave myself a quick check to see if I really was in one piece. How close had I just come to dying? To having no problems whatsoever? I even flashed on a headline: "Young Woman Killed by Centenarian."

Pearl Essie Anderson, no relation to Herb or me, was a subject for another paper. She held a distinguished place of honor as one of a handful of centenarians in this part of the state. At age 103, she possessed an amazing memory that connected to the all-important Colony time period that had begun in 1846 with the arrival of Bishop Hill's first Swedish settlers. Local historians considered her a national treasure.

Treasure or not, I watched helplessly as the ancient driver made a sloppy right turn into Herb's parking lot and miraculously came to a stop, seemingly unharmed and probably unaware of what had transpired behind her.

"I don't believe this," I said, and directed a couple of forceless hammer-fist blows at the steering wheel. "I don't need this today." I unbuckled my seat belt and tried the door. Nothing. I pushed hard against it. It wouldn't budge.

The stress of the last year had me up at all hours studying and writing papers. Fueling the crushing load had necessitated far too many late-night runs for pizza and high-calorie sugary snacks. I figured if the added weight could be good for anything at all, now would be the time. I had no other options. With a burst of adrenaline and a mighty shove, I got the door far enough ajar to squeeze out.

I climbed to the road and looked for anybody passing by. No luck. I detected the faint odor of engine oil. My bad luck may have gotten worse.

By the time I crossed the road and made it up to the minivan, Pearl had disappeared. I walked over to the main door of the shop and turned the knob. It didn't move. A quick peek through the glass revealed nothing amiss in the showroom. I took the well-worn path that led around back to the workshop. The large barn doors were closed, locked, and appeared normal. However, the smaller workshop door stood wide open. As I stepped closer, I thought I heard the sounds of a conversation. I turned my head to listen, but the words were muffled. Then the road noise of a car on the highway obscured them entirely.

I came to a standstill in the doorway. Herb's meticulously organized workshop looked like the end result of a wrestling match. Overturned chairs and tools littered the concrete floor. As I looked closer, I saw the crumpled figure of a man sprawled face-down in an unnatural position. I clamped a hand over my mouth. I felt my fingers turn to ice as the pressure welling up in my chest pushed past my lips. My strangled scream made Pearl jerk back from her kneeling position next to the body. She held a blood-stained hammer.

"Pearl! What have you done?"

CHAPTER 2

Pearl loosened her grip and the hammer clanged to the floor. The metallic ringing echoed in the silence and made both of us jump. With considerable effort, she straightened her back as much as she could and announced, "I must find the painting."

"What?" I couldn't choke out much more than that because I was fighting the first wave of nausea and the overwhelming urge to run.

I pressed my lips together and admonished myself: no running, no fainting, no throwing up. I instantly regretted that last thought. I kept upright and unsoiled by a force of will I hadn't known I possessed. After a few panicky heartbeats, I made myself look around again. Pearl couldn't have done this much damage. Someone else did— a much bigger, stronger, and more dangerous someone else. I held my breath and peered into the shadowy corners to see if anyone was hiding just out of sight. Seeing no sign of movement, I pulled my cell phone out of my jeans pocket, flipped it open, and punched in the emergency number. A professional sounding voice came on with a brisk, "911. How may I help you?"

"Help. Yes, I need help." My gaze shifted over to the dazed, unsteady Pearl and changed it to, "*We* need help."

The voice asked for my name and location. I had to squeeze my eyes shut in order to concentrate on the essential facts. "I'm Shelley Anderson. I'm at the Varnishtree Antique Market. The barn on the corner of Highway 34 and the Bishop Hill Road. We need an ambulance and—"

"And what?" the dispatcher asked with sharpened interest.

"Sheriff. We need the sheriff. Someone is hurt." My voice wavered and broke with a sob. I fought for control by taking some deep breaths. I don't know how I formed the next words. Inside my head they echoed distant and alien. "He isn't moving. Not breathing. It looks like Herb Anderson . . . I think he might be . . . dead." I couldn't stop the tears and pulled the phone away.

The dispatcher's tinny voice tried to give me instructions and urged me to keep talking. I opened my eyes and lowered the phone. I started to place it on a nearby cluttered workbench but recoiled. I mustn't touch anything. But I had to help, do something, so I set it down anyway. I stepped closer to Pearl and slipped off my denim jacket. It wouldn't be much comfort for the old woman, but I bent down and draped it over her shoulders. I managed a fast glimpse to confirm that the gray-haired man on the floor was indeed Herb. I returned my focus to Pearl and tried to coax her up so I could guide her away. We both needed to get some distance away from Herb.

"Help is on the way," I crooned softly over and over.

I finally got the unsteady Pearl up and over to the far side of the room and into the last upright chair. It had a clamp still affixed to one leg. I choked up thinking that the job would never be finished. I positioned myself to block out the view of the body. I worried about how long we would have to wait.

"Pearl, did you see who did this? Why—" She didn't let me finish.

"The old man made the cross. I followed. It led me here. The painting is here." Pearl spoke in a surprisingly strong voice for someone who looked feeble enough to fall over with the least amount of wind. "Why is he sleeping in my barn?"

"Ms. Anderson. Pearl . . ." I faltered as I tried to steel my nerves and will my heart back into a normal rhythm. "This is Herb's barn now." My eyes filled as I spoke.

"No. This was my grandfather's allotment after the dissolution of the Colony."

"Honey, Herb bought this corner lot years ago. He fixed up the barn for his woodworking and antique business."

"I do not sell land," Pearl scolded. "And I am *not* your honey."

"I'm sorry." I paused to think back and draw on the

facts I knew. "Herb bought this barn from the family trust. I interviewed him and took pictures of his restoration work. He did such a fine job, don't you think? Look how he put in those new trusses." I paused again, dabbed at my eyes to wipe away the tears, and pointed upward. "They blend in so well. You can hardly tell they're not original."

Pearl looked up at the rafters as if considering any number of possibilities for a moment. "No. The old man hid the painting. I promised not to tell. To protect it."

"Old man? What old man?" I couldn't make sense of what I was hearing. Then a faint glimmer of recognition produced a spark of illumination. "Do you mean Krans? Olof Krans?"

"I was a child. I watched him work."

"Yes, but that was in Altona. I interviewed you for a school paper, too. You told me all about that summer in 1915. You were ten years old. Do you remember me at all?"

"I talk about the old days with lots of folks," Pearl said without any trace of recognition.

"I'm Shelley Anderson. Christina Colberg's my . . . my mom." I hadn't meant to stumble over the last bit, but classifying Christina's status as "my adoptive mother" didn't seem like the best thing to do just now. Neither was trying to explain that she hadn't taken my Uncle Roy's last name when they married. I hoped something from Pearl's long-term memory would push through and help me.

Pearl worked hard to process the names I'd given her. She puzzled a bit more, then formed a thin, crooked smile and said, "You do look like Teeny's little girl. How is she?"

I was glad some shred of information clicked. "School's out and I was on my way home to see her."

"Well, you say hello from me," Pearl said. She relaxed just enough to begin wobbling.

I kept her steady and talking until at last I heard the wail of the first siren. More followed. Soon we both shook uncontrollably.

CHAPTER 3

I sat in the open end of an ambulance wrapped in a blanket, trying to rub off the lingering smudges of fingerprint ink. My nerves had settled a bit and the dazed feelings that must have been shock had receded enough to allow me to make some sense of the activity that swirled around me. I had no idea that Henry County could field so many deputies and emergency personnel on such short notice. It felt like half the county had converged on this little section of my world. And it bothered me to no end that none of them seemed familiar. I had grown up here, after all. I didn't think I'd been gone all that long.

Still, I was okay. I patiently answered all questions and repeated my story of what happened. "I was on my way home. That would be north of Bishop Hill. I got forced off the road by a near collision with Pearl. No, she isn't related to me. No, Herb's not a relative either. It all happened so fast. I don't see how she could have done that to him. No, I didn't see anyone else in there." I would wave a hand in the general direction of the workshop and its crime scene. It started to sound pretty lame by the time they finally said they were done with me and I could go. But stay in the area, they cautioned, there may be more questions. I wanted to laugh but couldn't muster the strength. I didn't have any other place to go, not just yet.

Nearby, the EMTs had a blanket-clad Pearl on their stretcher with an IV in her thin arm. As they prepared to transport her to the hospital in Kewanee, she continued to ramble on about a cross in the sky to an invisible Olof Krans standing next to her. I went over and gave her a gentle squeeze on the shoulder. Words failed and only a feeble, "There, there," came out. I remembered not to call her honey.

Pearl spoke of omens, a mysterious mission, and driving around the farm in her father's flatbed truck while the EMTs went about their business. As soon as they took a few more steps away, her ink-stained hand found mine and held onto it as she focused on my face in the present. Her brow furrowed from the effort. "I know you," she said. "I know you."

"Sure you do. I'm Michelle Anderson. Everyone calls me Shelley. Christina Colberg is my mom. You told me some great stories about Olof Krans. They got me noticed by a lot of important people. You helped me so much."

Pearl forced a little more volume from her weakened voice. "That's right. Give my best to Teeny. Come see me."

She glanced over to the EMTs and smiled when she saw they were still busy filling out forms and talking to the dispatcher. She motioned for me to lean closer. *"Promise,"* she pleaded. "We must talk."

The request sounded so urgent and needy. I nodded my head in agreement, made a pledge to see her again, and stepped away as they prepared to load the stretcher. A middle-aged woman came running up to Pearl's other side. Amy Anderson, a grandniece-in-law, appeared beside herself with distress.

"I just left to go to the post office," she explained to anyone and everyone multiple times. "I was only gone for a couple of minutes."

I knew full well that a trip to the Bishop Hill post office could eat up a big chunk of time. It all depended on who you ran into and how long you discussed the fresh news topics of the day. As a major information hub, the post office only had The Lutfisk Café as a main rival. "I'm here," Amy said repeatedly. She climbed into the ambulance and seated herself as close as possible to the stretcher and clung to Pearl's hand as the doors closed.

I started to walk away from the ambulance when I caught sight of another familiar face, one I hadn't counted on seeing until tomorrow morning, when I was due to start my summer job. What was my boss doing here? I had to look a sight and reflexively took a step backwards.

To my relief, David Ekollon, director of the brand-new Nikkerbo Museum and Conference Center, made his way toward the workshop door rather than in my direction. It gave me a minute to take a longer look at him. The man was far less than average all the way around: less than average height, with less than average blond hair on his head, and far less than average patience. He tried to make up for his deficiencies by growing a distinctive mustache and dressing smartly in dark tweedy coats and pressed khakis. Now, instead of his dapper self, he appeared rumpled, coatless, with his paunchy belly hanging over his belt.

Upon his arrival at the doorway, he found his passage blocked by a dark-haired female sheriff's deputy attentively performing her assigned task of securing the crime scene. He demanded to be let in so he could inspect his museum's important artifact for damage. He must be referring to the hand-painted wooden trunk I had seen on Herb's main workbench. I'd gotten a good look at it, along with everything else in the shop, as I waited with Pearl. Anything to avoid the bitter reality of Herb on the floor.

Ekollon's pale complexion began to glow red as the deputy calmly asked him to explain his business and show some identification. Ekollon didn't suffer perceived insubordination well, and this was no exception. The deputy flashed a glint of mischief in her dark eyes and formed a subtle smile as if she suddenly found a way to add a smidgeon of enjoyment to her job. She patted a couple of pockets before pulling out a notebook and pen. With a significant flourish, she prepared to write.

At that moment, as if the cosmos truly wanted to further complicate my life, a black BMW sedan pulled in behind Ekollon's aging Mercedes. A distinguished-looking, gray-haired, bearded man exited the car. Curt Hemcourt V, owner of Bishop Hill's new museum and mega cultural complex, strode confidently onto the scene.

My hands went instinctively to my face to wipe my eyes again before flitting up to smooth my rumpled hair. So much had happened this morning: a close encounter with a wayward minivan, my car in a ditch and possibly damaged, and a reluctant witness to murder. Way too much real life on no breakfast. My remaining strength drained down my legs and ebbed away through my feet. Ancient Pearl had held up better than this. I felt too shaky to face any critical inspections.

I turned and tried to inconspicuously slip away from the parking lot. Heading in the general direction of my car, the means of my salvation appeared before me: a tow truck from Galva. It had pulled my car out of the ditch already. I had to talk to the driver anyway and surely he'd offer me a ride. I approached the driver's side door. No one was there, only an Australian cattle dog staring out the opposite window so intently that it missed detecting my presence. The driver must be over there checking straps or hooks or whatever important things these guys did. I started around to the other side and walked straight into a face that sent me reeling back in time.

There in front of me stood Michael Anderson, the blond-haired, blue-eyed mirror image of my twin brother. He'd been an unpleasant thorn in my side during all my school days in Galva. On the first day of kindergarten, the teacher placed him between Marsha Ellen, my cousin and best friend, and me. Alphabetical necessity or not, it was very inconvenient. Even at the tender age of six, I knew that nothing good could come when a boy introduced himself by saying, "Hi, my name is Michael J. Anderson. The J stands for Jurassic." In nearly every school line-up from then through high school graduation, he was on hand to make stupid wisecracks, bad jokes, and rude noises. I groaned out loud. The irony of making the rude sound wasn't entirely lost on me.

"Nice to see you, too," he said.

I felt so very flustered. "That's my car," I managed to say.

"That's my truck," Michael said and gestured to the large vehicle in front of him.

Now I really felt small and sensed a warming in my checks that might herald a full-out blush. I couldn't make anything intelligible come out of my mouth and must have looked like a stricken fish.

"Are you okay?"

Was that genuine concern? I struggled to force out, "Good enough. I guess." I shrugged. "Sorry, I'm not myself right now."

He nodded toward the crowded Varnishtree parking lot and said, "It would be a wonder if you were. Looks like a circus over there. Not the sorta action we usually get around here."

"Yeah, and there's no end in sight. Ekollon and Hemcourt, the boss and the boss's boss, just showed up.

The investigators told me I could go. They fingerprinted me and everything. Took my statement, several times I might add." Aggravation began to creep into the sudden deluge of words. "Look, I need to get away. Could you give me a lift up to The Lutfisk? I need to eat something soon or I'll never make it home."

"You read my mind. I've worked all night and I'm starving. This is my last tow. Too bad it had to be you."

"What?"

"I mean," he paused, clearing his throat, "too bad this had to happen to you and Great Auntie Pearl." His own discomfort surfaced with a slight flush of color in his cheeks.

The ambulance carrying Pearl and Amy swung out onto the highway with its lights flashing. I couldn't stop myself from flinching when they started up the siren.

"I graduate from college and this happens before I even get home. Not a very auspicious beginning for the rest of my life."

"Get in. My stomach is saying, 'Feed me, Michael. Feed me.'" He grinned and motioned to the cab of the tow truck and the face of the waiting dog.

"So now the J is for Joker," I said with a forced smile. "What about your dog?"

"I was thinking J for Jester, and Sadie won't mind sharing. She's cool with riders. I take her with me all the time."

The prospect of company made the dog dance about the seat. Michael walked around to the driver's side window and reached through to grab the dog's collar. He stroked her ears in an attempt to calm her down. No luck. The dog eagerly anticipated making a new acquaintance.

"Is she for company or protection?" I wondered out loud.

"I figure with a dog sitting next to me and a Beretta under the seat, I'm good in all kinds of weather. And, in case you're wondering, I have a license for both."

CHAPTER 4

The three-mile drive up to Bishop Hill started out with an awkward stillness growing between us humans. Sadie was just fine. I had my arm around her and rubbed the sweet spot under her chin. The blue speckled dog held her eyes shut in blissful contentment. It looked like she could never get enough. I wanted something polite to say and had given up the search by the time Michael mercifully broke the silence.

"You're going to spoil her," he said.

"No way," I shot back. I started to croon to the dog in a baby-soothing voice. "She's a *good* girl."

As the petting continued, I felt my body relax as some of the tension drained away. I regretted my snappish tone and commented on the obvious. "Actually, this is a great dog."

Michael merely nodded.

We were halfway to the village when a flash of fluorescent paint caught my attention. "Will you look at that?"

"What?"

"That purple 'I heart U' on the sign post."

"I missed it."

"I saw that all along the highway from Galesburg this morning. Some demented high schooler has a crush on someone. An idiot with more spray paint than sense. Reminds me of something you might've done back in the day."

"I had my moments. And the day wasn't all that long ago. Or maybe it was." He rolled his eyes. "My memory is getting selectively bad all of a sudden."

I sighed. "I'm sorry. I wish I hadn't said that." I stared dissolutely out the window. "Now I can add feeling old and awkward to today's list of wonderful experiences." I turned to face him again. "Let's change the subject. So, how long have you been back? Are you still with the National Guard?"

"Haven't been in town too long. Uncle Bill has me driving the night shift. It keeps me out of trouble. And, yes, I'm still with the Guard." The renewed silence made it clear that I needed to drop any more discussion on those topics.

After a long stretch of me petting the dog with nothing else happening, he asked, "What got you up and out so early this morning?"

My turn to sit in stony silence, not wanting to talk about

sensitive issues. I didn't want to discuss why I hadn't bothered to comb out the new perm. Hadn't eaten anything. Hadn't said goodbye to Marsha Ellen, my Knox roommate. We'd been inseparable since kindergarten. Now I wished I hadn't been in such a rush to get away this morning, but I couldn't trust myself. As seniors, we were supposed to stay late last night putting the final touches on the annual art school showcase. We had everything in place for tonight's opening. Then my former boyfriend walked in looking for Marsha Ellen, not me. Talk about awkward. Every time I started to say something, total garbage tumbled out of my mouth. It was so embarrassing. They obviously wanted their own company and froze me out. I couldn't stand the thought of a repeat this morning, so I threw the last of my stuff into my already-packed car and left at first light.

"I saw your mom get into the ambulance with Pearl," I said after I'd cooled off a bit and built up my nerve. "She looked frantic. I'm glad she got there. It relaxed Pearl and made her more cooperative." I pushed Sadie's nose away long enough to get my cell phone out of my jeans pocket. Getting my phone back from the deputies had taken a lot of explaining. I made a call using speed dial. After counting out six ring tones and getting no response, I ended the call and found a new train of thought. "You know, they actually believed Pearl might have done it at first, like, you know . . . killed Herb." I had a hard time getting those last words out.

"And you didn't?" Michael shot back.

"Well, maybe for a second." I tried to find ways to justify myself. "It was such a shock. I walked in and saw her next to him like that, holding the hammer. I wonder if he tried to defend himself with it. Pearl must have come right in and picked it up." I paused for a moment and wished I could make that memory fade away. It stayed with me clear and sharp. I continued with a sigh. "She kept talking about the barn like she still owned it. She definitely slipped back in time. And she seemed confused about some other things, too." I stalled some before adding, "She wants me to come see her. She sounded so serious. Made me promise."

"We'll have to talk about that later. I imagine Mom will want her to get back to some kind of normal first."

"And what is normal for a centenarian? Or is she a supercentenarian?"

"She's not a supercentenarian." He stumbled over the first pronunciation, but improved for the next attempt. "I looked it up once. A supercentenarian is someone over 110 years old. She's got a way to go yet."

"I stand corrected," I said. "So again, what is normal for Pearl?"

"Got me. Great Auntie had slowed down so much lately. Had us worried." Michael shook his head. "Her new doctor decided to change her meds and took her off nearly everything so she could have a clean start. Kind of like a system reboot. But no one ever expected her to come back around so suddenly and so strong. Taking off in Mom's minivan. Getting involved in something like that."

He gestured back down the road to the Varnishtree. "I think for a tiny old lady she sure kicked butt today." He glanced over to me. "You didn't do too badly yourself."

"I didn't do anything."

"You held it together and called for help. That's huge."

I started to say something and was cut off.

"It sounds weird, but I'm glad you were there."

We drove the rest of the way without talking, but the quiet interlude didn't hold as much strained tension as before.

After we passed the southern Welcome to Bishop Hill sign, I watched the Krans portrait museum go by on the left side and the Swedish archive building on the right. Both had the look of modern brick buildings and could never be mistaken for the deeply aged Colony-era brick and stucco structures that came up next. We passed those and found our destination across the street and down a way from the fire station. The Lutfisk Café, a modest wood-framed, one-story building painted white with red-trimmed windows, looked warm, homey, and inviting — just the ticket for the bone-weary.

I still had my phone in my hand and tried to make another call. Again with no luck. "That's odd. I haven't been able to reach Christina all morning. She's not answering either number and I can't get her to use text messaging."

Michael pulled off the main street into a large parking space up from the driveway of the fire station.

"Let's get something to eat and then you can try her

again. I find the world works a whole lot better after one of Talli's cheeseburgers."

As I climbed down out of the cab of the tow truck, I checked out the half-dozen vehicles parked in front and across the street. The crowd seemed rather light for this time of day, and nothing looked familiar. I figured it had to be a good thing for me.

We stepped onto the porch and walked past the picnic tables that made up the outdoor seating area. To my surprise, the door opened in the opposite direction from what I remembered. It was hard to tell if it made an improvement. Inside, I got a warm blast of fresh Folgers aroma from the big Bunn coffeemaker. It was still in the same place, front and center, convenient for everyone to help themselves. Any local resident who waited around to be served was just asking for an order of mock abuse from the owner, Talli Walters.

CHAPTER 5

A stout bundle of energy with intense dark eyes and black hair showing the first few streaks of gray at the temples, Talli Walters called out from the kitchen, "Well, good God, it's about time you showed up. How the hell are ya?"

I wasn't sure whom she was speaking to, Michael or me. I was too busy pivoting out of the way of a large farmer getting his coffee refill. He gave me a quizzical look as I slipped past him. I wanted to talk to Talli in a normal tone and tried to get closer. I needn't have bothered. Talli, who had been making meatballs, hurriedly cleaned and dried her hands and came out to me. Marcella Rice was left to the business of scooping out small, round globs of blood-red meat and arranging them in orderly rows in baking pans. I felt a nasty queasiness creep up my throat. I made a tight-lipped smile and turned my head away as

Talli enfolded me with a compassionate hug. I couldn't resist.

"You've heard about Herb Anderson already?" I said, after surfacing for air.

"The Bishop Hill grapevine works fast. Poor Herb. Things like that aren't supposed to happen out here. And to get mixed up in that awful business . . ." Talli didn't finish. She held me out at arm's length and studied me. "What are you doin' here? You should be home."

"I've been trying to call Christina and she isn't picking up either phone. Have you seen her?"

"I haven't seen anything of your mom. Marcella and I have been up to our eyeballs in Swedish meatballs all mornin'. What can I do you for? Are you hungry?"

"Just starving," I said, nodding to Michael, and added, "Both of us."

Talli took charge and told Michael to get the coffee and find a table. She ducked briefly behind the counter and came up with a couple of clean dish towels. "Here, take these into the restroom and get yourself straightened up. You'll feel better."

I took the towels and headed for the restroom door labeled *Flickor*, girls. I knew I needed a few private minutes to clean and freshen, but judging by Talli's reaction, I must certainly be a sight. Had I made a mistake coming here? My reflection in the mirror confirmed massively tangled hair, eyes puffed up and blotchy, and a face streaked from wiping away tears with fingerprinted hands. I ran some hot water in the sink and proceeded to perform facial triage. I had to fix the damage as best I could and figure out a way to make a graceful exit.

When I came out, I found Michael sipping his coffee under the blue and white enamel sign that announced SORRY, NO LUTFISK TODAY. Tourists had brought it over as a gift during the big surge in visitation that the 350th anniversary of Delaware's New Sweden colony caused in 1988. It moved from place to place whenever a new coat of paint went up, but it never left the building. My cup sat across the table from him.

That sign always made me think about the only lutfisk I'd ever tasted. It was the creamed version that Aunt Betty cooked up for the Christmas smorgasbord. Everyone assured me that it was the safest and most palatable. I agreed for the sake of diplomacy, but since I'd never tried anything else, I would never know for sure. In culinary matters, I never considered myself overly adventuresome and definitely not what I'd call a professional Swede. A professional, in my opinion, lived and breathed everything Swedish all day long, and probably all night long as well. The perfect exhibit A: David Ekollon, my boss. I felt more comfortable in the camp that favored the American immigrant experience, with all things Swede in moderation. I suspected someday it might place us at odds with each other.

"Need a warm up?" Talli asked Michael as she came up and swirled a half-full coffee pot in the air. He nudged his cup closer to the edge of the table in order to minimize stray drops coming in his direction.

It looked like Talli wanted to join us, but at that moment the other waitress came by with two plates of food. Talli made sure we had ketchup on the table and left. On her way back to the kitchen, she stopped to exchange a few hushed words with some other customers. The topic had to be poor Herb. They glanced furtively in my direction.

"I hope you don't mind," Michael began, "but you were in there so long I just went ahead and ordered two cheeseburgers with fries."

"That's fine. I wouldn't have gotten the special anyway." I couldn't be sure what I would've ordered if left to my own devices. I had been hungry and knew I needed to eat something, but now I didn't seem to have the willpower to do more than pick at my plate. Michael, on the other hand, made his food disappear at a steady pace. Soon, he looked longingly at my unfinished stack of fat French fries. I made him suffer as long I dared before finally telling him, "Oh, go on. Help yourself. But move them over to your plate. I can't stand it when you put pepper on them."

Talli returned to our table offering to pour another round of refills from a freshly-brewed pot. This time she settled herself into a chair next to me. "We heard from the hospital. Pearl is gonna be just fine. More than fine. She's bossin' everyone around and demanding to go home. Your mom will have her hands full." She directed the last comment across the table to Michael.

"I think she can handle it. It'll be good to have Great

Auntie back in fighting form."

"Did they say anything else?" I inquired.

"Oh, sure. They're all amazed at how alert she is. And coherent. She told how she woke up this mornin' and felt like she did back in her 80s." Talli laughed. "Can you believe that? My, she must be tough. I can't imagine."

"Did they say anything about Pearl seeing something in the sky? A cross?" I asked, with halting caution.

"That's what she claimed set her off. 'Had to drive toward it,' she said. Your mom's minivan was sittin' in the driveway with the keys in the ignition, and away she went."

"I'll have a talk with Mom later," Michael said.

"It was probably just a couple of contrails," Talli said.

"Does that mean you saw it, too? A cross in the sky?" I asked. If that part of Pearl's ramblings turned out to be the real thing, then maybe some of the other stuff she told me might be true as well. Like a painting. A Krans painting.

"Sure, I saw some wispy clouds. Contrails. It coulda been a cross. To tell you the truth, I only glanced up for a second as I got into my car. I was gettin' a late start and needed to get down here to open up. The natives get restless if left alone too long. I didn't give it any more thought. Just some skinny old clouds as far as I know."

"Pearl went on and on about the cross she saw in the sky and how it was a sign from Olof Krans," I said. "I thought she might have been hallucinating."

"No, the part about the clouds was likely real enough," Talli said. "I wouldn't hazard a guess about the rest of what she had to say."

"While we were waiting for help to arrive, she mentioned a painting. A special painting. Hidden away. She wanted to find it. She couldn't understand why she didn't still own the barn or why Herb was there. I saw a painted trunk that he must have been working on. She also went on and on about a promise to protect a secret." I paused. It dawned on me that I had started rambling. But I couldn't give up and added in a weaker tone, "I wonder if any part of it could be true, like, you know, real."

"Oh, I doubt it," Michael said. "Come on, you've seen all her Krans paintings and the Lander paintings, too. Nothing is hidden."

"No, not in her home," I said. "She was convinced the painting was there, in that barn."

"That would have been the Hemcourt family immigrant trunk y'all saw," Marcella Rice spoke up with her distinctive Texas drawl.

After getting the meatballs into the oven, she had come into the dining area and settled her ample frame at another table, keeping her quad cane in hand as she eavesdropped on the conversation.

"David, I mean Mr. Ekollon, persuaded Herb to clean it up some, make it presentable for the fancy new exhibit. One of the many important artifacts that were going to show off the family's valuable Krans painting. The highlight of tomorrow's grand premiere of the new museum. Oh, excuse me, the *gala* grand premiere." Marcella's added emphasis pointed out her obvious disdain for the whole matter.

Marcella's story, as I knew it, had her traveling far from Bishop Hill in her younger years. She lived in Texas long enough to acquire an accent she couldn't shake. It was there a car accident damaged her left leg severely enough that she had to come back home to her mother's house to recover. When she was strong enough to start working again, her mother had the first in a series of minor strokes. Marcella stayed. She gained weight over the years, but made it a point to keep her hair in a well-styled bob in just the right shade of golden blond. Always a hit when she guided tourist groups about the village, she delighted the children by jokingly claiming her family's Colony ancestors came from a province in far western Sweden.

"I thought y'all had a hand in designing that display." Marcella directed her question at me. "Didn't ya recognize the trunk?"

"No. I don't know too much about the trunk. As an intern, I primarily worked with photographs of the smaller pieces. The insurance company supplied the prints. I'm due to see the actual work tomorrow when I check in for my first day as a summer hire."

"So, ya haven't seen the painting yet?" Marcella said.

"Nope. Not in person," I said.

"Get yourself ready for a real treat," Marcella said, adding a sticky sweetness to her drawl.

An uneasy feeling told me I shouldn't ask, but I did anyway. "What do you mean?"

"Just wait and see," Marcella said, before switching to a

new topic. "By the way, have you talked to your mom or your Uncle Roy?"

"No. But thanks for reminding me to try calling Christina again." I watched Marcella frown. Marcella and Talli considered Christina my mom, adoptive status notwithstanding, and neither had liked it when I started using her first name.

While I listened to unanswered ring tones, Marcella asked Talli, "Y'all hear about the scene at the village tavern last night? It seems that Roy and the very rich Mr. Hemcourt the fifth had drinks together and got into a heated argument. Roy had to be shown the door."

"What time was that?" I asked, giving up and snapping my phone closed.

"About midnight," Marcella said.

The answer didn't sit well. I'd overheard the investigators speculate about the time of Herb's death — sometime after midnight.

Roy Landers, my birth mother's much older brother, worked odd jobs around the village and Herb often found things for him to do. As a self-taught artist and direct descendant of one of Olof Krans's most famous apprentices, Uncle Roy came as close to being a Krans expert as the college-educated Ekollon or anybody else. Another reason Herb often had him around. I imagined the sheriff wanted to talk to him. That would certainly upset the often disharmonious balance that passed as marriage between Christina and Uncle Roy. I had to get back to the red brick house.

"Look, Michael, I've got my shoulder bag. I'll just grab my backpack out of the car. They're all I really need for right now. I can cross the bridge and cut through the meadow. It'll be faster on foot then you driving clear around with the truck and all."

"Are you sure?"

"Yeah, I'll get the rest of my stuff tomorrow."

"And how are you going to do that?" he asked and waited a couple of beats. My exhausted brain attempted the mental gymnastics of figuring out how I could retrieve my stuff and check in for my first day of work without a car. Nothing came to me.

"Okay, I give. It's impossible. I'm doomed."

"Look, I'm sorry. You were too easy. I'll bring your things over on Sunday. I can't do it any sooner. I've made plans for tonight and I promised to take my mom to some *gala* museum premiere on Saturday night."

I'd have to wait. What else could I do?

CHAPTER 6

I watched my poor car disappear. The trip to Galva wouldn't take too long. The real trick would be getting someone to look at the damage caused by the ditch. I hoped they might find time and check it out today, but it depended on how backed up they were. The Anderson Brothers had a long history in the area and enough customers to keep their garage going all day, every day. Having Michael pulling the night shift for his uncles had to help out a lot.

After adjusting my backpack and shoulder bag into more comfortable positions, I inhaled deep breaths of fresh air and started north toward the two-lane concrete bridge over the Edwards River. Out of habit, I paused midway across to check out the water level below. Down there lay my secret childhood hiding spot. It probably looked like a meager pile of rocks now, but back when it mattered, it became a fortress. I spent many summer afternoons down there listening to the sounds of the trees, the water, and the birds, a peaceful world far removed from grownups and my brother. The fishing had never been very good, so I had it all to myself most of the time. A perfect place for daydreaming. In my peripheral vision, a flash of blue with a fleck of red caught my attention. A female kingfisher had landed on the sagging utility line that spanned the river below the bridge. It stayed a brief moment before it dove down to the rippled water. The fishing must be better than I remembered.

On the left, just past the bridge, a gravel driveway led to an alluvial field entirely enclosed by a painted wooden four-rail horse fence. The white paint had begun to show the inevitable signs of weather by peeling away here and there, mostly on the edges of the boards. The weed and brush of the river bank spread their untamed growth right up to the driveway's southern edge. The drainage ditch on the other side contained mats of reedy cattails and bushy clumps of New England asters still a spring-fresh shade of green. Above the ditch, clusters of corn lilies crowded together, unprepared for their sunny summer displays. In between a practiced eye could spot bunches of what some people took as weeds, but what others identified as wildflowers. A few of those still blossomed, showing subtle touches of yellow and white with an occasional hint of delicate blue. Wildflower blossoms tended to be understated. The bolder, brighter borders that showed a domesticated human touch appeared further away around the red brick house on the hill.

The flattest spot of open ground close to the road served as the main parking lot for The OK Art Fest in the Meadow held every August. The pressure of thousands of automobile tires over many years left the soil compacted and not good for much more than year-round pasture. I looked over the gate and counted two full-sized and three miniature horses, plus two calves. I made sure the gate was securely latched after passing through.

This wide expanse of meadow stretching from the river, sloping upward toward the red brick house, gave us the best view of Bishop Hill. The northern end of the Colony Church's gambrel roof poked through the heavy mass of trees that shaded the river bank and seemed to crawl up into the village. Further to the left, we could make out the distinctive shape of the Steeple Building's clock tower and just a corner of the Blacksmith Shop's hip roof. Far to the right of the church, the cupola from the Bjorkland Hotel rose majestically above the foliage. Taking in the view on a clear morning became a ritual I savored each time I returned home. Maybe this time I could use it as an opportunity to open the difficult conversation I had to have with Christina. I wasn't looking forward to discussing my plans for going away. The prospect of earning another degree looked reasonable enough on the outside. I would probably leave it at that. No need to talk about Marsha Ellen, the former boyfriend, or the deeper issues between Christina and me. Am I a big chicken? No doubt about it.

I continued to walk and mull over the multitude of feelings I had about the red brick house on the hill. Like many, I believed that Bishop Hill's greatest asset lay in its collection of original buildings dating back to the Colony period of the mid-nineteenth century. They ranged from the modest wood-framed buildings to the massive brick and stucco public structures created in the Greek Revival style popular in Sweden at the time the Colonists left for the new world.

The red brick house would never find a place in any traditional architectural category. Its builders, the Westblooms, had succeeded in creating an Americanized original. Its piecemeal collection of hallways and rooms offered a labyrinth of nooks and crannies, excellent places for me to seek privacy. Now, it seemed old and rickety, an impractical monument in need of constant upkeep and repair. But no matter how my opinion of the house changed, the allure of how it came to be, and the story of the Westblooms, still captivated me.

Nils Westbloom and Cilla, his younger sister, were true children of the Colony. Their parents, devout followers of the Prophet, the charismatic Pietist preacher Karl Hemson, made the treacherous journey from Sweden to the new world only to arrive in time for a cholera epidemic. The exhausted adults succumbed to the disease, but the children survived. Like many other young orphans, the siblings were taken in and cared for by members of the communal society.

For the Westblooms, Bishop Hill, the New Jerusalem on

the banks of the Edwards River in western Illinois, comprised their entire world. They grew up, attended the one-room school house, and found meaningful work that helped the Colony as a whole. Nils learned many skills and eventually settled into brick making. Cilla also helped out in many areas until eventually she went to work at the looms weaving linens. The fruits of their labors usually went for use within the Colony, but in hard times the staples they made were peddled to outsiders for much-needed cash.

After the dissolution of the Colony in 1861, Nils and Cilla shared an allotment of farmland and a wooded lot located on the other side of the gravel road that years later would be called the Smoketree Road. They worked the land together in the beginning and established a single household.

Their house started out small. Size didn't matter as much when most of the food preparation took place in a separate structure, a summer kitchen. The multiple additions came much later in response to their growing needs. Even though the siblings never married, the front door of their home always stood open to other orphaned children. What began with necessity and kindness became a tradition, a new kind of extended family.

Naturally, Nils built with brick. He and his young wards added rooms and hallways as needed. The red brick house on the hill grew to impressive proportions.

Later, the enterprising builders turned their attention to the wooded area across the gravel road. They cleared the undergrowth and created the six Ox-Boy cabins, so named because of their location on the Colony's Oxpojke Trail, a main route the young boys took when driving teams of oxen between fields.

Christina's grandfather, one of the many orphans, spent years helping Nils develop his campground. Unlike the other boys, he never left the farm. He inherited the land and its traditions.

I only thought of my childhood from the point when Christina took in John and me and gave us the security of growing up on a farm, even if it was a different sort of farm. Having the cabins across the road meant a constant stream of new people from a wider outside world.

Usually, the artist types came in requesting a quiet spot to paint or write, and kept to themselves. Occasionally some came with their children. John and I welcomed the newcomers no matter how long they stayed. We went on grand adventures as we roamed the fields and woods. Sometimes we shared personal stories. Other times it was more fun to make things up.

Mindful of all the personal history surrounding me, I walked up to the back door still determined to leave it all behind after this summer.

CHAPTER 7

I found the back door locked and couldn't imagine why. Christina rarely locked up during the day. I peered through the glass panes and saw no discernible sign of movement in the cramped but otherwise neat kitchen area. Two coffee cups sat on a small oval table that was wedged into the only open space available.

Puzzled, I started walking around to the front of the house. I got out my phone and prepared to make another call when I spotted two figures in the distance coming up from the cabins. I could easily identify Christina by her short salt-and-pepper hair that barely moved in the breeze. She adjusted her glasses, smiled, and waved as she neared the gravel road that separated the cabins from the main house. The indistinct person walking beside her gradually morphed into the dark-haired female deputy who had the encounter with Ekollon at the Varnishtree's workshop door.

I waved back and looked up the road. The deputy's squad car sat parked in the shade of one of the oak trees planted by the Westblooms nearly 150 years ago. To me and most of the village the stately giant had become known as the Smoketree, because of its unfortunate reputation. As luck would have it, the tree had been planted in just the right spot that automobiles speeding over the top of the hill had a hard time missing it, and often didn't, leaving smoking wreckage under its sheltering canopy.

I waited by the house as the deputy said her goodbyes and left going south, probably headed to the Varnishtree to make her report.

"So that's why you haven't been answering my calls," I said when Christina was within hearing range. "She sure got here fast enough. I just found out about Uncle Roy and the bar."

"Deputy Dana Johnson showed up about an hour or so ago. I thought she came to tell me about you, but then she started asking questions about Roy. Did I hear him come back last night? Had I seen him this morning? Had he been acting differently lately? What kind of question is that? That man has acted differently his whole life and Vietnam sure didn't do him any special favors."

Those types of questions didn't sound good to me. My anxiety rose right along with Christina's. I bit my lip as I waited for her to wind down and take a breath.

Christina stopped waving her hands long enough to

plant them on her hips and assume a posture that reflected her exasperation. "She wanted me to show her the cabin Roy uses for a studio. I couldn't say no."

I felt parts of myself slipping away as I thought of each loss. Herb was dead. Pearl was in the hospital. Uncle Roy was in trouble.

Christina stopped again and her face softened as she studied me. "Oh, never mind all that." She dismissed it with a flick of her hand and opened her arms wide, inviting a hug.

What remained of my defenses utterly collapsed and I welcomed the embrace. The stress of the morning melted into tearful sobs.

"Come on, sweetie," Christina murmured. "Let's go inside."

We sat at the oval kitchen table with fresh coffee in front of us. It had the wonderful aroma of almonds, but I cradled my cup and merely went through the motions of sipping it. I'd already had my fill. Now, I just wanted to smell it and let its warmth spread through my hands into the rest of my body.

"I'm sorry about that," I said after I'd begun to relax. "I guess it all finally got to me."

"Don't apologize. You've been through a lot today. I've fielded plenty of phone calls, plus the deputy," Christina said as she leveled a scrutinizing gaze. "You're looking surprisingly good. The shorter haircut suits you. So does the perm." She reached out to straighten some wayward tresses. I pulled back just enough to discourage any help.

"Thanks. I thought it would be good for the art show tonight. But I'll be missing that," I said as I finger-combed my own hair. "Talli helped me clean up a bit at The Lutfisk. I couldn't eat much, but that little bit helped." I hesitated. "So there's no sign of Uncle Roy?"

"None that I could see. Everything's in its usual state of chaos with the exception of his files. He makes an effort to keep those in order." Christina sipped her coffee. She tapped the rim with a fingernail while waiting for me to say more.

"I just don't want to believe something like that could have happened to Herb. He was such a nice guy, a basically good person who would help out anybody. All he wanted was to fix things. Broken things. Make old stuff whole and useful again."

"He had a real gift for that," Christina said softly as she stared into her cup.

"How could this have happened? Who would have wanted to hurt him? And please don't say Uncle Roy. He can be difficult, but I always thought his drinking made him more of a danger to himself than to others."

Christina sighed. "I think you're right about that. He wouldn't hurt anyone."

"Marcella said he'd gotten into an argument with Mr. Hemcourt at the village tavern last night and for his own good had to be escorted out."

"Oh, I bet she enjoyed telling everyone that story," Christina said. As former friends, they had a long history of being at odds with each other's opinions and quick to pounce on weaknesses.

"How could a hassle between Uncle Roy and Mr. Hemcourt have involved Herb?"

"Well, from what I've heard," Christina said, "Herb came in looking for Roy, but didn't approach him when he saw who he was with. He told the bartender to have Roy meet him outside. Later, after the argument, Roy was ordered to leave. No one knows what happened next. Needless to say, folks are very eager to find out if Roy ever talked to Herb, and, if so, just what did Herb have to say."

"So, everyone's looking for Uncle Roy," I said, and watched Christina's reaction. She shrugged and said nothing. There had been plenty of times over the years when she'd let Uncle Roy have a full dose of her anger after he'd done something stupid. It wasn't like her to be pensively nervous and silent.

"Do you have any ideas?" I asked as I pondered my limited list of possibilities.

"No. In the old days, before tourism, he'd sleep it off in the park and come back here with some wild, fanciful story. But now, I don't know. It'll have to be wait and see."

"I suppose you could check with his friends," I said.

"Honey, he has drinking buddies," she snapped. "I'm not sure how else I'd classify them. You know how he can be when he's on a roll. How he uses his intellect to punch holes through someone else's opinion. 'I'm just being harshly realistic,' he says. Well, you and I can take it, we're family, but others don't have to. Anyway, I imagine the usual suspects are being questioned as we speak."

I leaned back in the chair and offered my best off-the-cuff suggestion. "If it was me and I didn't want to be found, I'd go hide out like Karl Hemson did when the mob of outsiders came searching for him. Oh, and I remember seeing that old dairy cave once when Uncle Roy tried to teach me how to hunt squirrels. It was dirty and spooky, but maybe . . ."

"Very funny," Christina cut in with a shake of her head.

"What are we going to do?" I asked.

"There's no 'we' to this problem. You have a job to get ready for. Plus, there's a whole stack of important-looking mail waiting for you on the counter. I see you've been busy and very ambitious with grad school applications. You can tell me all about it later. Now isn't the best time for either one of us. You need some rest and I need to think."

"Sure," I said with a selfish sense of relief. "When things calm down a bit." Having a little extra time worked for me, since I still hadn't figured out how to explain my desire to get away from small-time Bishop Hill without sounding childishly spiteful and ungrateful.

I excused myself from the table and headed upstairs with my shoulder bag and backpack. I surveyed my room and had to admit it contained much of the same disorder that Uncle Roy leaves in his wake. The piles had a little more order to them and the floor was maybe a little cleaner. Christina must have made a run through with dust cloth and vacuum.

I sat my things down on the bed to unpack, but got no further. I studied the corner that served as my private photo gallery. I often roamed around taking pictures of whatever caught my eye: people, buildings, and animals. At first it made me feel important, like I was the new Olof Krans, creating portraits with my camera instead of oil paints. I walked the streets documenting everyday village life. Several empty spaces on the wall marked items I'd removed for the senior art show.

I walked over to the window and stared blankly at the old tree across the road. As a little girl, I'd picked this room because I could see the big tree I'd heard so much about. I developed a notion that my mother would appear down there one day and everything would be as it had been before, only better. I waited day after day, studying the shifting shadows and attempting to memorize the patterns in its branches. But nothing magical ever happened. Mornings would invariably come with Christina calling me to breakfast.

I'd been so small; my mind struggled hard to tell one person from another. It was beyond me to process new titles like adoptive mother or aunt. I wanted a *mom*. That's when I came up with calling Christina by a new name, Teeny Mom. She had said nothing when it started, and, likewise, had said nothing when it suddenly stopped when I turned fifteen.

CHAPTER 8

I only meant to lie down for a few minutes and awoke hours later to the lengthening twilight of early evening. I lay there listening quietly for some sound either from downstairs or outside, something to give me a clue to what might be going on. Hearing nothing like the movement of a human, I focused instead on some birds and their scolding chatter. People often commented to me on how nice it must have been to grow up in a quiet place like Bishop Hill. They needed to be around on the days the wind roared across the prairie just before a thunderstorm, or when the calls of impatient livestock left no room for any creative thought, or, like now, when two tom cats directly below my window began vying for territory. The escalating yowls got me up and moving.

Downstairs I found a cleared kitchen table and a note: "S— Running errands. Will be late. Feed horses, etc. Lock up the barn."

Sure, not a problem. I knew the drill.

Seeing no use in waiting for it to get darker, I headed out the back door toward the barn with its two-part side door. The top half already hung open. I unclasped the bottom half and pulled on it with enough force for it to swing back and bang against the side of the barn. Hoping it would draw attention, I made it smack the side once more. If the dominant horse came in on its own, the others would follow. It worked like a charm and the animals formed a meandering procession up the hill. I ducked into the combination tack room and storage area to fill a bucket with oats. In no time, I had them in their respective stalls and munching away. I climbed the ladder into the hay loft and gave it my best guess as to how much to throw down into the feeders.

While brushing off bits of leaves and stems from my jeans and preparing to climb down, I thought I heard an odd noise in the distance. I hadn't heard Christina's Volvo come back and no one else but Uncle Roy had any business being out by the cabins this time of year. I made my way through the loose hay and peered out the window that overlooked the Smoketree Road. Below me, a large black dog had its nose to the ground and appeared to be heading in the general direction of the barn. "Oh, for Pete's sake, get a grip," I muttered. "It's just Flicka coming in for a cat food snack."

By the time I climbed down, the neighbor's black Labrador had polished off the leftover crumbs from the cats' metal pan and looked plaintively at me, expecting some more. "Look how fat you are," I admonished playfully. I led the dog outside and closed both parts of the barn door behind me. "You don't need anything else."

Again I heard a muffled, out-of-place sound. I looked down at the dog, but she showed no sign of having heard anything interesting enough to divert her attention from the begging at hand.

"Okay," I said softly, "you get to earn your treats tonight." I petted the willing dog enough to keep her close by as I reopened the top part of the barn door and reached inside for the flashlight that always hung there on a nail. "Let's go take a look over there, shall we?" I said. The two of us crossed the road to the lane that led to the cabins. We walked up to the closest one.

Enough light lingered to make the flashlight unnecessary. Soon the gloom would turn the muted landscape into dense gray shadows. The dog cooperated and stayed close as I checked out the first two cabins. I tried the doors, but everything seemed locked and normal. I stood in the middle of the lane trying to decide which ones to check next. The two across the way were closer, but the two down at the far end probably needed my attention the most, one being Uncle Roy's cabin. I assumed he had returned while I slept. Without my Chevy in the driveway, he had no clue about my being home. I chided myself for becoming spooked at nothing but a routine noise.

Flicka, apparently having her fill of intrigue and treats,

padded away toward her real home. I tried to coax her back. She just shot me a bored glance that conveyed the message: Kid, you're on your own.

The rapidly growing darkness and the lack of canine backup didn't inspire much bravery on my part, when this time I definitely heard the scraping sound of furniture moving across a wooden floor. It sounded like it came from Uncle Roy's cabin. All the cabins had tree names and officially his was known as the Hawthorne. In one of his darker poetic moods, he had painted over the sign next to the door and rechristened it the Hemlock Suite. His flair for cleverness went entirely underappreciated. I couldn't make out the name now because no one had turned the porch light on. Inside the cabin, the illumination was too faint to come from the regular overhead fixture.

What could be worse, hearing strange sounds, or having the strange sounds suddenly stop and the place go completely dark when I called out, "Uncle Roy, is that you?"

The abrupt change to pitch black and complete silence in the cabin sent a chill through me and made the hair on the back of my neck stand up. This entirely new feeling called for a hasty retreat to the road. I stepped backward cautiously and fought the urge to run. Until I heard footsteps that weren't my own. I stopped caring about how it might look, or how I would explain myself if it all turned out to be nothing. I just *ran*.

My lungs began to burn and my legs ached. Walking between classes on campus couldn't prepare a girl for sprinting. Sheer panic pushed me across the road until I could go no further. I reached the halo of the yard light and spun around while gulping air down my raw throat. I hefted the flashlight and tested its weight against the palm of my other hand. The words of a long ago self-defense instructor drifted back: "Aim for the bridge of the nose. Aim for the eyes. Ears. Do anything to stun their senses and buy time."

A car cleared the bridge at the bottom of the hill, its high beams a gorgeous sight. I turned to look back at the cabins, but the car lights left me too blinded to see if anyone might be in the shadows. The car slowed down and pulled into the driveway just in front of me.

I stared in disbelief as my own car lurched to a halt and the door opened to reveal Michael J. Anderson. At least for now, the J stood for Just In Time. Sadie followed him out with tail wagging and started toward me, probably expecting an extension of the petting she had gotten earlier in the day. The dog paused a moment, raised her ears, and then took off like a shot, straight across the road toward the cabins.

"Oh, great," Michael said, and started to yell for his dog to come back.

"No! Wait," I shouted. "Someone's over there. Not Uncle Roy."

"Are you sure?"

I took in more air between each mouthful of words. "I heard noises. I saw light inside the cabin. I called out. The place went totally black. I heard someone following me.

I'm so glad to see you."

Sadie began barking in the distance. "Is that your only flashlight?" Michael didn't wait for an answer. He grabbed it out of my hand and followed the sounds coming from the trees past the last cabin.

The abruptness startled me and it took me a moment to consider the folly of standing there all alone. I ran to catch up. This Michael J. Anderson bore no resemblance to the pain-in-the-butt, J for Jerk I remembered from high school.

I caught up with Michael as he neared the Hemlock Suite. Sadie stood off to the side barking into the woods. The dog wouldn't advance any further without a command. Michael called to her and she came to his side. He knelt down to rub her head while looking up at me. He started to say something, but I didn't let him get any words out.

"That wasn't open before," I said, pointing at the cabin door. "Someone was here."

"And it wasn't your uncle?"

"I called his name . . . and nothing."

Michael moved the flashlight's beam around the immediate area. I judged by Sadie's more relaxed stance that the place was in the clear. He walked over to the doorway and reached inside to switch on all the lights.

It took a few seconds to adjust to the brightness. When we could see, Michael said, "Wow, whoever was here sure did a number on this place. Must have been searching for something. Any idea what?"

I saw mounds of art supplies lying in jumbled heaps

next to empty pizza boxes. Papers were strewn about. Even the mattress appeared partially pulled off the bed.

"I don't know. Uncle Roy functions in his own world of disorder, but this seems extreme even for him. What bothers me most is that." I pointed to the old wooden office desk Uncle Roy used for sketching, painting, and assembling collages. The desk was massive and had plenty of room for a row of hanging file racks along the back outfitted with a colorful assortment of file folders. A few had been pulled up and their contents partially exposed. Others lay open on the desk and obviously rifled. I walked over to inspect one decorated with black angular Scandinavian runes. Without touching it, I could tell it was empty.

"We should call this in to the sheriff," Michael said.

"No argument here."

"I'll make the call," he said, and pulled out his cell phone as he started for the door. "I have to corral Sadie, too."

I started to follow but was distracted by a stack of unopened mail. The envelopes lay face down with one notable exception. Peeking out from under the pile was the elaborate logo of the grad school that was my top pick. With no time to wonder why it was out here, I had no qualms about quickly sliding it out and tucking it into a back pocket without being seen.

Deputy Dana Johnson responded to the call. She did her own sweep of the area before coming back to where

Michael and I stood.

"I've called for backup," she said. "We'll check the next few roads over to see if anyone saw anything suspicious or out of place." She took out her notebook, wrote down a couple of items, and then turned back to me. "Now, you're sure it wasn't your uncle?"

"It couldn't have been him."

"How can you be so sure? You said you didn't see anyone."

"Uncle Roy wouldn't have made me feel that . . . scared." I couldn't say anything more. Just recalling the panic made my throat tighten and my palms begin to sweat. I refused to cry. So I steadied myself, took a breath, and tried to look confident while rubbing my hands dry on my jeans.

The deputy directed the same question to Michael. "Are you sure it wasn't Roy Landers?"

Before he could answer, I blurted out, "Why do you keep asking if it was Uncle Roy? He wouldn't break into his own place. Mess up his files. Take something."

Deputy Johnson looked at me. "Something's missing? What, exactly?"

"I don't know what, exactly. His filing system is whimsical at best. All I know for sure is there's an empty folder on the desk. I didn't want to touch anything." I heard the pitch of my voice rising all on its own. I hadn't meant to sound angry. I couldn't stop myself.

"You've got to understand. I have to ask these questions. They're necessary." The deputy looked from me to Michael. I saw him nod. It didn't help.

Christina returned from her errands to find Henry County Sheriff's Department squad cars parked in the driveway and on the road. She quickly got filled in and took charge, leaving Michael and me free to go.

I knew Michael had plans, but the thought of him leaving left me with a sinking feeling. It must have shown on my face.

"Look," he said, "Sadie and I need a ride back to Galva. It's my night off and I'm meeting up with some guys at McKane's. They offered to help me with my computer class. There'll be live music from a new local group later on. You're welcome to come. You might know—"

I didn't let him finish. "Anywhere but here." I held out my hand for the keys. "*I'll* drive."

CHAPTER 9

I could tell Michael felt relieved to get back to his apartment in one piece. It was my car and I had every right to drive, but I still had the back seat packed with my apartment. Fitting two people and an active dog into the front seat took some doing. I heard him take a sharp intake of air the first time I used the brakes for a turn. I'm sure we both shared a gross mental image of a mashed Sadie dog in his lap. I slowed down and did my best to go easy on the brake pedal after that, but I could tell he was holding his breath a lot. It made for an extremely unpleasant ride to Galva.

After having a little difficulty finding his apartment, I was quite relieved when he said, "You go on to McKane's and I'll catch up as soon as I get Sadie settled in for the night."

When he caught up with me again, I was already well

into a beer and obsessing over the menu's pizza possibilities. He paid for my cheeseburger at The Lutfisk this morning, and even though Sadie ended up with most of it, I figured it was my turn to buy. I pointed out a couple of recommendations.

"Sure, either of those would be good for me." He ordered his own beer.

His cool tone and detached attitude made me realize he regretted his impulse to be a nice guy by inviting me to tag along tonight. My new goal: getting this evening over as fast as possible.

While waiting for pizza, we sipped on our beers in silence. I began to feel the buzzing effect of alcohol on an empty stomach. I liked the gentle haze that began to cloud my mind and obscure my recent accumulation of harsh memories. I couldn't help myself, I actually smiled at him.

"You should slow down," he warned. "It's been a long day for you."

"You're absolutely right," I said, with the slight slur already creeping into my voice. "I have to show up for work bright and early tomorrow." I took another sip. "And be bright." I tried to stifle a giggle behind my hand.

"Showing up hung over on your first day isn't a good idea. Trust me, I've tried it."

"Shortened your career?"

"You betcha." His thin smile didn't convey any happiness as he kept glancing in the direction of the door.

I bet he wished his buddies would hurry up. "So, where are these friends of yours?" I asked.

"Alan and James are always late. They're likely glued to a computer screen blasting aliens in a make-believe galaxy far, far away."

"I do know them." I pointed a finger at Michael before tipping my beer back again. "This should be good."

"How so?"

"Because I've had the occasional run-in with them at the computer lab on the Knox campus. Usually late at night. I'm there to pick up a printout or whatnot, and there they'd be, typing away. I know they go to Urbana-Champaign, so I assumed they'd slipped in quietly for a little extracurricular work. Very hush-hush." I flashed a sly grin.

Michael leaned back out of the spray of those last words. He sighed and allowed an unsubtle shake of his head. Back in school he always made me out as some kind of diva. Since I knew what he was thinking, I continued with my train of thought anyway. "The perfect opportunity for a bit of blackmail. This'll give me a chance to ask them about the little project I dreamed up."

"Okay, I'll bite. What project?"

"Well, last summer I worked the front desk at the Krans portrait museum. I can't begin to tell you how bored I got. It occurred to me on one inter—intermin—interminably long, rainy afternoon that there should be a way for a computer program to come up with a composite image of Karl Hemson." I took another drink before refocusing my attention on the intended point. "You know, the Prophet, the fearless leader of our fearless Bishop Hill Colony."

"Yeah, I've heard of him," Michael said. "I grew up here. Remember?" From there he issued a challenging, "So what?"

"Sooo, no photos or paintings of our beloved founder exist." While holding the bottle in my right hand, I ticked off my list with on the other. "There are Krans portraits of a brother, a son, and a daughter." I took another sip. "Combining those images somehow seemed do—doable to me. Alan and James told me in great tor—tortuous detail how difficult it would be. Give it your best shot, I pleaded." I attempted to form what might pass as a cute smile, failed, and gave up with a shrug. "Anyway, I can ask about it again." I proceeded to empty my bottle.

"I guess there's no harm in asking," he said.

I could tell his heart wasn't in it and his thoughts went elsewhere. Probably wanting a quick end to the evening as well.

CHAPTER 10

Saturday, May 31, 2008

Christina went out of her way to set up a lovely breakfast for me. I could tell because she bypassed the crowded kitchen in favor of the sunny dining room.

What we called the dining room was my favorite room in the house. It had a set of three six-over-six windows facing east with a view of the Bishop Hill road as it entered the village on its northern edge, while another similar set faced south toward the Edwards River. The abundance of early morning sunlight made it the most pleasant room in the house virtually year-round for both humans and plants. Lush foliage and bright blossoms added color and texture to every bit of space not otherwise used for active living. Dried flower arrangements adorned any extra wall space devoid of mirrors, art prints, or family photos. A nightmare to clean, but the overall effect blurred the line between inside and outside.

The perfect place and the perfect moment to initiate an important conversation about my future. However, I found myself far removed from any capacity for constructive thought. The straight-backed carved oak chair couldn't quite hold me upright. I deeply regretted that bottle of beer—and the one after that. The late night with Michael and friends, regardless of how enlightening it had been, was exacting a heavy price today. My head ached in ways I never knew were possible.

I could see Christina through the narrow slits that were my eyes. She was assessing the situation. Motherly advice was sure to follow.

"You should eat something, take two aspirins, and be sure to use some mouthwash before you leave." She waved the air away after I failed to stifle a heavy yawn. "A whole lot of mouthwash."

"Yup, you read my mind." She was stating the obvious and I just couldn't hold back the sarcasm.

"Was it really worthwhile?" Christina asked as she placed a mug of coffee in front of me.

"What?"

"Staying out late last night. Drinking to excess. And driving in that condition . . ."

Another stab of pain coursed through my brain as I tried to remember how I got home. "There was some coffee . . . somewhere in there . . . I think."

"Really."

"And yes. It was worthwhile. Actually," I said, between noisy sips, "it turns out that Michael was meeting up with Galva's premier geek patrol." I paused for effect. "It was illuminating."

Christina settled back into her chair and prodded, "Do tell me more."

"Okay, Alan and James are brothers, Galva grads, and engineering majors at Urbana-Champaign. They have solid reputations for knowing all things computer. Michael needed their help with a computer literacy class he's taking out at the community college. I, on the other hand, wanted to remind them of a project I'd dreamed up."

"What kind of project? Something for school? I don't understand. Isn't school over?"

"Not for school. Purely for personal curiosity. You know how there's no verifiable image of Karl Hemson?"

"Now you have my attention," Christina said, and she leaned in to hear more.

"Well, one rainy afternoon I had to take my break inside the portrait museum. No visitors, so I started walking around counting the Krans paintings of Hemson's closest relatives. The museum had three: a brother, a son, and a daughter. My first thought went to DNA testing, like they do on some TV shows. Then it hit me, there should be a way to take the dominant physical characteristics of those people and morph them together to come up with a serviceable composite image of what Hemson *may* have looked like."

"Michael's friends could do that?"

"It seemed like a good idea at the time. So, anyway, I asked about it again last night. Most of what they said escapes me now. Alan and James may have been humoring me, but they promised to try." I massaged my forehead in an effort to relieve the pain the sudden burst of mental activity elicited.

"You know," Christina cautioned, "there are a few people out there, descendants, who really wouldn't want you doing something like that. If he didn't want his image captured during his lifetime, for whatever reason, they're good with it. They'd want the Prophet left alone out of respect."

"But we're descendants, too. And it would be in the noble pursuit of truth," I countered. "With the right technology, the right program, I'm sure we could make something passable happen right now." I leveled my gaze at Christina. "Aren't you the least bit curious? Don't you want to know?"

"I'm just saying that some people are very touchy about Hemson. His memory, his reputation as a spiritual leader … those things are important to them. They'd want things left as they are. Not knowing more is fine with them. As for me, I've gotten myself into enough delicate situations over the years, I'm not about to jump at more. And this smells like something to avoid to me." Christina rose and went into the kitchen, leaving me alone with the remnants of my hangover.

I cradled my aching head in my hands and quietly berated myself as I watched Christina walk away. I didn't get why this business about the Prophet's image was such a big deal. Now I let this chance to talk to her about grad school slip by. I continued the mental harangue as I traipsed upstairs. Why did I have to tell her all about last night? Now she's mad at me.

I had to make myself presentable for work. Fortunately, my closet still held a standard Bishop Hill museum interpreter's costume of a long denim skirt and chambray shirtwaist top. An ensemble that only flattered the most feminine of figures. I had it as a leftover from December's St. Lucia festival, when I volunteered at the Colony Mercantile. Going down to empty out the car could be put off a little longer.

My car, still crammed with the contents of my campus apartment, showed few signs that the towing had done any real damage. It looked like my head felt—jumbled, disoriented, and a mess.

I opened the door and wrinkled my nose as soon as I caught a whiff of a faint unpleasant something. I took a cautious sniff.

"Eew. Dog." I tried to wave the odor away. "This is just the perfect way to start a summer job. Not."

CHAPTER 11

Landing a job at the Nikkerbo Museum and Conference Center had been quite a coup. As far as summer jobs went, this one had the advantage of minimal travel time by car. In fact, I could've walked it, and might just try it on another day when I had the time for a workout. Part of my general plan for the summer included losing a few of those extra pounds before showing up for the fall semester of grad school. But not this morning. I needed to make the best entrance I could manage. I had enough problems without coming in all hot and sweaty from hiking nearly four miles.

The east to west terrain along Highway 34 could lull a driver into thinking everything in Henry County stayed fairly flat and level. The north-to-south roads revealed the deception by dipping and rolling as they transversed the gentle hills and valleys that provided drainage for the

Edwards River. As a result, drivers needed to be alert for moving farm equipment and wildlife, or, in my case, wayward old ladies in stolen minivans. My aching head didn't keep me from paying close attention to my driving.

The advance team for Curt Hemcourt V had failed to put together a large enough land parcel south of Bishop Hill near Highway 34 for his desired development. So, for Plan B, his team maneuvered its way into a larger section of farmland north of the village near a secondary paved road. This spot lay well past the location of the original Nikkerbo, a Colony outpost. The building plans held no risk of interfering with the archeological site.

When Hemcourt's project was still in an early design stage, a few locals campaigned for it to resemble a red barn with white trim, typical of those of western Illinois. Others suggested a look reminiscent of a more traditional Swedish farmstead, again painted red with white trim. Hemcourt's architects chose to do a modern interpretation of an old barn with a steeply pitched roof already on the property. They claimed to have taken apart the basic dynamic elements of the original structure, added the cylindrical shape of the ubiquitous Midwestern grain silo, and then recombined them to attain new ground in functional design.

Most of the county waited patiently over the last three years as construction proceeded at a slow pace. The start on the main building had been delayed so Hemcourt's private residence could be finished first. The great man wanted to be present as his grand vision unfolded in steel and concrete. For the house, the architects employed the strong horizontal lines of log structures still found in Sweden and seen in a few early Krans paintings over here. But one couldn't miss the hints of the well-known regional style of Frank Lloyd Wright that also emphasized those same attributes. However, the size of the garage produced the most tongue wagging over local coffee cups. Newspaper articles had him pegged as an antique car enthusiast. It looked like he would have ample storage capacity for a sizable portion of his fleet of vehicles downstate from his Chicago mansion.

I headed for the museum, a large building in its own right but, in fact, merely the western wing of the newly constructed complex. The actual conference center to the east enclosed a great deal more real estate. The two wings lay at an obtuse angle to each other, connected by a central hub area, which contained administrative offices and a well-appointed kitchen. A long covered entranceway led from the shared lobby area to the parking lot and ran at a similar angle to the other two wings. The aerial view gave the impression of a large capital letter Y. And indeed, more than a few locals wondered aloud, "Why was this being built here?" They thought it was an outsider's intrusion and a waste of good farmland.

I gave Hemcourt and his designers points for giving all the buildings an overall low profile. A nice benefit from the half-buried, earth-sheltered aspect.

I turned into the main drive and circled behind the private compound until I came to the parking area designated for employees. I parked well away from the two closest spots to the back entrance. Each had been marked "Reserved for Director." The one closest to the door held Hemcourt's black BMW; the second slot had Ekollon's venerable Mercedes.

As I walked past the cars I noticed ragged strands of prairie grass hooked underneath the bumper of the Mercedes, a memento from yesterday's visit to the Varnishtree. The bumper of the BMW likewise held a clump of the same prairie grass, along with shredded cattails and some other bits I didn't take time to identify.

My initial participation in the morning staff meeting was mercifully brief. Director Ekollon handed me a pile of employment forms and told me to take them out to the front desk and fill them out. He'd collect them later when he gave me the day's assignment.

Sitting alone in the front lobby was a little spooky at first. The large desk with its banks of lights, push buttons, and video monitors made me feel more like a security guard than a museum interpreter. On closer inspection, I noticed that some of the electronic controls weren't hooked up yet and a couple of walls hadn't been completely finished. I expected the building to be closer to completion than this. I dismissed it as contractors missing their deadlines. To help settle my nerves and get a feel for the place, I sat there with my eyes closed, enjoying the smell of *new*, a welcome change from all my other experiences in Bishop Hill.

I'd grown up with worn wooden floors that could never be swept completely clean. Anything I'd ever dusted got recoated almost immediately. I'd worked in brick buildings that were too hot in the summer and too cold in the winter. The change of seasons, spring to summer and summer to fall, brought near-perfect temperatures, but only for a few days. I enjoyed watching old black-and-white movies, but I sometimes felt I'd grown up living in one—the same one day after day. I knew it wasn't fair. Bishop Hill couldn't help be anything other than what it was. It had been a special place in an earlier time, and I appreciated other people's passion to preserve it. My passion, the future I hoped for, would take me in another direction.

I opened my eyes and began working on the first form. But it didn't take long for my attention to wander off again. I picked at the polish on a fingernail as I imagined going to grand places where the artifacts sparkled and shone, made of silver and gold, not just wood, rope, and broomcorn. I'd have the degrees. Write the papers. They would trust me with great works of art. The likes of Ekollon would work for me. Ask me what to do next.

"That must be some daydream y'all got goin' on there, Missy," said Marcella Rice as she came up behind me.

Her sudden appearance made me jump in my seat and brought a protective hand to my chest. "You nearly scared me to death. Where'd you come from?"

Marcella was the only one to ever call me Missy. I never liked it much. Every Bishop Hill kid grew up with a chance to play one of three basic roles for our festivals: St. Lucia, Pippi Longstocking, or a gnomish tomte. Any of those characters could have yielded a far worse nickname than the one she settled on.

She walked around to the front of the desk and hooked her cane over the edge before using her meaty arms to take some weight off her bad leg and to prop up her smiling face.

"I came in through the kitchen. I'm helping Talli with the catering tonight and she sent me to check in with His Highness. I have to give him our meatball count and see if it meets with his approval."

"Oh, right, I saw you guys working on them yesterday."

"Well yes, Talli helped get them ready to bake, but those little Swedish cocktail meatballs are my specialty. I don't share my spice recipe with *nobody*, not even Talli."

Not sure who His Highness might be, I opted for all-inclusive safety and said, "I haven't seen Mr. Hemcourt yet today and Ekollon is still in the morning staff meeting, issuing everyone's marching orders."

"What are ya doin' out here all by your lonesome?" Marcella inquired.

"The ever popular paperwork, federal forms and such." I fanned out the sheaf of papers for her to appreciate.

"No wonder ya drifted off," cooed Marcella.

Slightly embarrassed, I shuffled them back together and had a thought. "Marcella," I asked, "didn't you go to school with him, Ekollon?"

"No, not me. He was closer to my younger brother's age."

"What was he like back then?"

"Oh my, let me think." To aid her recall, Marcella shuffled around the desk and settled herself into an extra chair. She filled it up and hooked her cane over the arm. "Let's see, all us Bishop Hill kids got teased some back then. David Lee, I remember he got some extra grief on account of his name."

"Ekollon is Swedish for acorn."

"Right. It didn't take long for that to become a joke."

"He claims his ancestors chose that name out of respect for the red oak trees they found growing here," I said.

"That's very possible. Some Colonists did change their names. Quite a few kept the names the Swedish army assigned to them. After all, the world can only take so many Andersons in one small place." Marcella chuckled at her humor loudly enough to produce a slight echo.

"That doesn't seem like a big deal." I took a quick look around before leaning forward. I hoped Marcella would take the hint and lower her voice.

"Kids can be cruel. But make no mistake, David 'The Dragon' Ekollon did not take the teasing meekly."

"What?" No one had ever mentioned that before. I couldn't help but grin over such a juicy tidbit. Marcella had a clever way of turning a phrase and could assign some interesting nicknames. I was again thankful that "Missy" seemed to be the limit for me.

"Even when he was small, he had that great booming

voice," Marcella continued. "If he didn't like something, he roared. It saved his butt on more than one occasion." Marcella chuckled again.

I nervously checked the staff room door. Still closed. "I could almost feel sorry for him," I said as I chipped away at another fingernail.

"Well, don't bother yourself. It wasn't long before he discovered that a skinny branch of his family tree brushed up against some minor Swedish royalty. He's been a pompous ass about it ever since. Nobody, but nobody, can be more Swedish than he is or more true to the spirit of the Colony." Marcella snorted. "And he's still waitin' to become a mighty oak."

Now the door opened and people were coming out. I gave Marcella a little wave and a quick shake of my head. She just assumed a Mona Lisa smile. Nothing seemed to fluster her composure. She certainly knew more, but there was no time to ask. Ekollon made his appearance. Marcella rose to smoothly continue with her meatball mission. I dove back into my W-4 form.

With the last form completed, I tapped the stack of papers back into an orderly pile and looked around. Marcella had apparently left. Ekollon stood in the center of a small knot of full-time employees and summer hires like me. The group was in the process of breaking up as people left for their day's postings. Ekollon stood close to a young man I had never seen before. Ekollon appeared relaxed and, dare I say it, friendly. His smile disappeared when he glanced over to me. I started to return a polite, closed-mouth nod to indicate a "Yes, I'm still here" reply when the young man also turned to look in my direction. His neatly-trimmed golden hair and shadow of a blond beard made his blue eyes all the more intense. Obviously Swedish and possessing their classic good looks. I could do nothing but stare like a deer caught in the high-beams of an oncoming car. I made a mental check to see if my mouth hung open. No. Good. I collected myself and rose to walk over and join them, self-consciously careful not to misstep or stumble.

"Ah, Ms. Anderson," Ekollon said with a curt nod. "May I introduce Lars Trollenberg. He will be with us this summer as a representative of a Swedish cultural society that has long been interested in preserving Bishop Hill."

"Then you must be based in Biskopskulla, Karl Hemson's birthplace." I put on my best smile as I shook his hand.

"My small group is from Stockholm. You wouldn't have heard of it."

"Oh, I see."

Actually, I didn't see, but it would have to wait. The wooden doors of Mr. Hemcourt's private office swung open and he swept out, followed by two men in gray suits. I recognized Les Patrick, a respected attorney from Galva and a family friend. I didn't know the shorter, pear-shaped man who stepped up to Hemcourt's right elbow.

"Good morning, ladies and gentlemen," Hemcourt called out as he approached us.

I had trouble forming a polite smile as we exchanged pleasantries. My eyes were unwillingly drawn to Hemcourt's mouth. It gave me a prickly sensation that only resolved itself when I realized that he now sported a modest mustache. He had shaved off the full beard.

He acknowledged my surprised look and those of the others by rubbing his chin and saying, "Yes, I decided to lose some of the facial hair this morning. All the better to look more like my ancestor for the reception tonight." He gave us a camera-ready smile. "I'm afraid the sideburns will have to wait a while. Eh, quite a while, actually." Ekollon began to say something that became lost when Hemcourt cut him off. "David, I think it's unnecessary and wholly inappropriate for Ms. Anderson to be here. After her recent experiences, she needs some time off to recover." Ekollon started to speak and again Hemcourt intervened with a wave of his hand. "Ms. Anderson, please take a few days on us. Let's say until . . . until Wednesday. And if that isn't enough, please feel free to contact us and we'll give you whatever time you need. Isn't that right, David?"

Ekollon merely nodded stiffly, obviously stifling his true thoughts.

I thanked him, handed over the employment forms to a sullen Ekollon, and proceeded to gather my things. I felt everyone's eyes on me as I made my way to the back door and the employee parking lot.

My mind spun in circles. What had just happened? What did he say? "After all her recent experiences?" What did that mean, exactly? He knew about Herb; could he already know about the incident at the cabins last night? I wanted to pinch myself to see if this windfall was real. The thought of paid time off to sleep overwhelmed any other sense of caution I might possess. I returned to a quiet house and needed no other invitation to go upstairs and collapse into my bed.

CHAPTER 12

I awoke hours later to sunshine. A vast improvement over yesterday. I heard footsteps downstairs and got up to investigate.

While changing clothes, I came across the envelope I'd stuffed into my pocket yesterday. I placed it on my desk. It was fairly skinny, so odds were high that the news inside would not be good. All the more reason to put off opening it.

Coming into the kitchen looking sleepy and disheveled, I really surprised Christina. "You're back," she said, "and before noon?"

"I got back a long time ago," I said, stifling a yawn with the back of my hand.

I squeezed myself into a kitchen chair. The red brick house had a lot of room elsewhere, but none to spare in the kitchen. The insufficient space was an unfortunate byproduct of a past retrofit that tried to give the old house some new amenities. The breakfast table had to make do with the sparse leftovers.

"Did you get fired? I'll have a talk with them. Don't worry, I'll get this fixed. They can't do—"

"No, no," I said. "Everything is fine. In fact, everything is *better* than fine. I was sitting in the front lobby, filling out employment forms, when Mr. Hemcourt and his entourage came in. I recognized your lawyer from Galva, but not the other guy. Though he might pass as the lawyerly type. Mr. Hemcourt couldn't have been nicer or more generous. He seemed surprised and concerned about me coming in so soon. After finding Herb." I choked up a bit and had to stop and swallow to clear my throat before continuing. "Even made Ekollon be nicer to me. Gave me paid time off. Just like that." I snapped my fingers. "Until Wednesday, no less," I added. "Beats me why he did it."

"Wow," Christina uttered as she let go of the steam she'd built up. "He's not known to be so considerate. It's nice to have some good news for a change."

"Shall I take that as still no Uncle Roy?"

"Nope. Nothing."

"That's so strange. I didn't think anyone could go unseen for this long. When I was a kid, you always said everyone had their eyes on me no matter where I went."

"You were a cute little kid," Christina reminded me. "A blessing of the village was an abundance of moms. Watchful moms."

"Jeez. No wonder I never got away with anything," I

said as I slid a little further down in the chair. "I couldn't have been that bad. Now John, he had to have been a handful."

"Well, I remember the time you walked through the ballpark practicing some choice new words you'd picked up on the school bus. I heard all about it within minutes."

"Thankfully, I don't remember that, but it does go to prove my point. Uncle Roy couldn't just drop off the Bishop Hill radar without help . . . or reason." I bolted upright. "Do you think something could have happened to him—like Herb?"

"There, there," Christina said with a soothing voice. "There's no reason to think that. It hasn't been that long. I've known him to be gone far longer than this and show up just fine. Let's hold onto that thought, shall we."

"Okay," I said and settled myself back into a slight slump, mollified but still worried.

"I've still got chores to do. There's fresh chicken salad, but stay away from the cake."

"You're *not* taking cake to the opening tonight?" I said.

"Oh, no. They have Talli and her crew in charge of a nice Swedish-style buffet. No potluck for this event," Christina said.

"You mean the *gala* grand premiere," I corrected with dramatic inflection. I could still hear Marcella draw out the words in her distinctive accent and mocking tone.

I wasn't sure if my humor had sailed over Christina's head or not when she said, "Sure thing. I may even wash my car."

"That seems a bit drastic. Afraid the old Volvo wagon won't fit in with the Saabs, BMWs, or the odd Mercedes?"

"Don't be silly. David Ekollon's Mercedes has way more mileage than the Volvo—or even me." Christina produced a smile for that one.

"Oh, did I mention I met a Swedish *god* this morning?" I said. "Introduced himself as Lars something or other, I don't recall what exactly, I was too busy picking my jaw off the floor." I turned serious. "It was, like, totally embarrassing. Someone should have *warned* me." I tried my best to glare at Christina, like it was her fault. It slid right by her.

"That must be Lars Trollenberg. Is he here already? I thought he was coming next week. He's dividing his stay between host families, the Lowells down here and some other folks in the Quad Cities."

"Now, come on, Trollenberg can't be his real name," I said.

"Really? Why not?"

"Really?" I parroted. "Because Trollenberg translates to Troll Mountain. It's an old Nordic legend for one thing, and it's the title of a black-and-white horror film from the late 1950s, for another. I can't believe it's anyone's actual name."

"All I know is what they tell me," Christina said.

"And who might *they* be?" I asked.

"I guess that would be David. He made all the arrangements for the visit. No one else seemed to know much about it."

"That's certainly not typical," I mused. "Any visit from Stockholm is usually a big deal around here. Do you know anything about this small group he's supposed to represent?"

"Afraid not," Christina said.

"More oddness." I let the mystery go as I made my way to the refrigerator and the chicken salad. My appetite had returned and took the upper hand.

CHAPTER 13

That evening, I entered Nikkerbo by the front door and walked past the front desk to the soft strains of live music. A three-piece group had set up on the left side of the first and largest meeting room of the conference wing. Buffet tables decked out in blue and maize, beckoning with intriguing smells, lined the right side. Round tables draped with fresh white linen and accented with blue cloth napkins filled the center. Each table held a lavish centerpiece composed of an amber glass fairy tea light surrounded by blue and yellow flowers. Between the golden mass of flickering candles and the subdued overhead lighting reflecting off crystal wine and water glasses, the functional room had been transformed into a sparkling delight.

"Nice," I whispered, remembering the last museum to hold a grand opening in Bishop Hill. I'd been a young student excited to have an afternoon's outing away from the fourth grade. The only significant thing I recalled was the dignified and elegant presence of the King and Queen of Sweden. They made a lasting impression. Curt Hemcourt V had to take his shot at being memorable. No afternoon speeches and photo ops would do for him. After all he'd gone through to see his vision come to life, he would not be denied this moment to quite literally shine.

Christina stood at a nearby table chatting with the young Swanson family. They had their toddler, Marilyn Violet, in a high chair. I could tell Christina had been getting caught up on the baby's progress and heard her tell them, "You're so brave to bring her out tonight."

They assured her that they had chosen a table close to the exit expressly to ensure an early, easy escape.

"I won't be so lucky," Christina commented before turning to see me. Excusing herself, she looped her arm around mine and said, "I'm so glad you decided to come after all." She steered the way over to a reserved table near the podium. "I see you found something from my closet. I've always liked that suit. And wearing it with a reproduction of a Colony work shirt is a nice touch. But you could have gone with plain, unbleached muslin. Really, did you have to pick the one made out of fabric with tomatoes on it?"

"I couldn't stay home by myself," I said as we nodded to the other guests already seated, "and I always wear these ripe tomatoes to festivals and celebrations. This is a bit of both. Do we have to sit up here so close to Mr.

Hemcourt?" I whispered.

"I regret ever having Aunt Betty sew that up for you. It's so loud." Christina let a soft sigh slip through her fixed smile. "Curt wanted me close. So, yes, we are up here with Mr. and Mrs. Fisher and Curt's personal attorney and chief financial whatever in from Chicago."

I greeted the Fishers, Bishop Hill's mayor and his wife, and waited for the formal introduction to the CFO, chief financial officer. I recognized the small, pear-shaped man from the morning and struggled to keep a polite face as I tried to keep from staring at his graying reddish hair and bland grayish suit, the same one from this morning. Pondering how a day's worth of creases only added to the baggy shapelessness of an otherwise expensive garment prevented me from catching his name. I found it impossible to believe anyone this drab could come from Hemcourt's Chicago inner circle of influence. He seemed preoccupied with his own thoughts and didn't have much to say to anyone.

Christina exchanged pleasantries and polite small talk with the mayor and his wife. When our table got the cue, we rose to converge into the buffet line. While I browsed, I quietly quizzed Christina. "Curt? You're on a first name basis with Mr. Hemcourt?"

"Honey, he needed allies and I did what I could to help smooth the way, to build all this." Christina gave a small wave to our surroundings. "Some people had to be convinced. Some just had to be calmed down. We, the county as a whole and Bishop Hill in particular, needed the infusion of money and jobs this development brought in." She leaned over to me. "And that would be for you, too."

"You arranged for my job?" I hissed back.

"No, of course not. You were the most qualified and they needed another person with a degree," Christina said. She looked nervous and added, "Do try to smile. People are watching."

"But you pulled some strings?" I struck a pose with the practiced synthetic smile I had to learn when trying out for extra-curricular activities in high school.

"Oh, honey, the teeth are fine, but less chest," commented Christina.

I wanted to throw something, but passed on the impulse. Instead, I settled on piling more food on my plate than I really wanted. I knew I'd suffer tomorrow. Tomorrow was on its own.

The evening began with an opening prayer after which the pastor called for a period of silence to honor Herb Anderson. Herb was well-liked and missed by a great many people. All the speeches, including Hemcourt's, expressed that sentiment. Most of the formal remarks remained mercifully short. Hemcourt looked over at our table several times. With a sideways glance, I noticed Christina didn't shy away from the attention.

I tried closing my eyes during Hemcourt's speech; not helpful. I still hadn't adjusted to his new beardlessness. I looked forward to slipping away from the older crowd. I wanted to mingle with my own kind.

I spotted Michael across the room, seated with his mother. Since I hadn't felt comfortable enough to ask for his cell phone number yesterday, I had to wait until he looked in my direction. When he did, I glanced sideways to Christina and raised my wine glass in a silent toast to mothers. He returned the gesture and then smiled at his own mother, who never stopped chatting with her tablemate, an old friend from her quilting group. I wondered if J now stood for Juvenile. I certainly could connect with that one. The chance to commiserate couldn't happen soon enough.

Hemcourt presided over the ceremonial parting of the velvet ropes and finally everyone got a chance to enter the new museum wing and view the Hemcourt family's esteemed collection of artifacts, proof of their Colony connection. I considered it sad if someone measured their worth in terms of whether they were Swedish or not, whether they were a Colony descendant or not, or if they had a Krans painting on their wall. Last summer's job at the portrait museum had me answering the phones and handling information requests from the general public. I could refer inquiries for genealogical information to other organizations. However, when someone called to find out how they might acquire a genuine Krans work of art, I was at a total loss. No amount of money could produce a painting out of thin air. I had to assure far too many people that museums were not in the business of selling the art they were commissioned to preserve and protect for the public.

I found most of the exhibits much as I'd expected. My position last semester as an unpaid intern had gotten me into a few meetings with the consulting firm hired for the design work and installation. I considered it a privilege to be asked for my opinion, but I knew full well it wouldn't matter in the end. They would do whatever the senior partner wanted. That was how it worked.

As I walked the planned circuit through the halls and rooms, I marveled at the professional presentation. Everything was clearly labeled and the explanations understandable. Not always an easy task with some of the more sensitive issues surrounding the religious aspects of the Colony.

I stood in front of a lone Bible table, handmade to hold little else except the Swedish-language Bible centered upon it. To me it symbolized a person's right to read the Bible, to pursue individual piety, and to create a religious experience that came more from the heart than the head. A perfect demonstration of the Pietist movement as it began in Germany in the late 1600s and which had spread to Sweden by the early 1700s. The Bishop Hill Colony, founded in 1846, was late coming onto the scene, but it made up for its timing by inspiring the immigration of a great many Swedes wanting to live a better life on the American prairie.

Whatever one's interpretation of the communal group's beliefs, the founders came to the New World seeking religious freedom and the opportunity to carve out a place in what they considered a wilderness. They built on a grand scale for the time and the region, and a significant portion of it survived into the modern age, a marvel envied by many other historic communities. The Colony's second centennial would come up in my lifetime. I wondered how Bishop Hill would fare by then. I wondered where I would be.

I neared a cluster of spectators and figured that this had to be the Hemcourt Krans. The handsome Lars Trollenberg stood in front of the portrait surrounded by a group of adoring females. Lars performed gallantly and appeared to be enjoying himself. The smile he beamed in my direction was unexpected, but seemed genuine enough. I reciprocated as I buttoned my suit jacket over the garishly red tomatoes and merged into the little group.

"How nice to see you again, Miss Anderson," Lars said with his singsong Swedish accent. He added a quick, "Please excuse me, ladies."

I was surprised by this sudden shift of his full attention over to me. The group of ladies moved somewhat reluctantly toward the next exhibit while shooting disappointed looks at us from over their shoulders.

"How interesting," I said. "You're almost as popular as . . ."

I stepped closer to read the label that listed the portrait's title, *Curt Hemcourt I, 1897*, on the first line, with *Olof Krans (1838-1916)* on the second line. The other pertinent information followed: oil on canvas, 24 x 18 in., and a long list of Hemcourt family names as provenances.

"You're surprised that I'm popular?" Lars asked, a little too brightly.

". . . As the first Mr. Curt Hemcourt here."

"*Ja*, so what do you think of the painting?"

"Hold on a minute," I said, "I have to get my art expert hat on."

"Hat? I don't know what this means."

"Sorry, a figure of speech I've picked up. You see, here in Bishop Hill there are so few of us and there are so many jobs to do, we are forced to wear a great many hats. A different hat for each job. *Förstå*? Understand?"

"*Ja*, I see."

I leaned in to get a closer look and study the surface of the canvas. The wet-on-wet brushwork appeared consistent with the Krans style. The colors fell within the known range of his paint box. The condition of the canvas neared perfection. A great example of a painting preserved under ideal conditions. I wondered what Marcella had to complain about; it looked like the real deal to me. I stepped back and declared, "It looks like a fine example of his mature period."

"That's my opinion also," he said with satisfaction.

"You're familiar with this kind of art?"

"Before your portrait museum opened, members of my family helped with the cleaning and restoration of the Krans paintings taken to Sweden. The paintings had been stored in the Colony Church for many years. *Ja*."

"*Ja*. I mean yes. A less than ideal situation. I've heard stories from people. How they played among them as children. They even picked them up and moved them around to suit whatever game they had going on. We're so lucky to have as many as we do. Nearly a hundred in the portrait museum and quite a few others in private collections such as this." I gestured to the painting in front of us.

"I don't think we'd be so fortunate if today's children had a go at them. My nieces and nephews never sit still and their toys don't last long." He made a disapproving face.

"You come from a large family?"

"*Ja.*" There was no time for more talk. Ekollon came by to collect a reluctant-looking Lars and escorted him over to mingle with a group of more distinguished guests. "A pleasure to see you again," Lars said, and took his leave with a formal bow.

I turned back to the display and with a heavy heart took note of the space left vacant in the foreground. I had a clear image of the trunk on Herb's workbench. A placard explained that the family's immigrant trunk would join the display when restoration work could be completed. I knew it also involved the sheriff releasing it from a crime scene. But then what? Who would they find to finish Herb's work? Not many woodworkers measured up to his standards.

CHAPTER 14

During a lull, the crowd parted and I spied Michael standing with the techie brothers, Alan and James. I made my way in their direction.

"Good evening, gentlemen," I said, addressing the group. Thinking I knew the answer, I turned to Michael and asked, "So, what does J stand for tonight?"

"JPEG," Alan said, speaking up before Michael could answer. James pulled a wad of papers from the inner pocket of his black leather jacket and said, "*Viola!*" in his best attempt at a French accent before he unfolded them.

I could see a black-and-white male face peering out of the top page and assumed there were more versions underneath. "Awesome. You guys have made my day."

"We're so pleased to be of service, milady. Might I suggest we adjourn to a quieter location for a private viewing?" James said.

In my own poor excuse for a French accent, I said, "Definitely. I don't think my presence shall be missed one wee bit."

"Take care with what you say," Alan chimed in. "Strange forces are afoot in the village on these dark and somber nights."

"Oh, go on." I opened the door to an empty office. "Let's go in here before my feet start sticking to the floor."

The office looked more like an unfinished storage room with a haphazard assortment of boxes stacked along the wall opposite the door, with one lonely desk in the center. I put the papers down on the desk and proceeded to smooth them out. I quickly examined each printout before moving on to the next. My goal had been to combine the facial characteristics of the three known Hemson relatives painted by Olof Krans and possibly come up with one common image that might hint at what the Colony's leader had looked like. There was nothing else to go on. Stories handed down through the years said that Hemson had been disfigured by an accident. A few other accounts had him leery of being taken back to Sweden on legal matters. Whatever the truth, he had never sat for an artist, nor had a photograph taken during his lifetime.

Despite their similarities, each page in front of me held a new composite face that was very different from the next.

"Thanks for printing these out. I haven't had time to get my computer set up. Christina is still using that old relic." I found myself speaking more and more slowly, finally pausing with a sigh. "This isn't as helpful as I'd hoped." I continued to spread them further apart, trying to get a better overall view. What emerged was a rogue's gallery of dour-looking Colonist wannabes.

"We tried to tell you this wouldn't be easy," James said.

"Yeah. Like, when you use three faces there's a seriously large number of possible permutations," Alan added. "Two would have made it easier."

"Wait a minute, guys," Michael started to say. "That one over there looks like a possible—" A commotion outside drew his attention to the door as it opened and Christina entered the room.

"I've been looking all over for you," Christina said.

"What's going on out there?" I asked.

"Herb Anderson's cousin, Gordon, has had too much free wine and has gotten weepy and emotional. He wants to finish Herb's work on the trunk but can't get anyone from the sheriff's department to let him into the Varnishtree's workshop." Christina surveyed the contents of the desktop. "This one," she said as she pointed to the same one Michael had just expressed interest in. "You'd better clean this up before someone else finds you." She stared at me and added, "A certain someone who won't be so broad minded." I guessed she must have meant my boss, David "The Dragon" Ekollon.

"Right. We were just leaving, ma'am," the brothers said in unison and headed for the door. They bumped into each other as they both stopped short to hold it open for Christina to exit first.

"Come on, I'll show you what I mean," Michael said as he picked out his page and left the room. I gathered the rest together and looked for a way to get them out of sight. The sooner the better, but I didn't have my shoulder bag handy. A large, leafy planter in the hallway right outside the door would have to do. I rolled up the pages and inserted them among the foliage.

I caught up to Michael as he stood in front of the Hemcourt Krans. He discreetly held up the printout so we could compare the two without drawing too much attention.

"See," Michael said. "It could be him. Look at the eyes."

"Okay, maybe. I'd like to have better light," I said.

"Can't y'all see it for what it is?" Marcella said. She had been policing the area and held a small tub of empty wine glasses and dessert plates under her arm as she leaned on her quad cane with the other. When neither of us volunteered anything, an exasperated Marcella said, "Oh, come on, Missy. You've been around Krans paintings your whole life. Been to college and all. Take a good look at it and tell me that's the real deal."

I had no chance to answer her challenge as the regal visage of Curt Hemcourt V approached with Ekollon at his heels. Marcella spied a stray plate nearby and deftly continued with her duties. I watched her walk away, gingerly favoring her bad leg. Making meatballs and waiting tables had taken a toll on her, but taking it easy was out of the question. I never knew Marcella to ever slow down.

"Ms. Anderson," Hemcourt said smoothly. "I'm pleased you felt well enough after all your adventures to join us tonight. How do you like my family's Krans?"

This felt a shade more like a command than a question and it had me stumped for a moment, so I led with what I had already.

"The somber colors of the suit and background focus attention on the face like most of his portraits. I think the subtle blending of light and shadow around the eyes is its most striking feature. It looks like a fine example of Krans's later period, probably when he worked in Altona," I said as I regarded the details of the stern face. "What I love most is its excellent condition. That, for me, sets it apart from other pieces I've seen in museums and private collections. Whoever performed the restoration did a quality job."

"Of course they did. My father had that done in the late 1960s. Well before the time I came to appreciate my roots in the Old World. I was a callous youth back then and couldn't be bothered about my heritage. It took years and some maturity before I came around and began serious scholarly study." He flashed a photo-op smile briefly before growing more serious. "I'm sorry my father didn't live long enough to see our family's return to Bishop Hill, the place in America where it all began for us. This would mean so much for him." Hemcourt reached into his tuxedo pocket to produce a small object, silently gazed at it for a second, and then slipped it back in. I hadn't gotten a good look at it. Ekollon, at his elbow, offered to take yet another publicity photo.

"Not now," Hemcourt said, and curtly excused himself to continue with the business at hand, mingling with potential museum patrons and future customers, Ekollon behind him like a silent shadow.

"Wow," I whispered to Michael. "What was that all about?"

"You haven't heard the story? It's been everywhere."

"No, so sue me. I've been up to my eyeballs in studying, finishing papers, and trying to graduate."

"Sorry, my bad," he said. "The callous youth he just referred to was probably responsible for a fire in the family home in a posh Chicago suburb. That charred coin is a memento."

"Where was this painting?"

"I think they said it was hanging somewhere else, in an office. Maybe. I'm not sure. Lucky break. Lots of smoke damage to the house."

I looked at the painting and then stared thoughtfully at Hemcourt's receding back. Across the room, Marcella caught my eye and nodded. I shrugged my shoulders. Marcella must be seeing only what she wanted to see.

"What are you doing tomorrow?" Michael inquired.

"Gosh, I don't know. Sleep in. Make blueberry pancakes. Catch up on things. Sleep some more. Why?"

"How about coming over tomorrow afternoon for a visit with Great Auntie? She still wants to talk to you. Mom's okay with it. As long as you're up to it. Around one?"

"Sounds fine. I can make it."

After the crowd had thinned out, I went looking for Christina to let her know I was exhausted and couldn't stay any longer. Finding her talking with Hemcourt, Ekollon, and the doleful little man in the baggy suit, I decided to hang back and wait for a better opportunity to get her alone. I didn't have to wait long before Hemcourt continued his rounds with his little entourage tagging along a pace or two behind.

"That little man with Mr. Hemcourt, do you know his name?" I asked.

"It's something Swedish, but unusual. I can't remember what it was."

"It sounded like Goober, but that can't be right. He certainly doesn't talk much. What does he do, exactly?"

"His law firm has something to do with the financial side of Curt's business. I only heard him referred to as chief financial something or other. Curt wasn't expecting him. That's how he came to be at our table. Both Curt and the goober man seemed stressed out this evening."

"Hmm, chief financial officer, that means money," I said. "Do you think Mr. Hemcourt is having money problems? Like, maybe that's why he's making such an effort to promote the conference center tonight."

"He told me that he'd like to break even in five years."

"Wow," I said. "That seems kind of ambitious. We *are* in the middle of a cornfield."

Christina showed no sign of appreciation for the humor and asked, "Are you getting ready to leave?"

"Yes. I wondered if you were, too."

"Maybe in a bit. I still have someone I need to talk to."

"About Uncle Roy?" No answer, but the sour expression said to leave it be. "Okay. I'm going. See you later."

I reached my car and fumbled in a jacket pocket for the keys. Nothing in that pocket or the other. I balanced my shoulder bag on the hood of the car and continued the search. Finally, success. I fished the elusive keys from a bottom corner. I held the car key in my hand, ready to put it in the lock, but something nagged at my subconscious. I stood there slowly poking at the contents of my bag. Something wasn't right, but I couldn't make it out. My mind worked like that occasionally. It seemed more difficult to puzzle out the something that should be there but was missing. I gasped when I realized the search had been for the computer printouts. Of all the things to lose track of right under Ekollon's twitchy nose. If Christina was right about some descendants not understanding about my little project, he would be at the head of the line. I had to go back in and find them before he did.

I hustled along the corridor and turned a corner only to find Ekollon materialize in front of me. "Ms. Anderson. Where are you going in such a hurry? Is there a problem?"

"I've, uh, lost track of something. Nothing important, but I didn't want it thrown away by the cleaning crew," I said, slightly out of breath and disappointed by my lack of luck.

"Looking for something. Hmmm. Perhaps it could be

these?" He pulled the rolled-up printouts from inside his coat, watching my reaction the whole time. "Most interesting. They appear to be variations on a common theme. Krans paintings, perhaps? Although none I can ever recall seeing."

I felt defeated and small with no ready lie coming to mind. "Yes. My friends and I were exploring the possibilities of what other Krans portraits might look like," I said, trying to mask my nervousness with a weak attempt at evasion. "They know a lot more about computers and programming than I do. There are ways to merge and morph images. It's all beyond me, but—"

"Spare me the details. It seems like a frivolous endeavor for a serious scholar. You are a serious scholar, are you not, Ms. Anderson?"

"Yes, sir. You see, I collect old photos and such and this seemed—"

"I found this one quite interesting," he said as he held up a page by its corner. "It bears an ever-so-slight resemblance to the distinguished Hemcourt ancestor over there in the Krans painting, or maybe it could be one of mine. I can't decide. What do you think?"

"Oh, I don't know . . ."

"Take your time and examine it closely," he said coolly. "What do you think?" He held the page closer this time.

"Well, maybe a little." I tried not to physically squirm. "They all have such serious expressions. It's hard to say. But really . . . honestly . . . no, not so much."

"And what do you think of our museum's fine example

of serious-looking primitive folk art?" He gestured toward the still-lit Krans display. "Do be frank, Ms. Anderson."

I could feel the blood rush to my cheeks as I stammered, "Well, it's interesting—"

"Interesting!" He nearly spat the word. "That's not a very high recommendation from an expert. You are an expert, are you not, Ms. Anderson?"

"Hardly, sir." I could feel the hot breath of his disdain bearing down on me.

"Come, come, now. You're poised on the ladder. You can't wait to climb to the top of your field. You want to become *the* expert, don't you?"

Bracing myself, I felt his hissy fit building momentum.

"Well, young lady, you're correct about one thing, you certainly *aren't* qualified to be considered an expert. And the way you're going with these silly pictures, you'll never be taken seriously. I can't believe I spent so much time on your training last summer. What a waste." He let the pages slide to the floor and stalked away muttering, "*I'm* the one everyone turns to first. It'll never be *you*."

I stooped down, gathered the papers, and exited as quickly as possible. On the drive home, I tried to figure out what had happened. I was still alive. Probably still worked there. But what was that last bit about wasting his time on me? Sure, he gave me extra work to do, but I figured it was more about him wanting a break. And wanting his job . . . he couldn't be more wrong. I would do so much better.

CHAPTER 15

Sunday, June 1, 2008

I woke up in a panic and a tangle of bed linen, the disturbing dream already unraveling around the edges and fading. The clock told me I'd slept late and needed to get up and going if I was to make my one o'clock appointment with Pearl. I showered and rummaged around my closet until I found something agreeable enough to wear. The pickings were light. My car had to get unpacked and soon. I couldn't keep borrowing from Christina.

Walking into the kitchen, I stepped on a moist clump of something dark and foul-looking. "Did you forget to take your barn boots off again?" I asked Christina, who stood at the counter fussing with a large mixing bowl.

"That's from weeding the flower bed next to the back

door. When I heard you were up, I rushed to get these muffins started. I didn't pay attention to my shoes until I noticed the trail. I'll clean it up later."

I assumed my usual spot at the oval table. "Any sign of Uncle Roy yet?"

Christina shook her head and kept herself busy.

"Have you been looking for him?"

"No," Christina said with a distracted tone. "I'll walk around the cabins later. Maybe go down by the river."

"Maybe we should—"

"Honey, I don't need your help with this," Christina snapped.

"Yeah, right." I shrank back from the blast. "I'm sorry," I said with a sulking tone.

"Oh, let's not start the day this way. Please." Christina took a muffin pan out of the oven and replaced it with another. "Deputy Dana Johnson has been driving by on a regular basis. It's very unsettling. I decided to give her a couple of muffins on her next pass. If nothing else, it might make me feel better. At least, I can hope so."

I regretted my lack of patience. A few fragments of the dream still clung to me and I decided to use them as a peace offering of sorts. "I woke up having a really weird dream. I was trapped in an old building, an old Victorian house maybe, one with a lot of rooms. I couldn't get out because the doors kept changing shapes and sizes and wouldn't open. I think they started out as doors. They transformed into more box-like things with lids that wouldn't open. Anyway, it all shifted back to a house before I woke up." I left out the part about the house having a hidden secret space. How I had to climb up a twisty flight of stairs looking into a lot of creepy spaces before catching a glimpse of a dark scary figure at the very top. That's when I was jolted awake.

"Have you had dreams like this before?"

"Yeah, but not quite this intense and never anything with boxes and lids." I always assumed the main symbolism involved a searching journey. And I had a pretty good handle on what to do about that.

"Sounds like something fresh-out-of-the-oven muffins will fix right up." Christina set a plateful in front of me.

"Awesome, blueberry." I smiled and recalled warm memories of muffins past as I broke one apart before Christina could supply the knife and butter. After eating one and feeling revived and more relaxed, I decided to ask a benign question. "What did you think of last night's gala?"

"I thought it went quite well," Christina said as she continued working at the counter. "They had a good turnout and everyone left happy. With the exception of Herb's cousin, Gordon, that is. His wife coaxed him out not too long after I found you in the office. What was your take on the *gala* event of the season?"

"Like you said, it seemed like quite the social hit. But it turned kind of strange for me. First, the Hemcourt Krans. I can only describe it as . . . too perfect. I don't know why it bothers me, but it does."

"I'm sure it's nothing," Christina said, probably

sounding more cautious than she'd like to.

"Second, Ekollon. I tried to hide the computer printouts the guys gave me, but he found them and went ballistic."

"Oh, dear," Christina said with her worried-mother look, and sat down across the table. "What happened?"

"You were so right about some people still being sensitive about anything involving Hemson. Even though Ekollon didn't mention Hemson by name, he was mega-peeved and really chewed me out for trying to come up with Krans-like images. I'm going to have to be extra careful the rest of the summer. I'd like a solid reference."

"Sounds like a good plan. So, you're not a fan of the Krans portrait of Curt's ancestor?"

"The brush work and technique looked good enough, genuine, but again, its condition seemed so utterly perfect."

"You make it sound like a bad thing," Christina said, fussing with the crumbs on the table. She swept them off into her hand and rose to walk them over to the waste basket. She took the opportunity to check the oven before sitting back down.

"According to Michael," I continued, "the Hemcourt family home suffered a lot of damage from a fire. He said newspaper articles placed the painting somewhere else. I certainly didn't see any sign of smoke damage, but the lighting wasn't meant for close inspection."

"The fire started in an electrical outlet in the den," Christina said. "Curt doesn't like to talk about it."

"He had something in his pocket. Small. A coin, maybe?

It seemed important to him. Sentimental."

"Oh, yes. Curt's shown it to me. Not much to look at. Just an old nickel he found in the ashes of a burnt desk. His father's health went downhill afterward and I get the impression it still weighs heavy on his mind."

"Yeah, he mentioned his father last night. I suppose that's why he's here."

"Okay, for the sake of argument, if the painting had been in the house during the fire," Christina pondered, "could it have been cleaned up so well that no one, not even a professional, could tell?"

"Maybe, but I have my doubts. Such as they are." My burst of enthusiasm slumped along with my posture.

"What do you mean?" The oven timer went off and Christina had to get up again to remove the pan from the oven.

"Oh, nothing," I said with a sigh. "It's just that Ekollon made it crystal clear last night that I was a small-time nobody and would probably stay that way."

"Really." Christina had exasperation in her voice. She walked over to the spot on the counter piled high with accumulated mail and picked out a couple of pieces. "A small-time nobody wouldn't be getting letters from places like these." She waved the unopened envelopes in the air.

"About that, I've been meaning to talk to you. I really want to go to a good grad school. I know it'll probably be far away and expensive, but I'll look really good with an advanced degree in museum studies. I've been working with the financial aid office from one in particular . . . to straighten out the money situation. I know I can make it happen with enough help."

"Okay, show me your numbers," Christina said.

I'd been dreading this moment for so long that hearing a simple "Show me your numbers" totally took me by surprise. A quick look at the time threw me another curve and forced me to beg off. "Can it wait until this afternoon? I promised Pearl I'd be there at one and I need to get going. The old schoolteacher in her still likes people to be punctual."

"All right, but tonight for sure." Christina went back to her muffins.

"Yes, ma'am." I pushed my chair back and inadvertently stepped on another clump of dirt. I looked at the smashed clod. It didn't look right; the wrong color for any of the flower beds I knew of.

Christina had her back turned as she prepared the care package for the deputy and didn't see the suspicious look that came across my face.

Again, I didn't have the time or energy to face my packed car, so I opted for a brisk walk into the village instead. I needed the air and, after last night's buffet line, the exercise.

Retracing the path I took on Friday presented little trouble, since it hadn't rained again. I heard the sound of a lawn mower and assumed someone had gotten a head start on their neighbor. Sure enough, off in the distance another mower echoed the sounds of the first. I smiled; life in Bishop Hill went on as usual.

The Lutfisk Café had a healthy after-church crowd, but most of the shops in the village still hovered in a peaceful pre-tourist lull.

As I passed by the café, someone waved at me from a crowded picnic table on the front porch. Even though I couldn't make out the face, I returned the friendly gesture and stayed my course toward the old brick sidewalk by the Colony Church. This section had interested me ever since I noticed the variations in the brickwork. While not random, the pattern shifted enough to make me wonder how many hands had been at work here, perhaps a whole crew, or merely one person over four or five days. If only one, then he had gotten a little lazy or distracted. Or perhaps an ever-practical foreman insisted on an increasingly frugal use of materials. Whatever the story, I now had to watch the walkway for another reason. A brick here or there would mysteriously pop out of place. I likened it to natural selection at work in the world of brick sidewalks: only the fittest survived.

My head popped up as a distant voice finally registered. I looked back to see Lars hurrying to catch up. I nervously looked around to make sure he indeed called to me.

"Good afternoon," he called out again in his rhythmically accented English.

"*Hej! God dag,*" I replied in my clumsy Swedish.

"Please, English," he said when he had caught up to me. "I need the practice."

"Sorry," I said. "You've heard just about all the Swedish

I've got anyway. I took evening language classes in the basement of the Swedish archive building as a kid, but I was there more for the snacks and coffee laced with lots of cream and sugar. It's a wonder I ever got to sleep on those nights." I felt pangs of embarrassment and regretted spewing out too much information.

He smiled broadly, "*Ja*, very good. I'm on my way to the archive building now, to help with translating a letter. We can walk together."

I reciprocated his smile. He didn't appear to sense my discomfort, or, if he did, he chose to ignore it. A kindness or a gentlemanly act, either way, it offered pleasant relief from feeling flustered by the attentions of such a good-looking guy. "Sure. I'm on my way to Pearl Anderson's house."

"Is she the elderly lady from that bad business out by the highway?"

"Yes." I hoped he would let it go without wanting any specific details.

"Where is her house?"

"Not far. In fact, it's past the archives and around the corner from the water tower. Anyway, isn't it a nice day for a walk?"

"*Ja*, very much so." Lars fell into step with me. "I hope you find her well."

"She must be doing well or I wouldn't have gotten this chance to visit."

"It's terrible what happened to her. And to you also. Finding that poor man dead. How are you doing after such a terrible shock?"

I was taken aback enough to pause and admit I really couldn't say for sure. Certainly, getting caught up on sleep helped. But wasn't I inventing ways to keep disturbing memories at bay—waking up in a cold sweat from a weird dream, thinking Christina might be up to something involving Uncle Roy, counting bricks in the sidewalk. Such things might not be considered normal. Last night at the reception, whenever anyone asked me that question, I gave a stock "I'm fine," as I wanted to do now. I changed my mind and said, "Well, I guess I'm getting by as best as I can." I would have to give it more consideration. Later.

Across the street, a display of boxes in the Blacksmith Shop window caught my eye, and I used it to steer the conversation in another direction. "Gordon Anderson has a studio space over there. Did you meet him last night?"

"Mr. Ekollon introduced me to so many people. Too many to remember. That's why it's so nice to see you again. You I remember."

I willed myself not to make anything of that last bit. "Gordon is Herb's cousin. Or was his cousin." I felt a flush of heat rise up my neck and hoped my cheeks weren't turning red as well.

"The gray-haired man with the weary eyes who had to leave. Too much to drink, I think. He got very loud about his sadness."

"That's a good way to describe it." Struggling to wrestle my feelings under control, I forged ahead. "Gordon's an excellent woodworker in his own right. He's also a painter who's shown tremendous improvement over the years. I'm told his paintings are selling much better since he adopted a Krans-like style."

"He copies Olof Krans paintings?"

"Oh no, I didn't mean it that way. He uses the simple, less sophisticated technique of someone who's self-taught, *like* Krans. Several artists around here have tried primitive styles over the years. Usually the landscapes sell very well, but not the portraits. But you'd expect as much."

"Why is that?"

"Come on," I chided. "You know how those portraits look. There's a limited market for that kind of dour seriousness." I sucked in my cheeks and glowered sternly.

Lars chuckled. "*Ja*, but not for the original Krans paintings. There's always keen interest in those."

"Very true. All the local families who didn't keep their originals are not happy campers."

"I don't understand." Lars looked confused.

"During his lifetime, Olof Krans gave a lot of his paintings away as gifts. It's said that when some folks grew tired of their paintings, they just threw them away. After he died, some of his paintings sold for as low as a dollar each at the estate sale. Rolled-up canvases went for a quarter, if they sold at all."

"How sad. They are so valuable now," Lars said. "The close and familiar cannot always be appreciated until it's too late." He shook his head at the thought of the waste.

A vague sense of personal uneasiness signaled a need to change the subject again. "Have you been in that building?" I pointed out the imposing stucco façade of the Steeple Building.

"Not yet."

"Be sure to check out the wooden floor boards in the first floor hallway when you do."

"Why look at a floor?"

"They used coffee to stain some replacement boards to make them look old," I said.

"*Ja*, we do that too," he said as he led the way across a nearly vacant Main street. A single car turned at the corner and made its way toward The Lutfisk. "Ah, coffee. Where would we be without it? Asleep all day, I think." He grinned at his joke.

"I certainly would," I said, chuckling as we walked on. "Seriously, I may laugh, we may laugh, but the records show the Colonists placed the highest priority on having ample supplies of coffee."

"All that and you still can't make a good cup."

"Ouch, that hurt," I said, donning a pained expression. "Oh, of course, you're one of those people, aren't you?"

"What do you mean?" he said, with an air of distress.

"You're one of those Swedes who *adds* instant coffee to what Talli makes. She keeps a jar tucked behind the Bunn machine just for you people." I playfully bumped my fist at his muscular arm.

He held his arm in make-believe pain. "It's true. I confess. She found it for me. I think it's time for a truce. I'm here."

"It was nice seeing you again," I said with sincere

warmth. "Good luck with your translation."

Lars seemed to respond with an equally warm tone. "Thank you. Until we meet again, my best regards to your family. I hope your uncle is safe. And your brother, John, is also well."

I thought it cute that he pronounced John's name with the Swedish Y in place of the J. I smiled as I watched him cross the street and disappear into the archive building. Turning right and going down the side street, I got to the wooden water tower before it registered; I hadn't talked about my brother last night or now. Lars would certainly have heard gossip about Uncle Roy at the opening, but not about John. I puzzled on it for a bit and then dismissed it. Someone must have mentioned I had a twin brother awaiting deployment to the Middle East. If he could remember extraneous bits of information like that, he'd make a great politician someday.

╬ PEARL ╬

Summer 1915

"They call me Painter Krans in newspaper stories," he said, with a flourish of his brush. "*Ja,* a house painter by trade. A portrait painter by duty." He pointed the brush at Pearl Essie. "I set the story of the Colony in paint for all to see, to remember."

Pearl Essie often heard him testify about the need to record the severe faces of all the silent old ones, those who sacrificed so much to come to this new country, to verify their existence as fact. She wondered what it would be like to see through the eyes of a newly arrived immigrant. She looked out the window and tried to imagine the houses and streets of Altona looking foreign and strange. The effort failed. She couldn't distance herself from the familiar landmarks of her life.

Krans spoke again of his satisfaction that his paintings of the Colony's struggle to establish itself on the American prairie found approval by the other old settlers. For this, the Galva newspaper called him "Genius Krans."

"Too many titles." His hand formed a fist around his brush and the studio echoed his words.

"What do you mean?" she asked, worried that he'd lost his temper. Momma told her to leave if she began to annoy him.

"I'm sorry, my *liten Pärla*. I didn't mean to frighten you. I was just thinking how strange life can be. We must do our best. *Ja*. The Prophet would demand no less of us."

She sighed to herself. Not another lecture about Karl Hemson. Another thing to be endured.

To her relief, he launched into another retelling of his trip to Chicago and meeting the rich patron. He lived so far away. Yet this important businessman had heard about Olof Krans and the paintings he'd created for the Colony's first reunion gathering that marked its fiftieth anniversary in 1896.

CHAPTER 16

Sunday, June 1, 2008 — 1 p.m.

I turned south again at the next corner. The county museum on my right once served as a school building with multiple classrooms and a gym. It was the modern successor to the original Colony School located a couple of blocks away.

Pearl's teaching career had begun with all of her students lumped together into the one main room of the Colony School building. She taught there until consolidation closed that school and all the other small rural schools. At that time, the closest students came into the village to the larger modern building. Years later, when the powers that be decided the students had to move on again, this time to Galva, Pearl chose not to go with them. She retired to a small house down the street.

I stopped in front of the neat blue bungalow and took a moment to take in the view. Past the house, a pile of tree trimmings signaled the abrupt end of the street. Further on, the fields opened up to a panorama of flat, fertile Midwestern farmland. From where I stood, I could just barely make out distant traffic passing on Highway 34. Closer in, a tractor traced a geometric pattern cultivating the rich black soil for this year's crop of corn, or maybe soybeans; I couldn't tell at this distance. At least the farmer wasn't spraying. Just out of sight to the far left, Varnishtree's barn stood vacant. I experienced a dull ache in the middle of my chest, as if my heart had dropped out, leaving behind a hollow void. Why Herb?

I dabbed at moist eyes and nose with a tissue and turned to the house. I hoped I'd arrived close to the appointed time. It would be a shame to annoy the old teacher by being tardy.

Amy Anderson, Pearl's grandniece-in-law and main caretaker, met me at the door and escorted me into a living room comfortably furnished with overstuffed chairs, a sofa, and a small TV set. The book-lined walls might have given the room a too-dark aspect if not for the many floor lamps. Amy politely inquired if she could get me a cup of coffee. Coffee, the cure for all things. I kept the secret of my amused smile to myself and extended one last opportunity to gracefully back out of this meeting, "Are you sure she wants to see me?"

"She's talked about nothing else since Friday. When is that little girl coming? Is she here yet?" Amy said.

"Actually, it's been a blessing. She's been so alert, so much like her old self, it made a great diversion. It kept her mind off what happened to Herb. I really didn't want to talk about that."

I nodded in agreement and let Amy guide me over to a table set for three. Each delicate bone china cup and saucer set had a different floral pattern, as if they were souvenirs collected at different times, in different places. A tray of spritz cookies shared the center along with a vase of flowers that glowed in the sunlight of the nearby window. "Has anyone been here to take her statement?" I asked as we settled into carved walnut chairs.

"Sheriff Henry came himself."

"What did Pearl say? Anything different?"

"Not really. She repeated the same story I've heard since Friday. She woke up to see the cross in the sky and it drew her out of the house. She thought she was driving her father's flatbed truck down to the old barn. She's still suspicious about someone else owning the barn. She doesn't recall the sale and thinks something fishy is going on. She told the sheriff to investigate that." Amy shrugged her shoulders. "I guess that's good. I don't know. Anyway, the sheriff thanked us and left his card in case something new popped into her mind."

I thought I caught a glimpse of movement in the bedroom. A hospital bed had been added for Pearl's comfort and convenience. Her head was propped up by a couple of pillows. She appeared to doze peacefully with a log cabin quilt covering her legs. Her thin, frail chest slowly rose and fell with each shallow breath.

"She usually takes a nap now," Amy explained.

"I hate to disturb her."

A familiar voice called out from the bedroom. "There's no need to fuss over me. I'm awake. Come help me with this cover and find my slippers."

Soon Pearl emerged from her bedroom in a pink floral house dress and white cardigan, her thin white hair swept into her signature top-knot bun. A few wisps escaped to hang limply over her collar. She pushed a walker under her own power with Amy a hovering shadow beside her. Pearl made her way to the table. However small and frail she appeared to be, she still had an underlying reserve of strength and stability.

"I don't need this walker," Pearl said as she sat down. "They won't give me my cane back."

"The doctor wants you to wait a while," Amy said patiently. She obviously had repeated the same line many times already. She nudged Pearl's chair into place before retaking her seat.

"I had that dream again, just now," Pearl began as Amy poured the coffee. "I'm ten and visiting old man Krans."

"That would have been the summer of 1915, in Altona," I commented more to myself than anyone else in the room.

If Pearl heard, she didn't acknowledge it. She continued, "He didn't mind my coming. Others were a bother, but not me. I watched quietly. Stayed out of his way. He loved to talk and relive the past while he worked."

"Did he speak in English or Swedish?" I asked with a little more volume.

"He used English to tell how the fancy patron found him after the Colony's fiftieth anniversary reunion. The patron paid for Krans to travel to Chicago. By train. Bought everything: canvas, brushes, fat tubes of paint. Quite the experience for Krans. The man even sat for his portrait."

"It must have been a special treat," I said. "By necessity, he usually worked from calendar pages and early photographs. That's one of the reasons I got interested in black-and-white photography." I fell silent and hoped I hadn't said too much. I had to encourage Pearl to keep talking.

"You're right. I forgot about his photos." Pearl paused and reflected for a moment before continuing. "He was making another painting of the same man. Boasted how well the eyes turned out this time. Deep, soulful eyes . . . mesmerizing." Pearl tapped the table with her finger. "His boasting made him worry. Too much pride is a sin according to the Prophet." Pearl rolled her eyes and threw her hands up in mock exasperation. "I didn't want a lecture. I had such a time sitting still. But the portrait captured my imagination, so I pretended to listen. I was such a willful thing back then. Momma couldn't keep me out of the cookies." A distracted Pearl took a present-day spritz cookie, dipped it into her cup, and raised the softened morsel to her lips.

I wanted to ask questions about dates, names, anything

to pry out more information, but a slight head-shake from Amy stopped me. Amy merely waited, then offered a simplified, "What happened next?"

Pearl, ever the lady, politely finished the cookie, sipped her coffee, and wiped away some lingering crumbs before speaking again.

"Well, you won't believe what happened next," Pearl said. "Momma, *Mormor*, and old Auntie Sophia came in. She wasn't a real aunt, you know. *Mormor*, my grandmother, taught me to call her auntie on account of her being one of the old ones, a Colonist. Auntie Sophia always had her hair done up in tight braids that crossed over the top of her head. She wore the same shirtwaist and long skirt common to all from the old country. The only modern thing was a gingham apron." Pearl nodded to herself and chuckled.

Amy and I waited patiently for Pearl to resume her story.

"Krans greeted them in Swedish. He turned to the painting and began to retell the story of his grand adventure in Chicago." Pearl made a fist and struck the table hard enough to rattle the cups in their saucers and give Amy and me a jolt. "Auntie stopped right there, dead in her tracks, with her mouth wide open. Not a sound came out at first." She paused for dramatic effect. "She found her voice all right. It rose higher and higher, until it hurt my ears." Pearl demonstrated by placing cupped hands over her ears for a moment. "Then that old woman flung herself at the painting, scratching and clawing. Those perfect eyes looking straight ahead, seeing nothing." Pearl stopped to let the image soak in before pointing a finger at us to emphasize the finish. "She ran away with Momma and *Mormor* chasing after her, calling in Swedish, '*Stoppa! Stoppa!*'"

Pearl reached for another cookie while Amy and I exchanged baffled glances. Amy waited until the cookie disappeared and Pearl had sipped more coffee before coaxing her on with, "And then?"

"The old man shook. He stared at the painting for the longest time. Finally, he said, 'She was tormented by ghosts from long ago. No one must ever know.' I had to make my promise. Never to say a word about what I saw Auntie Sophia do." Pearl solemnly put a hand over her heart now as she must have done as a child back then. "He repaired the painting, brought back its glory. I was good to my word. I never told a soul—until now."

"And why now?" Amy asked.

"The cross in the sky means I have to find it." Pearl exhaled a heavy sigh. "Only I don't know where it is. The old man would show it to me if I begged. But one day he lifted the canvas off its frame and rolled it up. He died the next winter." She stopped the narrative and gazed wistfully off into the long-ago past.

Before she could draw Pearl back, Amy became distracted by a dog barking outside. "I'm sorry. That's Sadie. Michael leaves her here sometimes. Pearl really loves that dog. I'll see what she's gotten into. It won't take but a minute."

I sat at the table at a loss for what to say. Amy made it quite clear that she didn't want any mention of Herb or the traumatic events of Friday. However, I wished she had something more substantial to back up the story. Pearl had started out talking about having a dream.

At that moment, Pearl shifted back to the present as if she detected my dilemma. "I remember the name," she said with an impish smile.

"What name?"

"The fancy patron from Chicago," Pearl said with confidence. "Hencourt."

"How?" I gasped.

"I had a pet rooster back then. Ate out of my hand. That puffed-up bird held court in a yard full of chickens—hens—Hencourt."

I couldn't do anything but stare with unblinking eyes and bring my hand up to cover my gaping mouth. The similarity between Hencourt and Hemcourt was too great to be a coincidence. Pearl not only provided a link between the Hemcourt family and the portrait Olof Krans painted in 1897, but perhaps to another portrait painted of the same man, Curt Hemcourt I, in the summer of 1915.

As if instructing a student, Pearl said, "I'll be 104 in November. I can't get around like I used to. It's up to you, my dear. You must find that painting. Its time has come." The plate of cookies drew renewed interest. Outside, Amy had Sadie pacified and reached the back door. By the time she sat back down at the table, Pearl had switched the conversation to inquire about Christina, whom she still called Teeny. I had to give this old lady credit for an altogether inspiring performance.

CHAPTER 17

Monday, June 2, 2008

The next morning I stepped into The Lutfisk Café and leveled my bleary gaze on the three glass pots arranged on the Bunn machine. Trying to judge which pot might hold the freshest, most potent brew this early just wasted time; I did it anyway. After the late night, my brain was on autopilot. Michael J. Anderson came up next to me. His disembodied voice drifted into my muffled zone of awareness. "Don't look now, but the aliens who tried to abduct you last night need to come back and finish the job." It added an irritating new dimension to my bad mood.

"Oh, how funny," I said, and censored my thoughts on what the J stood for today. "What are you doing here? Is your night shift over already?" I picked the fullest pot, poured for myself, and offered to top off his cup with a nod of my head.

He held his hand over his cup. "I'm going decaf," he said. "I put in my time. I'm here to wheedle some lingonberry pancakes out of Talli before I go home to crash."

"She give in yet?"

"Yup, she did. I'll share," he offered. "Diet or not, you look like you could use some carbs." He motioned with his cup in the direction of my tousled hair.

I got his meaning and decided to join him for spite as well as Talli's version of Swedish pancakes. We made our way past the centrally placed rectangular farmer tables to a round one in the back corner. Out-of-the-way favored my ill temper this morning.

Settling into the padded chair, I began sipping my coffee and didn't stop until half the cup disappeared. Heaving a caffeinated sigh of relief, I volunteered some information to a mercifully silent Michael. "I was up most of the night doing research, mostly on the Hemcourt family's Krans portrait. I found a few pertinent online newspaper and magazine articles about it. There was a lot more on the fire, as you might expect with rich folks losing a big chunk of an expansive house. Reading between the lines, I'd guess our Mr. Hemcourt V may indeed have some atoning to do. Interesting point, as far as I can tell: all the articles placing the painting at the corporate headquarters were dated well after the fire."

I paused my report to stare at my coffee cup before

taking another deep drink. I didn't want to mention the additional hours I'd spent fretting over the collapse of all my immediate hopes for the future. I'd finally opened my accumulated mail. That included the financial-aid letter Uncle Roy had pilfered and I had stolen back. I read their meager offer. It might as well have been a rejection.

"I crashed sometime after three. Christina and I keep missing each other. She was gone again by the time I got up, so I came over here."

For once, I had welcomed the stillness in the house; it meant I had some breathing room and time to adjust to the bad news. As of yet, I had no alternate plans.

Talli came over and placed a plate of large, rolled-up pancakes before each of us. "I heard you guys talking. I had enough batter for two orders, but I'm out of lingonberries. Used 'em up yesterday. I asked Marcella to bring in her backup jar this morning. No luck on that. I'll bring the syrup by in a minute." Before leaving she pulled a sympathy card and a pen out of her apron pocket and placed them on the table. "The card's for Herb's family. He came in here most mornings."

After Talli walked away, I asked, "So, did you think you might run into me here?"

"Why would you think that? How would I know you'd be here?"

"This is the heart of the community. Talli keeps track of all of us for all kinds of reasons." I gave the card a little wave. It was already filled with so many names I had to sign it near the bottom before handing it across the table.

"Your mom put you up to it, didn't she? To see what I found out."

He muttered a noncommittal, "Oh?" as he added his signature to the card. "About what?" He looked totally innocent for Talli's benefit as she dropped off the syrup and retrieved the card and pen.

I wasn't taken in by his acting and whispered a challenging, "Oh, come on. You know all about Pearl's story, about Krans hiding a painting, a possible second Hemcourt portrait, back in the summer of 1915. He died the following winter, so it might have been one of his last ever."

"Mom never called it a Hemcourt Krans," he said in a subdued undertone and began to pour a generous amount of syrup around his plate.

"Aha! So your mom did tell you Pearl's story about the Krans." I caught myself and lowered my voice. "Your mom missed that part where Pearl remembered a name. Sadie was outside barking at something or other."

"So what?" he whispered back. "Great Auntie could be making stuff up because the names Hemcourt and Krans have been plastered all over the place. Instead of remembering something that happened, what?" He paused as he ran the numbers in his head. "Over 90 years ago? Her mind just did a cut and paste. How can anyone remember that accurately, over that length of time? It's not natural."

I kept my voice low as I explained, "Pearl remembered a name because it made her think about a pet rooster in a pen with other chickens—a court of hens—Hencourt. It provided a nice vivid image and that's the key." I opened two butter packets and spread them over my pancakes. "Hencourt and Hemcourt are practically the same. And I've actually worked at improving my memory. I found a book that taught me a few tricks. I made it a game. Making up visual cues is very old, very reliable." I took my turn with the syrup and poured a modest amount on the side of my plate. I was counting calories this morning, not that he should care.

Michael shrugged his shoulders with a look of feigned indifference. "Okay, sure, she told me about this hidden painting. It goes with what you said on Friday. But really, you shouldn't be buying into this story. There probably isn't anything to it, just another Bishop Hill legend."

"I reread some of my books on Krans last night and he did make duplicate paintings, maybe for sales or maybe just to get something right. He also had a few popular themes he revisited often. His work as a whole improved a great deal over the course of his career. So it's possible there's unknown and unsigned work out there other than his animal paintings." I cut into my pancakes and forked up a piece.

"Again, so what?"

"So, your mom wants it." I left the crude, brief statement hang there as I savored my first bite.

I watched his brow furrow and his jaw tighten as he fought to suppress his annoyance. "Well, who wouldn't? If something like that really turned up, it would be worth a truckload of cash."

Pacing myself between smaller mouthfuls, I continued to provoke him. "But only to the rightful owner. I bet there'd be folks coming out of the woodwork trying to lay claim to it. Or even a little piece of it. If it should ever show up."

Michael wasn't so busy with his own plate that he'd pass up making a point. "Okay, the Hemcourt family, especially if they can prove it's a second portrait of their guy, but who else?"

"Pearl, as an eyewitness, provides provenance, proof of origin, so that's your family. The first Roy Landers, Uncle Roy's great-grandfather, was the last documented assistant to Krans, so that's bound to draw my family in somehow. I don't know about any direct Krans descendants." I surveyed the bottom of my cup before swallowing the last sip of coffee. "Now, let's see . . . we can't forget the state. They have a significant investment in Bishop Hill in general and they're so deep in debt they'd be desperate enough to grab at any straw with a potential payout. And there's Ekollon."

"Why would he get into this?"

"Authenticating a colossal find like an unknown Krans would give him a golden reputation in his little niche of the art world."

"And wouldn't it do the same for your reputation?"

He had me with that. Game over. I hunched forward, hovering over the table with my head in my hand. "Yeah, and mine, too. If only I had a reputation to start with." My ego flat-lined once again and I pushed the last few fragments of pancake around my plate before continuing. "I got around to opening my mail last night. I didn't get the financial aid package I needed." I paused to collect my composure. "I don't see how I can go to grad school now." I sat back and gazed into my empty cup, wishing for more—more of everything.

Michael took in my news and change in attitude and went with it. "So, if you found this painting first, it would give you a ticket out of Hicksville."

"Don't make it sound so crass." I straightened up and squared my shoulders. "Haven't you ever wanted to get away from here? Check out the wide world that's just waiting for us to kick this dust off our feet and participate. Come on, we can make a difference. Leave a mark. We can show them we're not just any old small town . . . " Suddenly self-conscious, I let my tirade fade away. I scanned the room and was relieved to see we had the place to ourselves. A rare situation for any morning and deeply appreciated now.

He waited for my outburst to run its course before speaking his own piece. "Yeah, I wanted those things once. That's one of the reasons I joined the Guard." He spoke slow and soft. "I saw a big enough chunk of the world. Iraq. I saw what war can do to people. To my friends. My buddies. I saw . . ." As if under a deep current of hurt and grief, he surfaced and sucked in an unsteady gulp of air. "I saw too much. I need to come back from that. Here is better for me now."

I began to see how my words may have wounded him and felt his pain for the first time. Tears of regret stung my eyes. I reached over to place my hand on his. "I'm so sorry. Please forgive me."

"There's nothing to forgive," he said and pulled his hand stiffly away. "You don't understand anything." He got a handle on his raw emotions as well as his temper. "Look, I'll deal with my mom. I still think it's a lost cause, but if there's anything I can do to help your *mission*, let me know." Those last words didn't sound sincere.

I felt miserable and kicked myself. I've always known how to push his buttons, and here I'd done it again when I really didn't mean to.

The gloomy silence that settled between us was broken by Gunnar Olson coming through the front door and letting it slam shut. Michael and I looked up at the commotion behind the counter. The urgent conversation concerned Marcella.

"She was supposed to work for me today. I can't find anyone who's seen her since Saturday night." Talli's voice rose with increasing alarm. She called out to the back of the room. "What about you guys?" She looked at Michael first.

"I saw her cleaning up at Nikkerbo Saturday night, late," he said.

"Me, too," I chimed in. "She was picking up plates and glasses." I wondered if I should say anything about Marcella shooting sly knowing looks at me from across the room. I decided it wouldn't help.

Talli failed to note my perplexed expression and shifted her attention back to Michael. "You were driving around last night. Did you see anything of her big-ass Buick, like it was off the road, in a ditch, or something?"

"No. I had a call south of Kewanee and another east of Galva, so I wasn't over this way."

He rose from his chair. "I'm done here. I can check out some back roads on my way home."

Michael, Gunnar Olson, and Talli went outside, but stopped by the front porch. Their heads bent toward each other like a football team deciding on the next play. As they broke up to go their separate ways, Lars Trollenberg walked by and stepped onto the porch.

Inside, he filled his travel mug and fished the jar of instant coffee from its hiding spot. He saw me in the back corner and headed over. I was busy drawing a makeshift map on a napkin.

"Good morning. May I join you?"

"Yes, please do." I pushed the used plates aside and motioned to the vacated chair across from me. "I was sketching out a map of some of the back roads. Trying to remember something, but it isn't coming back fast enough." I decided to leave it at that. No use attempting to explain more. Not totally sure where I was headed with it anyway.

"Everyone looks so serious today," Lars said.

"They're concerned about Marcella Rice, the large lady with the cane. You would have seen her working Saturday night at the museum opening. She made those delicious meatballs."

"Ah, yes. Very good, but not like ours," he said. He dumped a heaping teaspoon of black crystals into his cup and swirled them into a now darker mixture.

I watched in amazement for a few moments before the first smirks escaped, then a short burst of laughter. I fought to regain a straight face and said, "Oh, thank you. I needed that. I had a rough night and this morning hasn't gone too well either. Everyone is worried about Marcella."

Talli returned to her post behind the counter. She shot an icy squint in my direction. The phone rang just then, or she might have said something. I heard the mention of Marcella's name and stared at Talli, trying to discern if the news was good or not. Talli shook her head for no.

Lars took a self-satisfied sip of his coffee and said, "You should smile more often."

I suppressed a snappy comeback to the trite comment and remained polite. "Wish I could. Are you going to work at Nikkerbo today?"

"*Ja*, I have the early afternoon tour, if anyone shows up. Ekollon is out today, so they have to trust me to lock up." He pulled a key ring out of his pocket and jingled it as he said with grave seriousness, "The keys of power." He placed them on the table. "I also have a car for the day. After work, a few of us are going to a restaurant in Alpha. I hope I can persuade you to join us."

I looked at the keys and was indeed persuaded. "I'd love to."

"Good. I'll pick you up after five." He snapped the lid

on his doctored mug of Swedish coffee.

After he left, I gathered the dirty dishes into a steady stack and carried them back to the kitchen, the sign of a local willing to help out. Talli used her close proximity to drop some unsolicited advice. "Now, that's a nice one for a date. Glad you didn't go pick another fight."

"Me, pick a fight?" I said sweetly. Talli flashed me an evil frown. "Okay, I'll be good," I promised.

An information rack by the door caught my eye and I slipped out a brochure for the annual Oxpojke Trail Bike Ride. Inside, I found a grainy reproduction of an old map. It showed some of the back roads west of Bishop Hill and answered the question I puzzled over with the napkin doodle. I tucked both into my shoulder bag before looking back at Talli.

"I don't really have a date, do I?"

"Uh-huh. Sure looks like it to me," Talli said.

CHAPTER 18

After pulling into the driveway of the red brick house, I couldn't help noticing the door to Uncle Roy's cabin stood wide open. My elation at the thought of his safe return didn't last long. As I watched, Christina came out and threw something to the ground. Her body language broadcasted her displeasure. She motioned for me to come over. I could only surmise that this Monday morning hadn't started well for anyone.

When I got close enough to hear, Christina said, "We had another visitor last night and it wasn't Roy."

"I was up until three. I didn't hear anything."

"Right. Nose in the computer screen and listening to music with your headphones."

"Yeah, right. Distracted, totally self-absorbed, but my light was on. I raided the kitchen a couple of times." I tried to remember what I did and when and had to give up because it wasn't coming. "What a lot of nerve." I started to grasp the sheer creepiness and began spinning new theories on the spot. "Or maybe it was something else. Like, he didn't find what he needed. Or he forgot something. He had to be desperate to come back."

"Desperate?" Christina considered the thought as she walked inside the cabin with me right behind. "I don't know. I'm not sure I know anything anymore. At least this time they didn't trash the whole place, only rifled through Roy's files. I'm trying to figure out if anything is missing. And look at this." She pointed to the desktop covered with old photographs and sounded completely discouraged for the first time. It presented a side of her I'd never experienced before. I'd always known her to take charge of every situation and know exactly what to do. To be the anchor for everyone else's rocking boat.

"I made a lot of noise feeding the livestock Friday night. So they, he, got interrupted, rushed, and had to come back last night?"

"Even if I could tell what's missing, what good are old photos? I don't get it," Christina said.

The array of photos bugged me, until it hit me. It felt reminiscent of the desktop filled with the printouts of the Krans portrait wannabes from Saturday night. I reached over to the row of hanging file racks at the back of the large wooden desk and combed through a few of the folders, recognizing most of the names. I thumbed through them again, slowing down and focusing on the selection of tabs that had an H or a K. I pulled them up far enough to glance through the ones denoting Heritage, Historical, and Krans. The photos could have come from any of them. Other folders could be missing from this break-in or from the one on Friday night. My gaze shifted back over the mass of black-and-white images. Someone took valuable time with Uncle Roy's collection without inflicting any real damage. A thoughtful thief?

I again noticed the stack of unopened mail that had partially hidden my grad school financial letter. I absentmindedly turned them over. It took a second for it to sink in: I was looking at more pieces of my own mail. I couldn't believe it.

"How did these get out here?" My indignation began to build.

"What?"

"How did these letters end up out here?" I wasn't happy and I wanted to share.

"Let me see," Christina said. I passed the letters over to her and she shuffled through them. "I don't know how they got out here. They're supposed to be on the counter with the rest of your mail. That's where I saw them last week."

"But why would Uncle Roy bring them out here?" I asked curtly.

"He wasn't happy about you wanting to go away to school."

"But I've *been* away to school. That didn't seem to bother him too much."

"This is different. It's further away and . . . well, there's the chance you might not come back. I'm sure that's what bothered him. He lost your mom. Losing you could be too much for him to deal with."

I had no comeback for that. I didn't think he would care all that much. I looked at the mail as she handed it back. I'd thought wrong.

"Give him time. He'll get used to it."

"Sure," I said and returned my attention to the assortment of photos on the desk. I thought to ask, "What about the deputy who's been driving by so much? Did she see anything?"

"I asked Deputy Johnson already. Nothing. I think she was too busy watching me."

"You? Why you?"

"Dana thinks I'm hiding Roy."

I wanted to rearrange the photos with my fingertips, but I knew I probably shouldn't. Distracted, I uttered a low, "I have to admit the thought has crossed my mind, too." Christina's indigent huffing, puffing, and narrow-eyed stare indicated it might be a good time to occupy a separate space. "Okay. Okay. Sorry for stating the obvious. I'm going."

Out on the front porch, I tucked my letters away and walked over to lean against the corner closest to the edge of the wooded area behind the campground.

I studied how the grass around the cabins and the walkway leading down to the small lake appeared freshly mown. I marveled at how blue the sky looked without urban pollution. A few puffs of clouds drifted in from the northwest. The breeze swayed the taller prairie grasses that formed the border between the manicured and the wild. From the porch, I could see the leaves of coneflowers, wild bergamot, and Queen Anne's lace interspersed among the waving stands of tall grass. They beckoned me to come closer.

The well-tended walkway down to the lake was lined with bushes, smaller Mulberry trees, and more wildflowers. However, I was drawn to a path often left overgrown and neglected.

On the fence near a hedge apple tree, two pieces of metal caught enough light to flash their presence: the top one, a round disk, and below it a crudely made arrow. Both were nailed in place years ago by a scout troop marking the point the Oxpojke Trail took off on its westward journey to the old Colony fields in the area of Red Oak grove. Beyond the markers, I could pick out cottonwood, oak, and walnut among other large trees that gave the trail a forested feel. Not so scary in the morning light. The scouts hadn't cleared the trail in ages, but Uncle Roy did it every year out of respect. I could see where the grass had been trampled down. I took the strap of my bag and lifted it over my head to secure it across my body. I walked over to take a closer look—and kept on walking. I followed the footprints: deer tracks of varying sizes, dog tracks—I hoped they were made by dogs, not coyotes—and those made by humans.

The trees crowded in on themselves and arched over the trail, meeting in the center like Gothic doorways. Their shade kept the undergrowth to a manageable height even as the trail came to the occasional clearing that allowed sunlight through to the pathway below.

Further on, the trail opened up on one side to restored prairie. A doe, startled by the intrusion, snorted, leaped to her feet, and fled with a dappled fawn close to her heels. I could see where they had flattened the grass to form well-padded beds. This was why Christina fenced off her rose bushes in an attempt to offer some protection from the hungry mouths that threatened to nip off tender leaves and buds.

Coming away from the woods and prairie, I faced a road that could have been the mirror image of the north-south Smoketree Road I'd just left behind. Gunnar Olson's farm house to my right was a white wood-framed structure with a roof of green asphalt shingles. Their driveway left the road and split in two with one fork going behind the house, the other leading off to barns and outbuildings that filled the cleared area between woodland and prairie. Their cultivated farm fields were further north.

I pulled the brochure from my bag and oriented the map so it lined up with the real world in front of me. The choice was to cross the cattail and wildflower-filled ditch and hike through the rough fields in my light walking shoes or take the road. The road won.

I followed it to the left until the first corner offered the chance to resume the westward trek. As I walked, I kept an eye on the approximate location of the original Oxpojke

Trail as it intersected the modern obstacles of new houses and fences. It didn't seem likely that any intruder would have followed what was left of that path. So, if coming by way of the road, where would they have parked?

Up ahead, an abandoned driveway led far enough into a group of trees that it might offer a screen to keep a car out of sight in the dark. I found some tire tracks but had no idea how old they were. My brother might have known, having been a former scout, but he was far away. I carefully backed out, trying to step in my own tracks. Someone else would have to investigate this. I kept walking. Another large mass of mature trees meant I neared Red Oak grove and even rougher terrain. The brochure related that the woods and surrounding fields constituted the original land purchase for the Colony and its heart, until they laid out the town of Bishop Hill.

I walked on, watching the light play through the gentle movement of the trees, when a shadow that overlapped the road moved in an odd way. I squinted, trying to make it out; maybe a black cat or a large crow? It finally revealed itself as a wild turkey. I'd heard they'd made a comeback. The bird disappeared into the brush, but a slash of darkness remained on the road. As I approached, the dark area turned into a gash, then two. I grew alarmed when the set of tire skid marks led to the edge . . . and over.

Leaning as far as I could over the brush-filled ravine, I could just make out the back end of what had to be Marcella's Buick. I pulled my cell phone out of my pocket and placed the 911 call, hoping they wouldn't think I was making this up. It had only been three days since I made the frantic call from Varnishtree for Herb.

I talked to the dispatcher and relayed my location as accurately as possible. This time, I wasn't asked to stay on the phone. I snapped it closed and put it away as I hovered by the edge of the road. The thought of staying put and playing it safe had immense appeal. But no cars came by. I took a couple of deep breaths and carefully began to pick my way down the side of the ravine, finding hand holds on branches and saplings as I gingerly tested for a solid place for each step. I willed myself not to panic. To keep breathing. This wasn't Herb. It was Marcella. She'd do it for me if she could.

Marcella sat slouched behind the steering wheel with eyes closed and blood matted in her dyed-blond hair. I hoped my courage wouldn't fail as I tried the door handle. It opened. So did Marcella's eyes. The shock sent me backwards into a sitting position in the dirt.

"Marcella," I shouted with equal parts amazement and relief as I picked myself up. "We'll get you out of here. Help is on way. Please hang on." I found a hand to hold and squeezed.

Marcella moaned and tried to speak. "Missy, is that you?"

"Yes, ma'am." I smiled through grateful tears. No, this won't be Herb at all. "Why in the world were you over this way? This isn't on your way home."

"Followed that crazy nut," Marcella mumbled.

"Nut?" I wasn't sure if I'd heard her right.

"Deer jumped in front..." Marcella's attempt at forming words overextended her remaining resources and brought on a fit of dry-throated coughing. "Water," she rasped.

"Oh, if I'd only known. I was just at The Lutfisk. They're all worried about you. Out looking for you. I bet they'll be here in no time." I couldn't stop myself from babbling on about nothing. I needed the sound to keep myself grounded and Marcella awake. "Nuts? Why look for nuts? Were you going to bake something?"

Marcella's face paled as she fixed her waning gaze out past the windshield and whispered, "He turned wrong ... me, too." Her eyelids fluttered closed.

"Marcella! Please, stay with me."

From above, the sound of gravel crunching under heavy tires filtered into the ravine. "Down here! We need help!"

Marcella's eyes remained closed, but her breathing seemed good. I had no time to waste. I had to get up to the road and flag down the passing car. After tucking Marcella's hand back inside the Buick, I started picking my way back up to the road.

I was trying to get a good foothold next to a strong-looking bush when Michael's voice came down. "Is anyone there?"

"Yes, we're here. Marcella's in her car. She's unconscious."

"Shelley? Hold on. I'm coming down." For a second time he seemed to know what to do and was willing to take charge. With intense relief, I watched him climb down the embankment. He kept his balance with one hand while clutching a first-aid kit in the other. How could someone change so much in just a few years? For a fleeting second I thought of J for Jekyll and Hyde. I kept my mouth shut; now wasn't the time for stupid jokes. He was all business and it made me wonder about myself. What kind of business was I good for?

He opened his kit, pulled out gauze pads, and with a bottle of water he produced from his pocket went to work on Marcella's face. "Has she been awake at all?"

"Yeah, just for a bit. Tried to talk. Asked for water."

"That's a good sign." He made sure to moisten her lips.

"How'd you get here so fast?"

"I was working a grid through the back roads when the 911 call came in." I looked puzzled, so he added, "The tow truck's radio monitors the emergency channels. I knew where to go."

Marcella's eyes remained closed, but some color returned to her cheeks and neck.

"I don't get it," I said. "How is it possible that no one saw her?"

"Believe it or not, this isn't the first time a car has gone down here."

"But a full-sized car like this? It's practically a boat. Going unnoticed for over a day."

"It happens. A ravine with steep banks and a lot of brushy growth can hide lots of stuff. Especially if folks driving by aren't looking directly at it."

"Or for it."

"Exactly." He gently dabbed at Marcella's forehead cuts and without looking away said, "Look, you did good here."

I felt a warm rush of pride quite unlike anything else I'd ever experienced. I ducked my head and averted my eyes, since they threatened to turn moist again.

Sadie had followed Michael and stayed close until some leaves rustled. She bounded off a short way but came back when he whistled. "Will you take her up to the road?" It sounded like a question, but wasn't. It was a dismissal. "Dana will show up soon. And the ambulance."

"Dana?"

"Deputy Dana Johnson. She's the closest. Been working this zone since Friday. I've talked with her already."

Sadie didn't want to cooperate at first. Michael gave his dog a stern look and the order, "Go to the truck." She charged upward toward the road. I wasn't about to emulate such obedience. I took my time and was careful not to slip or fall. The dog waited patiently as I finally made it to the top, panting and hot.

Deputy Johnson made good time and arrived on the scene just before the ambulance.

The wail of the sirens and the flashing lights brought palpable waves of fist-clenching panic that caught me by surprise. I retreated inside the tow truck to safety and slid down into the seat, glad for the comfort Sadie provided. I waited and watched, helpless to do more.

The rescue crews went about their business with skill and efficiency. By the time they had Marcella on a stretcher and up on the road a small crowd of onlookers, mostly local farmers, had assembled.

I climbed down from the truck when I saw Deputy Johnson head in my direction with her notebook out. Statement time. I wished I didn't know the drill. I nervously picked at bits of grass and weeds sticking to my jeans.

"Good morning," the deputy said before going through the prerequisite formalities. I answered all and waited for the million-dollar question. "How did you happen to find her?"

"I was having breakfast at The Lutfisk. Talli expected Marcella to come in this morning. When she didn't show, we were worried." I decided to skip past the drama-queen scene with Michael. "I got back to the house and saw Christina over by the cabins. We had another unscheduled visitor. One thing led to another and I started walking the trail. It comes out to the road over there." I pointed in the general direction.

The deputy took in the information and frowned. "You were just walking?"

"Yeah, just walking. I thought I saw something on the road. Turned out to be a turkey, but it got me to look over the edge. I called 911." I shrugged my shoulders and hoped the deputy had enough.

Over by the ambulance, Marcella complained about the deer that had bounded out of nowhere. In trying to avoid the collision with the animal her cane had slipped under the brake pedal, got stuck, and sent her off the road. She definitely sounded stronger, but I had to ask, "Is she going to be all right?"

"I can't say for sure, but it certainly looks promising."

No one got around to asking Marcella why she had driven so far out of her way to go home. I wondered if she would've started talking about crazy nuts again.

Michael and his Uncle Bill left the group of onlookers but waited for Deputy Johnson to walk away before approaching the tow truck. I noticed how Michael stopped to exchange a few words with the deputy as they passed each other. They certainly seemed to be on friendly terms, first names and all. Perhaps a whole lot more.

Michael's Uncle Bill approached alone. "How you doin', Miss Shelley? I came by to take over. Let Michael get on home in my pickup."

"I'm doing okay, Mr. Anderson. Sounds like Marcella will be fine, too."

"Oh, sure. She's a tough ol' bird. Way too contrary. She'll pretend to follow doctor's orders 'til she gets home."

"As long as her leg doesn't give her too much trouble."

"That is a fact," he said as he grinned.

Michael came over to fetch his dog and gather his personal items. He politely offered to give me a lift home and seemed surprised when I accepted.

CHAPTER 19

It appeared that Michael wasn't about to speak first, so I had to take the lead. "Thank you so much for giving me a ride. I wanted to apologize again for this morning."

"Not necessary. It was a bad morning for you. But seriously, you need to work on some new karma."

"I'll get right on it. Look, do you remember Friday at The Lutfisk?"

"Yeah," he said before really thinking, and then switched his answer to, "No."

"Marcella came over and started dropping snarky comments about the Hemcourt family's beloved Krans portrait. Later, at the opening, she came right out and suggested it wasn't—" I paused to dig out the exact words. "It wasn't the real deal."

"Still no," he said. Impatient now, he pulled out onto the road and turned south at the first corner. There were no crossroads to directly connect where we were to the Smoketree Road that ran between the red brick house and the Ox-Boy campground. We had to go almost to Highway 34 and then loop back around. I wanted to use that extra time to talk him into the detour I had in mind.

"Okay, the barbs were aimed at me. She was trying to get me to make a closer, more professional inspection of the painting. The last time I saw her, she was across the room staring at me, giving me a look."

"She gave you a look," he said with a skeptical tone.

"She thought I'd seen something."

"What?"

"I don't know," I said. "I mean, I'm not sure. Yet. I need more time."

"Well, that's helpful. Not."

"I've been thinking about that and some other stuff."

"Other stuff. What other stuff?" He paused. "I'm not going to like this, am I?"

"I need to go to the Varnishtree. See Herb's workshop again."

"What? No. Definitely *no*."

"Please, Michael. You said you'd help."

"Yeah, I said that, but it's probably still sealed off. Crime scene tape and the whole nine yards. I can't do anything about that."

"Just drive me there. I'll do the rest myself."

"I don't like this. Why don't you talk to Dana? She'd be happy to help."

"You mean Deputy Dana? And say what? That I just

need to poke around. Sift through their evidence. That's *so* not going to happen. Besides, I don't know what I'm looking for. I just need to see it again. It feels important."

Michael took his time, as if considering his options, and then grudgingly came around. "Okay, this might help me out with my mom. You were right. She's all hot to find the lost Krans of Great Auntie's dream. I think it's nothing but a fairy tale, but I could truthfully say I drove by the place. We'll see if anyone is there. No promises. Good enough?"

"Yes, good enough," I said. It was a foot in the door, so to speak.

We drove into the Varnishtree parking lot. It was empty of cars and crime scene tape except for a few tattered bits of yellow that had blown over to the edges. I tried my best not to show it, but being here again left me feeling daunted. I had to keep on task. I had my own mission now.

Michael must have sensed my apprehension and asked, "Why are we here?"

I put my hand to my chest and drew a slow breath with eyes closed. "It's Marcella. Finding her. Waiting for the ambulance. It brought back memories. I think they're memories. Images anyway. I have to get back inside and see it again." I opened my eyes and turned to him. "I can't let them down. Herb. Pearl. Marcella." I opened the truck door and found the determination to move forward. Again, I took the well-worn path around to the back. This time the shop door was closed. I tried the handle. Locked.

"Michael, reach up there and feel for a key. I'll look around down here." He had followed a couple of steps behind and now nervously scanned the surrounding area. He hadn't paid attention when I spoke to him, so I had to repeat, "Search up there above the door for a key. I can't reach that high."

"Herb kept a key up there?"

"There's one out here somewhere," I said.

"This is your plan?"

"Well, yes," I said. "Maybe not the best, but it is short notice."

He made a face as he probed along the door's gritty casing. "You know, if you're planning on becoming a career criminal—cat burglar, jewel thief, or whatever—I'd reconsider. This sucks."

"Okay, you do locks. Open things. Have a go at it."

"I don't 'do' locks. I open locked car doors—for the real owners. Anything else is breaking and entering."

"That's why I need the key. We'll be fine with the key," I said. I checked the cracks and crevices around the door frame and probed nearby flowerpots.

"You might get an argument on that. I'm taking a course at the community college and I think this would be considered—"

"Aha! Found it." I held up the key in triumph. "Herb wanted to protect his tool collection, but he was always misplacing stuff—eyeglasses, keys, whatnot. He got so fed up he made copies of everything he could. Look, if you need to go, then go. I'll be fine." I made a show of steadying my hands and prepared to put the key in the lock.

"Just do it already," he said. He had totally given up the moral high ground.

We walked into stark darkness. The only light we had came in with us. I flipped the light switch and closed the door. The overhead bulbs came to life reluctantly and gained in brightness over the next few minutes. They gradually illuminated walls fitted top to bottom with custom-built shelves. Herb's immense antique tool collection was on display.

"So you're taking a class. In what, exactly?"

"Criminology. My friend Mark and I started out together. I thought he got into it. We quizzed each other on everything, even ten-codes. But he dropped out. I stayed. Dana thinks I have a chance of getting on with the sheriff's department next time they test. If they ever get around to doing it again. Things are tight there like everywhere else."

"Uh-huh." I had stopped listening. I walked around slowly, looking at everything in a trance-like state, summoning up all the details I could from Friday morning. The wait for help had left me with little else to do but look around. My hands felt clammy, my brow began to sweat, and my breath came faster as it all swept over me again. Hoping for clarity, I pointed as I recited, "Pearl and I sat there. The big trunk was there. The smaller one there."

"Big trunk? There's no big trunk."

"The Hemcourt's painted immigrant trunk will go into the museum exhibit with the Krans portrait. Herb had it on the main workbench. I set my phone down next to it. Almost didn't get it back."

"OK. But what other thing? A small trunk, you said."

"No, smaller than a trunk. Like a bentwood box, stitched together on one side. More oval than round. Painted a lot like the trunk. It was . . . there." I indicated a bare spot on another workbench. "And it's gone, too."

The door opened and a man stood silhouetted in the light. He looked at both of us before staring directly at me. "What are *you* doing here?"

A surprised Michael managed to force out, "Nothing, man. We were just leaving."

Gordon Anderson took a step into the room. "You shouldn't be here." He continued to glare at me.

I started to protest but got hushed up with a subtle nudge from Michael and a quiet, "Save it for later."

"You're trespassing," Gordon growled.

"Where's the Hemcourt trunk?" I demanded.

"They released it and I took it to the museum this morning. Not that you need to know. I'm Herb's cousin. The only one with permission to be here."

"And the smaller one? The bentwood box, where did that it go?"

"There was nothing else." Gordon's pinched face and heavy hooded eyes grew darker under the fringe of gray hair.

"But there was. Right there." The memory started to waver and fade like a mirage or one of my dreams. "At least I think so," I said, suddenly unsure of myself.

"You must be crazy. Everything is right where Herb left it. Except for Hemcourt's trunk."

Michael whispered into my ear, "Let's go. *Now*." He tugged on my arm as he spoke to the increasingly agitated Gordon. "Sorry to have bothered you, man. She just had to come back. It must be the shock. She's not herself. We'll be going."

"Not so fast." Gordon stepped closer with a tense, threatening look.

"That's my line," Deputy Dana Johnson said as she entered the workshop with her heavy-duty flashlight in hand and a no-nonsense expression on her face. "Michael, care to explain what's going on here?"

"They're trespassing. Arrest them," Gordon ordered.

"Now, hold on a minute, sir. I'm sure there's a reasonable explanation," the deputy said.

"It's all my fault. I had to come back," I pleaded.

"You could have come to me," the deputy said.

A sideways glance to Michael's embarrassed face made me confess, "That's what Michael said and I wouldn't listen. I pushed him into this, to help me. Look, I'm sorry."

"Let's go outside and discuss this." The deputy motioned for us to walk around Gordon and pass in front of her to safety.

Gordon stood his ground. "Are you going to arrest them?"

"Do you really want to press charges after all that's happened here?" the deputy stated, with an official-sounding firmness. "She's the person who found Herb and

Pearl on Friday, and the car accident with Marcella Rice just a while ago. It doesn't look like any damage has been done here. Just a misunderstanding."

Gordon's mind clicked over the logic and the possibility of bad press and let his temper cool down a notch. "Fine. No harm done. Just make sure they stay away." He stepped back.

"You heard the man. Let's go, folks."

Deputy Johnson escorted Michael and me outside and watched as we got back into our vehicle. I checked the side-view mirror; she was still standing there, watching as we made the turn that would head in the direction of Bishop Hill. I guessed she really wanted me to go home.

By the time Michael dropped me off in front of the red brick house, my head throbbed with a nasty headache. My apologies elicited nothing but a few grunts and brooding silence. He drove off leaving me in pain and misery.

Not bothering to look for Christina, I slipped unnoticed up to my room to lick my wounds. How could everything have gone so wrong? Maybe Ekollon was right about me; I was nothing but a wasted effort on everyone's part.

I set my alarm before crawling under the quilt. I planned to call Lars to cancel our date. But not now. Now, there was only crushing exhaustion and surrender to sleep. Things had to get better.

CHAPTER 20

The tormenting dream transported me to a colorful, impressionistic approximation of Herb's workshop. I floated along bulging shelves as a disembodied Herb talked about each tool and artifact in his deep, rich voice. Each had its special use and story of how he came by it. He had inherited many from his father and grandfather, but the bulk of his collection came from traveling all over the country in his younger years. He kept them all in well-defined categories. Everything was where it should be, in perfect order. The scene transformed itself somewhat and I could hear Michael ask an urgent question. "Why are we here?"

The answer came through in the silky-smooth, ethereal bass of Herb. "Because with perfect order comes the ability to see what's out of place." I stared at a small oval box as it morphed its way to the top of four other boxes. The alarm sounded and they dissolved. I sat up convinced of the reality of the original bentwood box.

Checking the clock, I calculated I could make it to Nikkerbo before Lars locked the front doors. Based on last night's research, I had another piece of the puzzle to check out. I had to pull myself together one more time.

I flew down the road as fast as I dared. Lars would begin locking up Nikkerbo for the night by starting from the back and working toward the front, making sure no one was left inside. I had to get there before he finished.

I dashed up to the large glass doors just as he approached from the other side. He looked at me with surprise at first, which transformed to worry as I pushed my way through.

"Something is wrong? I was coming to get you in just a few minutes," he said.

"I need a favor from you. It's hard to explain," I gasped, "but *hugely* important."

"Let me lock the door first." Lars fumbled with the keys as he tried to find the right one.

"Good, the alarms aren't set."

"Not yet," he said.

"I have to see the Krans painting. *Now.*" With the element of surprise on my side, I took off fast.

"Um, wait. I'm not sure about this," he called after me.

I didn't slow down until I stood in front of the Krans exhibit. To Lars's horror, I climbed over the velvet rope barrier, went up to the Hemcourt portrait, and lifted it off the wall.

"You can't do that. *Gloves*. You must have gloves," he sputtered.

"I don't have time," I said.

"But you know what the protocols are."

His protests fell on deaf ears. With the painting off the wall, I got a good look at all the important things: the brushwork, the quality of the paint, and the craquelure, the fine network of surface cracks. I hefted the portrait around to see the wooden stretcher strips, the supporting framework for the canvas. They looked like solid wood, stained dark with age, just like Krans would have used. The bottom of the frame held the key, my real goal. And there they were—the initials of the first Curt Hemcourt followed by Roman numerals, the marks for each successive generation christened with the same name, crudely scratched into the wood and also darkened by age. I studied the vacant space where the missing V, representing the fifth generation, should have been incised into the old wood. "That's odd," I said.

"That you are acting like a maniac? Come down from there," Lars shouted in exasperation. When I started to step out of the display area with the painting still in my possession, he waved his hands and shouted again. "No, put it back!"

"Not without you looking at the first Curt Hemcourt's initials." I angled it for him to see. "Now, notice the marks for each of the following sons—two, three, and four. See the blank area? No Roman numeral five for our own Mr. Hemcourt. Why is that?"

"So what? He hasn't gotten around to defacing the painting's frame. Perhaps he chose not to keep going on with a bad tradition." Lars was turning pink and close to hyperventilating. "I don't care. Just put it back before anyone sees us."

"Who else is here?"

"No one."

"And the security system isn't on?"

"No." He shook his head to add emphasis.

"Then we're golden. Home free." I carefully replaced the artwork and stood back. I gave it another few minutes of my best professional assessment before climbing back down.

"Why did you do that?" he asked, clearly shaken by the stunt.

"I had to see the back. I stayed up last night reading up on this painting, its personal history with the family, and, more importantly, its location before and after the fire."

"Mr. Hemcourt's father had it in his office downtown."

"Not necessarily. I think those references appeared in print after the fire. Like someone made an effort to contrive a different backstory."

"That can't be true. And if so, you'd need proof." He paused as he hunted for an English word to convey his meaning. "Proof like steel."

"The internet is a wonderful thing. All kinds of information live on and on, forever. If you dig long enough, you find it."

"Leave this for now," Lars said. "I have to finish locking

up so we can go."

I volunteered to drive Lars to Alpha as a goodwill gesture. He accepted before looking into the still-packed back seat. I apologized and explained how busy I'd been since Friday.

He'd heard about Alpha's bowling alley and wanted the chance to absorb some local American color. We entered to find the place packed with children having a birthday party. Kids ran in all directions, their screams blending in with the loud music, producing a wall of noise that instantly surpassed our pain threshold.

Lars had a polite smile clamped into place. "This looks like a fun time, but with all these children it's too loud. I can't hear myself think." His well-meaning look slowly shifted to one of beseeching hopefulness.

"Our 4-H club came here a few times," I said, stalling as I mentally ran through the limited list of last-minute alternatives. I tried not to look desperate. "Let's go into the restaurant side and see how busy it is." I led the way to the adjoining dining area, which thankfully had a much lower decibel level. We chose a table midway between the clamor of the bowling alley and the drone of the TV set mounted head-high in the corner.

"*Ja*, this is much better." Lars relaxed and we turned our coffee cups right side up, the signal for the waitress to fill them up. We required some time to study the menus, so the waitress moved on to top off the cups of other diners.

"You'll have to call the others and let them know the change in plans," I said.

"Something came up and they can't make it tonight. It will be just we two."

"No problem. Things happen." But what I really wanted to understand was why Lars asked me to come in the first place. He seemed interested in me, but why? With nearly every able-bodied female in the county swooning over his good looks and his charmingly melodic accent, Lars made it obvious he wanted to spend time with me. Nice, but I've never had that kind of luck in dating before. This didn't feel right and I decided to keep my guard up.

We ordered sandwiches when the waitress came back around. I watched as she called our orders in through the large window-like opening that divided the kitchen from the dining room. She lingered there and engaged in some friendly banter with the cook. The humming fan masked their conversation.

"You're wondering, perhaps, why I asked to see you tonight."

I briefly thought about trying to hide my rueful expression behind the menu, but the opportunity zoomed past. "Ah, you have mind reading skills, too."

He gave me a thoughtful smile. Quite gentle. "You see, I'm having a marvelous time working over here this summer. I'm learning so much about Nikkerbo. Mr. Ekollon has given me so much freedom to see how all things work. Down to smallest details. But I also have another job, another purpose." He gathered his thoughts and perhaps some courage. "I was asked by my uncle to find out information about your mother."

"My mother?" My mind went blank. I froze.

"In Sweden, my uncle worked on the special project that restored the Krans paintings and came with them when they were returned to Bishop Hill. He was young and wanted to learn about American farming methods, so he stayed on for almost a year as part of an exchange program. Your mother, Nora, and he became good friends. They wrote letters to each other after he returned home. He knew she had married and started a family." Lars nodded to me.

"That's how you knew about John, my brother. And where I lived."

"*Ja.*" He paused to clear his throat and chose his words. "He worried about Nora. He worried much more when the letters suddenly stopped. He always hoped that she stopped writing because she was too busy with her new responsibilities. Her new life. Her new family. He only recently learned that she had died very young, very tragic. He would like to know more."

"My mother . . ." I began to form the words, but halted. My eyes went down to the table as I picked up my paper napkin. It felt good to have it in my hand. Without thinking, I slowly twisted it into a series of new shapes. I concentrated on how to explain Nora. "My brother and I were very young. We were told she died in a car accident." I was stalling, trying to judge how much to tell of a story I barely knew myself. "I'm sorry, but I don't know about any letters. I have some photos and yearbooks from school." I thought for a moment. "There's a nice photo of a group. Friends. Maybe your uncle is in there. I can bring it in to the museum."

"I'd like that. Please, tell me more."

So simple a request, yet it pressed on me like a heavy weight. I could sense the blood warming my cheeks, my head feeling lighter. How embarrassing. So many blank pages in my mother's life, yet I was unprepared to have one filled in just now. I unfolded the misshapen napkin and used it to wipe away the first tear. "You say your uncle knew my mom," I said, not expecting an answer. My voice softened to a whisper as I prepared to lower some of the defensive barriers I'd built up over the years.

"*Ja.*" Lars had to lean in closer to hear.

"The other day, I wondered how you knew so much about John. What else do you know?"

"Only a little. Please, tell me more."

"Okay, to start with, there's a huge age difference between Nora and her older brother, my Uncle Roy. Nearly seventeen years." I shifted my position in the chair but failed to find any more comfort. I pressed on. "When he graduated from Galva high school and joined the Army, she was still in diapers. He came back from Vietnam and she was this little kid who idolized him and his every move."

Lars smiled warmly at the mental snapshot. "That's nice."

I shared the feeling for a moment. "People told me she

followed him around every chance she got."

"He was good with that?"

"Oh, yeah. You see, it was rough for him to come back after serving. He said everyone was on his case about something. The way he looked. The way he acted. His friends. His job, or rather the lack of a decent job. College didn't work out. Nothing did. He barely got by most days. He told me Nora kept him sane. She gave him unconditional love and a reason to live."

"My uncle told me of her sensitivity, kindness, and grace. He never forgot her."

"Right," I said, with a little more confidence. "She graduated high school in 1982 and went to the local community college. Uncle Roy campaigned for her to go on to a four-year college, she had the grades and all, but she wouldn't budge an inch. She stayed here. Right here in dull old Bishop Hill."

"It's not so bad to live in a small place," Lars protested. His voice held a seriousness that softened as he continued. "So, she stayed here and married someone named Anderson. A fine Swedish name."

I appreciated his attempt to lighten the mood. "Yupper. Harold."

Lars pursed his lips before asking, "Where is he now?"

"My dear old dad? Don't know. Don't care. He was bad news from the beginning. Uncle Roy drinks too much, that's for sure, but my dad got into far worse things. When mom died he never came for us, my brother and me. No one has heard a peep from him in all these years." I discarded my used napkin for a fresh one out of the tabletop dispenser. "Uncle Roy stepped in and got temporary custody."

"He raised you and your brother?"

"Pretty much. We were four-year-olds and a handful. He tried his best. There was a big fight with my dad's parents. They wanted to take us away. But it never happened. Good thing, too. No one around here trusted them. Considered them outsiders."

"Is this when Roy and Christina, how do you say it, came together?"

"Hooked up," I said, deciding to simply lay it out. "Uncle Roy and Christina's fiancé at the time were best friends. I guess the three of them hung out together a lot. The guys enlisted in the Army together. As I said, Uncle Roy came back from the war. The other guy didn't."

"I'm so sorry," Lars said, with surprise that turned into sincere regret. "Such a terrible loss. A burden for both of them."

"I guess so." I had to stop, step back, and ask myself if I'd ever considered that before, Christina's feelings over a loss of that magnitude. The answer? Never. Uncle Roy carried his wounds close to the surface; everyone could see his trauma, his pain. But Christina, the organized, efficient engine of discipline, showed no cracks, no weakness, no outward sign of loss or grief. At least, none I'd ever seen. I twisted the napkin as I realized that as a child I only thought about my own feelings. Parts of me remained very much like that child. I felt ashamed.

"The loss brought them together. They fell in love and got married," Lars surmised.

"Well, that depends on whose story you want to believe: theirs, or the rumors and the whispered gossip." I'd gone past dodging the truth. "Some folks around here believe it was a marriage of convenience. They got together to make sure we kids stayed with Uncle Roy."

"And what about you? What do you believe?"

"I gave up wondering about it when I was fifteen."

"What happened?"

"What happened was," I said, as I summoned my courage, "I found out that Nora was declared legally dead when John and I were 11 years old. I found out about it when I was 15. By accident."

"No one told you. Tried to explain."

"Christina said they were waiting until John and I were old enough."

"They waited too long."

"Yes."

I dropped the second ruined napkin on top of the first. "Look, this is too hard for me. I've avoided this stuff for a long time. I know it sounds bitchy, but I'm not ready to deal with it now." I exhaled in resignation. "That's the real reason I've made so many plans to leave. I want . . . wanted to start over, reinvent a life without all these shadows from someone else's past hanging over me."

"But this is your home."

"It's familiar, people know me, but it hasn't felt right in a long time." I lifted my eyes to gaze at him and offer a weak smile. "I'll look for that photo for you."

The waitress delivered our orders and asked if she could get us anything else. We both gave her a polite "no."

CHAPTER 21

"Get a grip. It's not his fault," I told myself.

I repeated those words over and over, both in my mind and out loud, while driving south toward Bishop Hill. I should've stayed with Lars as he waited for the tow truck to come and get his borrowed car started, but I felt too wrung out to take a chance on facing Michael again. I should've turned right at the first crossroad and headed home, but I couldn't face that either. Instead, I let the pull of the softly glowing street lights guide me into Bishop Hill.

Drained and emotionally tender, I let the car roll to a stop next to the quiet park and sat behind the wheel repeating, "It's *not* his fault."

The real meaning had changed and expanded beyond Lars to include a host of other people I owed apologies to. I got out of the car and headed for the playground. The grass yielded under my feet. Old stories came back as I walked. The Colony's dugout shelters of the first harsh winter lay buried underground. People died down there. How strange to have a slide, swings, and a merry-go-round up here now.

Sitting on one of the hard wooden swings, I wished I'd told Lars about Nils and Cilla Westbloom. Their story sounded much more romantic than Uncle Roy's and Christina's. But were they really any different? At the heart of each was a common thread of war, lost love, and building new lives. Could the same story have essentially repeated itself over one hundred years later?

I let my feet push back and forth, giving the swing a gentle sway as I slid deeper into bittersweet memories and regrets.

"Why couldn't it have just been a real date?" I muttered.

There would have been fewer complications.

A dark figure stepped out from the shadows of the bandstand and got quite close before I became aware of its presence.

"You shouldn't be out here this late and all by yourself, Miss Shelley," said Winston Maskin with a curt nod. The former mayor of Bishop Hill tipped off his battered baseball cap, revealing a head full of springy white hair.

The light illuminating the playground area made his hair glow in the dark. It also flashed off the shotgun resting in the crook of his other arm. My involuntary spasm of shock threw me backward. My hands clamped onto the chains of the swing just in time to keep me from falling. "What's going on?"

"Sorry to scare you like that," he said, "but with all the shenanigans going on around here, some of us got together to see if we can catch the jerk breakin' into places. I got the park tonight."

"You mean the Ox-Boy cabins?"

"Them and the others."

"What others?"

"Places right here in the village have been broken into in the last two weeks. The Mercantile over yonder. Oakberry Antiques. Even Gordon's place showed signs of someone workin' the lock on the back door." He made multiple gestures to indicate the locations of the crime spree. Not that it mattered to me which way he pointed. I stared at the shotgun.

"I haven't heard tell of a crime wave like this in 80 years," Maskin continued, "back when the bootleggers used to pass through on their way to Kewanee and Peoria. Darndest thing, those crooks never killed nobody, leastwise nobody around these parts." He scratched at his head before resetting his cap. "Nothin' like old Herb out there. But we'll catch up with this jerk soon enough. Just like before. Then we'll find out what happened."

"Evening, Mr. Maskin," Michael called out from a safe distance. "I was driving through and thought I'd stop to see if anybody needed help."

"We're good here. Miss Shelley was just leavin'. Right?"

"Oh, yes. Going home. Right now." I lifted out of the

swing and quickened my pace to gain some distance away from the homegrown vigilante. I liked the old man better on those Sunday afternoons when he walked around the park with a vintage camera hanging from his neck, engaging tourists in idle conversation.

"Can you *not* get into trouble for five minutes?" Michael hissed into my ear. He tugged me along by my elbow as his long strides got us nearer to my car and safety.

"I don't know how it happens—it just does."

"Well, Lars is on his way home. Now it's your turn. There's too much going on tonight. I got a tip about the big stakeout action. Sheriff's deputies, geezers with guns, this *isn't* the best place to be right now."

"Awesome. Is Deputy Dana here?" I slipped out of his grip and slowed down to scan the area. I peered into the shadowy corners expecting to see sinister movements.

"Focus, Shelley, focus," he said, as he threw me a caustic look.

I reset my pace for the car. "Any ideas about what the thieves are after?"

"Not the time to worry about that stuff."

"What if . . ." I slowed down again. "What if they're looking for the painting?"

"What painting?" He opened the car door for me and waited.

"The missing Krans," I whispered.

"*That* again. It's not likely. No one knows about it except—"

"A very select few." I got behind the wheel and closed the door. Rolling down the window, I called out, "Meet me tomorrow morning at The Lutfisk. I bet we can figure it out."

"Are you sure you wouldn't rather have your good buddy Lars to help you out?"

"Oh, so now it's J for Jealousy?"

"No way," he spat and turned away.

"Oh, come on. The Lutfisk. Tomorrow morning. I'll bring muffins."

"I'll think about it. No promises," he said without turning. He took a couple more paces before swinging back around with his arms stretched wide. "You don't have the best track record, you know." He resumed stalking across the street toward the tow truck and the waiting dog.

"Great, I'll see you in the morning," I called out. I scrutinized the shadows again, wondering who else had heard. It's not paranoia if they're really out there, I reminded myself. I turned the key and was relieved when the engine turned over. Taking off, I turned right onto Main Street. On the way out of the village I searched again for any out-of-place shapes in the shadows.

I pulled into the driveway of the red brick house and parked under the yard light. I fumbled with my key ring looking for the house key, all the while vowing to become more organized and just a better person in general. In the distance, I noticed headlights cresting the hill to the south. I watched in mild curiosity to see if the car would turn off the Smoketree Road and go toward Bishop Hill. Perhaps on its way to the tavern. Though, this late at night, I'd expect people to be heading home. The lights kept bearing straight, crossed the Edwards, and headed up the hill to me. As it passed, the SUV slowed down as if to take a good look. There was no telling the identity of the driver, or even the true color of the vehicle; it just looked dark. However, instead of obeying my first fleeting impulse—to hurry into the house—I did the opposite. I stood my ground and glared back at the shadowy driver. The SUV sped up, passing the Smoketree before it disappeared over the hill.

I entered the front door and went directly to the kitchen, setting my bag and keys on the table. I gathered myself upright. "This is *my* life," I said. "I will have some degree of control over it." I went to the counter to make a muffin count. Six left. I sat down to write a note reserving four for tomorrow morning. I added a mental note to set my alarm clock and leave it out of easy reach. Morning would come too early and I had a lot to do.

CHAPTER 22

Tuesday, June 3, 2008

A sharp bang yanked me out of a sound sleep. I wondered what exactly I'd heard. The back door slamming? Voices downstairs? I peered groggily at the alarm clock and weighed the odds of getting back to sleep. Falling back onto my pillow, I stared at the ceiling, knowing it would be fruitless to try. I groped through the folds of the quilt for my robe, thoroughly despondent at the prospect of starting the day too early.

By the time I dragged myself into the kitchen, I found a robe-clad Christina as the sole occupant. "Did I hear voices?"

Christina ignored my inquiry. "I got your note and saved the muffins for you and . . ." She waited for me to fill in the blank.

"Thanks. I'm meeting Michael Anderson at The Lutfisk." I stretched and yawned. "I hope I'm meeting him. I have to be prepared with a peace offering. Things didn't go smoothly yesterday. In fact, I'll probably be lucky if he shows up at all."

"Care to explain?" Christina asked, with her worried-mother look.

"Well, to start with, Talli thought I picked a fight with him yesterday morning." I pulled out a chair and collapsed into it. "I guess I sort of did."

"You two butted heads throughout your school years," Christina said as she settled into her own chair at the table. "But that was a long time ago. People change."

"I'm finding that out. He seems to have changed a lot more than I have." I scratched my head and raked my fingers through the tangled curls, then gazed wistfully at the coffee pot, so close, yet so far away. "Between finding Marcella and thinking about the possibilities of an unknown, unrecorded Krans canvas, I got all excited and kind of went off the deep end." I didn't want to discuss the details of meeting up with Lars and the trip to Alpha just yet. My long-standing issues over Nora couldn't be resolved quickly and needed to wait. Stalling and being vague seemed like the expedient way to go.

"Marcella, I know about that, but back up to the part about a Krans canvas. I don't understand."

"Remember Sunday, I went over to Pearl's house to visit, to talk to her? No, wait a minute, when I got back you were gone again." I caught myself before I went too far out on a limb of sarcasm and took a second to remind myself to go easier on Christina. "I'm sorry," I said and started again. "I saw Pearl on Sunday and she had this great story to tell. It went back to her at age ten. That would put Olof Krans at seventy-five, the summer before he died. She used to visit his Altona studio and watch him work. She remembered a particular portrait, supposedly a repeat of one he had done years earlier. She witnessed an old woman, probably a Colonist, damage it, attack it in a fit of rage. It upset Krans so badly that after repairing the canvas, he took it off the stretcher strips and hid it. Made her promise not to speak of it to anyone."

She looked skeptical. "Okay, and why speak of it now?"

"That's a good question." I got up to pour myself a cup, and, with a look, offered some to Christina, who nodded. "Last Friday morning she saw a cross made out of clouds in the sky, contrails I'd guess. She took it as an omen, a sign from Krans. Anyway, the cross set her off on a quest to find this long-lost painting." After pouring, I set the pot back on its warming pad. "Lucky me. I got in the way."

"But no one has come up with any new Krans paintings in years. It's not at all feasible that anyone could do it now."

"She remembered a name," I said as I sat down again. "Her eyewitness account provides provenance, or would provide it if the portrait ever surfaces."

"What name?" Christina didn't seem to be all that much into what she was hearing.

"The man in both paintings—the original and second

one—the rich guy from Chicago, was named—Hencourt. At least, that's how she remembered it."

That jarred Christina into paying complete attention. "Hencourt? Or Hemcourt? Another Hemcourt portrait," she said softly, and not entirely like a question.

"Pearl expects me to find it." I smelled the aroma and savored the first sip. I used my peripheral vision to gauge the reaction. It didn't disappoint.

"You?"

"Yes, me. I stayed up the other night doing research, but I still don't know where to start." Not ready to come clean about the other reason I stayed awake, I opted for a dodge that might prove useful. "When Herb added that workshop onto his barn, didn't he salvage it nearly whole from somewhere else? Do you remember where exactly?"

Christina thought on it briefly and replied, "Sure, he found it in Altona. It had been a lean-to addition on another building that was getting renovated. The owners didn't want it and planned on tearing it apart and burning it. Herb thought it perfect for his needs, so he separated it from the other structure, jacked it up from the foundation, put wheels under the thing, and moved it over here. It turned into an event of sorts. They had to prop up some power lines and close the highway long enough to make room for the turn into the lot by the barn. Attaching it went smoothly. Herb always did first-rate work. Custom-made all those shelves . . ." Christina felt in her pocket for a tissue.

I finished her sentence in a near whisper. "For his

antique tool collection." I could still picture everything lined up by category and use. "I went back there yesterday. Yet another reason Michael isn't happy with me."

"Oh, honey. You shouldn't have done that."

"I had to. I needed to see it all again. I just hadn't expected anyone else coming in on us."

"What? Who?"

"Gordon Anderson. He totally freaked. Deputy Dana arrived in the nick of time to save us."

"When was this?" Christina looked lost. "After you found Marcella?"

"Yeah, Michael offered me a ride home and I talked him into the side trip to Varnishtree," I said, and hesitated; now seemed as good a time as any. "I didn't go looking for Marcella. Finding her was pure luck." I reached for my shoulder bag and pulled out the creased brochure. "See, marked on the trail map—Dairy Cave Site." I held it out for her to see. "Is Uncle Roy hiding out there? Did I hear his voice earlier?"

Christina's finger traced the rim of her cup. "Yes, he's been here. I don't know if he's still out at the cave or not. He doesn't say much. Just comes and goes. I never know when he'll show up." Her face paled and the furrows deepened in her brow.

"They won't stop looking for him," I said. "They have questions about Herb that need to be answered. Then there are the break-ins in the village. Like it or not, they'll suspect him."

"But he's not doing any of that. He just wants it all to go away."

"All what to go away?"

"He won't say. Keeping secrets must be a family trait," Christina said with a sigh.

"And we're one big, happy family," I murmured.

Worried or not, Christina got up, declaring the menagerie in the barn was calling for breakfast, and left to get dressed. I sipped my coffee and wondered how I would ever turn things around. I missed last week when my days were filled with sunny hope and optimistic promise. These days looked cloudy and bleak.

I needed to get going, too. Michael just might show up.

CHAPTER 23

The Lutfisk Café enjoyed a bustling morning crowd of locals and regulars. Folks who would normally only nod and smile at me, if they acknowledged me at all, gave me a polite chorus of "Good morning" and "Thanks for finding Marcella." It made me feel a little uncomfortable. This kind of fame could go as fast as it came, but for right now it did give me a warm and fuzzy glow.

Talli, behind the counter, called out, "Coffee's on the house." She spotted the paper bag in my hand and added, "Oh, goody, somethin' in there for me?"

I held up the bag. "Sorry to disappoint, but they're an offering for Michael. Peace muffins. Have you seen him?"

"An excellent idea, but no, I haven't seen anything of him. I expect he'll be by eventually."

I got lucky and quickly grabbed a newly empty table up front by the long, narrow window, a remnant of the building's former life as a gas station. I set the muffins to the side and gazed at the panoramic view. How much time to allow for waiting? Michael had every right not to show up.

Armed with two cups of coffee, Talli sat down. "I needed a break. Been hard at it since I opened the door this mornin'."

"What's up? I wouldn't have expected this many people this early in the morning."

"Oh, everyone's wound up over last night," Talli said.

"What happened?" I tried to pull off acting innocent and uncaring, but I really wanted to know what happened after I left the park. I tried not to tense at the memory of Winston Maskin stepping out from the shadows with a shotgun cradled in his elbow. I'd purposely avoided mentioning it to Christina. No need to add any fresh worries to the pile I was building. But if Talli knew, and everyone here knew as well, Christina wouldn't be far behind. I wouldn't catch a break on this one.

Talli took no notice of any unease on my part as she told the story. "Winston, Gordon, and a few other ol' boys got it into their thick heads that they'd be the ones to protect the village last night. They armed themselves and went out. Those fools managed to catch themselves two deputies who were tryin' to set up their own stakeout."

I choked out an incredulous, "Whoa."

"Our heroes got the drop on them behind the Blacksmith Shop." Talli couldn't hold the laughter in any more.

"What happened then?" I silently thanked Michael for getting me out of the park when he did.

"Thank God nobody got hurt," Talli continued, after she regained her composure. "But they got into all kinds of trouble. Sheriff Henry is *furious*." Before she could add any more details, she noticed a customer at the counter waiting to pay and excused herself. She left me wondering about the content of the conversations around me. I thought it better to study the scenery outside while I waited for Michael to show.

Over the next half hour the most interesting thing to happen was getting a short phone call from Lars asking me if I was home. I told him I'd be at The Lutfisk a little while longer before heading back home. He basically wanted to let me know he'd gotten home safe last night. An odd call to make; if I was talking to him, didn't that mean everything was fine? But who was I to say anything about odd behavior.

Not long after Lars's phone call, Ekollon's old Mercedes pulled up. It struck me as somewhat strange, since he wasn't a morning regular of The Lutfisk. I didn't feel at all uneasy until a sullen Lars exited from the passenger side. Alarmed, my thoughts went directly to the Hemcourt family's portrait at Nikkerbo. But how could there be a problem with that? No one saw anything, except Lars. Surely he wouldn't have sold me out. He had nothing to gain by doing anything so treacherous. I could do nothing but sit tight and wait for whatever happened next.

Lars entered alone. If he had wanted to be inconspicuous, he had no luck; all eyes were on him as he leaned down to my level and asked softly for me to come outside. Mystified, I gathered my few belongings together, more of an automatic response than conscious thought, and went out the door leaving a roomful of curious whispers.

Outside, I shot Lars a questioning look. "Don't expect any help from him," the puffed-up, pompous Ekollon said. "I've got you both. He may have diplomatic immunity, but you don't."

Now I had two questions to convey when my confused stare shifted back to Lars.

"Isn't that cute," Ekollon sniffed. "She's pretending not to know."

Ekollon's blatant, nasty attitude caught me off guard as I asked, "What's this about?"

"What's this about?" parroted Ekollon. He glared at me for another minute in order to magnify his dramatic delivery. "Just the little matter of a stolen painting." Ekollon couldn't restrain himself. He practically dripped venom.

Still mystified, I had to guess. "You mean the Hemcourt family's Krans? At Nikkerbo?"

"Oh, please," Ekollon said, after an ever-so-slight pause and a curious look before he went on with his tirade. "Of course I mean the Hemcourt Krans."

"It's gone?" I said in disbelief.

"Stop this pathetic acting," Ekollon commanded.

"But it was fine when Lars and I left. I saw him lock up.

He did it right. Then we took my car to Alpha." My brain kicked into high gear as I ran through last night's events. "People saw us. Lots of people saw us. Afterwards, I dropped him off at Nikkerbo's parking lot. Neither one of us went back inside. His car wouldn't start, so I called for help. Anderson Brothers, Galva, you can check with them."

"Well, I'm sure the sheriff's deputies will do just that." Ekollon said. "They're on their way."

I protested with a renewed air of urgency. "Winston Maskin saw me in the park last night. He'll tell you I wasn't carrying any large objects."

"You've got it hidden in your car." Ekollon stared right through me.

"My car is still packed from moving out of my Galesburg apartment. There's no room for anything else. Ask Lars." I pleaded my case while being hopeful that procrastination would work out in my favor just this once.

"Her car is quite crowded," Lars confirmed.

"I've got you on video taking the painting off the wall." Ekollon drew his shoulders back to assume a haughty, smug stance.

It didn't make sense. I asked Lars about the alarm system. It hadn't been activated. That would have been his last act before he locked the final door. "There was another camera," I mumbled. Then I realized there had to be a separate system. "Why? Who were you spying on?"

"That's immaterial," Ekollon said.

"Okay, I admit I handled the painting. It was improper

and against procedure, but I didn't take it." I rounded on Ekollon. I wanted to face him directly. "If you recorded me taking it off the wall, then you have a recording of me putting it back."

"Don't expect that to clear you." The pitch of Ekollon's voice began to rise as did the crimson color in his cheeks. "You committed sacrilege. Blasphemy. I won't stand for any more of such conduct. You won't get away with besmirching the honor of the Prophet."

I couldn't believe the crazy words I was hearing, and with such bitterness. "Sacrilege? Blasphemy? The Prophet?" Stunned, I watched a replay of his temper tantrum from Saturday night at Nickkerbo. Then Friday's crime scene at the Varnishtree flickered into my mind. Varnishtree. Herb's workshop. Where they gave me such a hard time about my cell phone. It gave me an idea so utterly far-fetched and impossible. I *had* to try it. I pulled out my phone and pushed some buttons.

"Calling mommy? Or maybe mommy's lawyer? How cute," Ekollon sneered.

I tilted the phone's screen so Lars could see it. Hardly daring to breathe, I waited. A ring tone came from Ekollon's direction.

"Not now," Ekollon grumbled. He reached into his jacket pocket and pulled out his phone, meaning to swiftly deal with the distraction. Only the ringing came from his shirt pocket. It continued uninterrupted until replaced by a low battery alarm. He froze in place and stared at me.

I returned his stare with every bit of steely resolve I

could muster. One beat, two. The next move was his.

A stiff and livid Ekollon began to inch his way backward toward his car. Putting ever more distance between us. "You're fired. Both of you. Finished," he hissed before getting behind the wheel and slamming the door. The spinning tires of the Mercedes raised a cloud of dust as he accelerated north across the bridge.

"What . . . what just happened here?" A confused Lars asked.

After a few moments of icy silence, I managed to tell him. "The number I called was Herb's." It was my turn to spit some venom. "He had Herb's cell phone in his shirt pocket."

As the information registered with Lars his face transformed and his mouth dropped open. "You can't be serious. Do we call 911? That's what you do here, *ja*?"

"Yes. I mean, no." I wanted time to think. "Let's go. We've given folks enough of a show. I think Ekollon was bluffing about the sheriff, but I'm not interested in waiting around to see who else turns up." I shepherded Lars over to my car and muttered "Diplomatic immunity?" with an incredulous shake of my head. He only offered a sheepish shrug of his shoulders. "Oh, just get in the car," I ordered.

"That was amazing. How long have you known about Ekollon?"

"I don't know. Suspected? Maybe a little. Hard to tell when he's an ass most of the time anyway. It just all came together in a flash," I said. "Where to? Back to the Lowell farm?"

"*Ja*, that will do. I must speak to them. He picked me up from there before he came looking for you."

"Did you see him make any calls?"

"No, he was too busy giving me commands."

"Good. Maybe we can catch a break." I leveled a stern look at him. "Diplomatic immunity," I scoffed. "You are so busted."

Still feeling the lingering effects of the adrenaline rush, I pulled out onto the Bishop Hill road heading south. As I drove, I tried to organize my thoughts to come up with an explanation.

"Okay, I've been noticing little things. Like Marcella acting strange and dropping sly innuendos about the Hemcourt family's Krans. While we waited for the ambulance yesterday, she mentioned following a crazy nut. I didn't get it at the time, but she meant Ekollon, the little acorn who was fanatical about all things Swedish and the Colony. That got me thinking of how he showed up all rumpled and disheveled at the Varnishtree on Friday. That's so unlike him. This is the man who thinks he's the expert everyone calls first."

"*Ja*, he does have a high opinion of himself," Lars said.

I continued with my line of thought. "It made me think about cell phones and how much grief I got over sitting mine down on Herb's workbench. They wanted to keep it. I had a hard time convincing them that it was indeed mine and, like, I had to have it. So, what if Herb *did* call Ekollon first? The way he reacted back there, the red-faced hissy fit, brought it all together in an instant. I just knew. I can't believe calling Herb's phone actually worked." I shook my head. "And keeping it with him . . . and on. Stupid."

"It proves his guilt."

I paused before wondering out loud, "You know, I'm not so sure. I would never have suspected he could do anything like that. A pompous windbag for sure, but physically hurt someone? Kill Herb?" I shook my head again, my conviction not so solid anymore. "That first break-in at the cabin . . . the feeling I had." It made me shudder just to think about it. "And why come back? It doesn't make sense." I released an exasperated sigh. "Maybe it wasn't him."

"Now you think he's innocent?"

"Oh no, he's not innocent. No way. But why come back to the cabin a second time?"

"I don't understand. Your cabins were broken into twice?"

"Yeah, the one my Uncle Roy uses. I happened upon the first one Friday night. It scared the life out of me. Sunday night late or early Monday morning, someone broke in again and combed through his files. Pulled out a bunch of old photos."

"He missed something the first night," Lars mused. "Something worth going back for . . . Photographs, you say? I've never seen Ekollon overly concerned about any particular photos or images. Now, Karl Hemson, that's another story. Get him talking about Hemson and he can turn into a maniac. I do not joke."

I did believe him, but I had to stay focused on real and present problems. "I wish Uncle Roy had better housekeeping skills. He sets a tool down and it stays there. But his files, he's always kept them in good shape. Still, it's too hard to tell what's missing."

"If Ekollon didn't kill Herb Anderson, are we still fired?"

I ignored him. "Okay, he was there at Varnishtree. We know that much. Herb probably called him. Ekollon missed it, got a message, came running as soon as he could. Herb might have already been dead by then." Such a cold thought. I was amazed I could say it out loud like that. Overwhelmed by the need to keep talking, I asked, "What would be so important that he'd fail to report a death, a murder?"

"Mr. Anderson was working on the Hemcourt immigrant trunk," Lars offered. "I helped get it over to his Varnishtree shop last week."

"Judging from what I saw its condition seemed pretty good, great even, given its age. Why commission Herb to work on it at all?"

"Ekollon had concerns about an area near the bottom on the right side. He talked Mr. Hemcourt into giving permission to take it in."

I summoned up an image of the workbench. The trunk rested roughly in the center with a variety of hand tools near one corner. "There may have been some cracks on that end, near the bottom. I paid more attention to the *rosemaling* pattern than anything else. It was continuous and intact." I knew that wasn't helpful. "Where is he anyway?"

"Ekollon's probably made it to the interstate by now."

"No, not him. Our Mr. Hemcourt the fifth. He was nice enough to give me time off this week. Maybe he'll give us our jobs back," I said, still pondering the strange assortment of facts I'd accumulated. "You know, there's another thing bothering me. Remember no Roman numeral V on the back of the painting?"

"What are you saying?"

"Maybe he never signed it because he knew it wasn't 'the real deal,' as Marcella would say."

"I went over that painting, carefully examined it. It was a genuine Krans. Everything fit—brushwork, pigments, stretchers, even the nails. It was all there. The OK signature, everything. I didn't consider the scratches on the frame significant."

"Didn't it seem too perfect?"

"*Ja*, exceptional." Lars shrugged his shoulder again.

I pulled into the driveway of the Lowell's neatly kept farmhouse. "Are you going to be all right?"

"*Ja*. No worries. How about you?"

"Not as confident. I have to go home to face the music. I'm not at all hopeful." I gave him a squinty look. "And some of us need jobs."

CHAPTER 24

The red brick house looked peaceful as I pulled into the driveway. No other cars. No lights. No signs of unusual activity. I took it as all good and hoped it would last a little longer.

Instead of going into the house, I headed across the road to the cabins. Seeing the barn a second time had sort of worked out. Another viewing of the Hemlock suite might yield something worthwhile as well.

The outside appeared the same. Rustic, rough-hewn boards provided a nice picturesque look in the summer, but had minimal insulation value. It had to be a brutal way to spend a winter. Uncle Roy craved his privacy and couldn't be coaxed into anything else. The temperature had to drop into the negative digits before we got him to come inside for a night.

I glanced over to the tree marking the Oxpojke Trail. It

appeared normal, too. I picked out my tracks from yesterday. Fresh signs of deer overlaid them. I surveyed the sky above the tree line and noted the gathering clouds; the current spell of pleasant weather would likely come to an end. Tonight was bound to be wetter and cooler. Good thing I found Marcella when I did. The rain might make the farmers happy, or maybe not. They complained about everything.

Inside, the cabin showed the positive effects of Christina's touch, file folders and photos all tucked away. Desk, table, and bed in tidy order. She had made the most of the opportunity and cleared out the piles of old pizza boxes and the general clutter that had accumulated in the corners. With the room dusted, swept, and cleared of cobwebs, it looked habitable and downright cozy. I sat on the bed and took it all in. Uncle Roy would absolutely hate it.

I cast an appreciative eye around the combined studio-living space. The walls held older, unframed paintings, landscapes mostly, with lots of pencil and charcoal sketches tacked up where he could study them and envision improvements. They displayed such promise, clearly a credit to his great-grandfather's name and his position as Krans's last assistant. Roy Landers, Sr., had learned well from the self-taught folk artist. He had combined that experience with his own natural talents for a comfortable local career. Early on, Roy Landers, Jr., had shown some of that same talent, but opted to stay focused on farming, as did his son, the third in line with the same name. The fourth time around was the charm, with Uncle

Roy inheriting the eye for color and composition along with the name. He had a steady hand with the brush, at least when he wasn't on a drinking binge. I liked his more recent diversions into Outsider art, or Oursider art as he took to calling it. I appreciated the not-always-subtle ways he used to make a statement or poke fun at a stuffy tradition. Great work with a pitifully small fan base of loyal customers. I wondered if the sheer waste of his talent out here somehow held a premonition for my life.

Thinking about my life reminded me of the handful of letters I'd found stashed on his desk. Letters I hadn't read yet. Bad news could wait a little longer. But I got to thinking, what if my letters weren't the first ones he'd pilfered? Lars mentioned his uncle wrote letters. What if ...

I stared at his colorful collection of hanging folders. If he had taken letters meant for Nora, they'd be in there, somewhere. I'd looked through those files on Friday. I'd pawed through them again on Monday. But I hadn't been searching for envelopes. And certainly not Swedish-looking envelopes.

I thought about using the gallery trick I picked up in a studio painting class. I got up and took a couple of paces away from the desk. I closed my eyes and counted to ten and then spun around. The trick was to pick up on the first thing you saw. Something that stood out: a line, a shape, or this case a color. Blue. Not just any blue, but a bright shade of blue. Swedish-flag blue. Maybe.

I pulled the folder up and found it held a handful of old lightweight airmail envelopes. They all had impressive

Swedish stamps. All were addressed to my mother, Nora.

Quick footsteps on pea gravel intruded into my confused thoughts. It only took a moment to ascertain Christina's style of walking. At that pace she must really be angry. I stuffed the envelopes in my shoulder bag, pushed the folder back in place, and sat on the bed. She'd heard about Ekollon and Lars in front of The Lutfisk. Bad news always travels faster than good. I flopped backward and braced myself for the explosion.

"Don't be mad," I called out as soon as the door opened. "I can explain." As I spoke, the irony struck me. What if at some point Ekollon had to say something like that to Sheriff Henry and his investigators? I snickered at the thought of his flushed chubby face and twitching mustache sitting in a room trying to come up with convincing excuses.

"What on earth have you got to be happy about?" Christina demanded.

"I was just thinking about . . ." I started to say Ekollon, but sat up and motioned to the artwork on the walls. "Uncle Roy. Look at all this potential. He never should have stopped."

"He hasn't," Christina said as she did a slow turn, "not completely. And you can't change the subject so easily this time." She looked down at me. "A public scene with Ekollon? I must say you keep yourself quite busy. How do you do it?"

I could tell she really didn't expect an answer. "We had a disagreement. That isn't a crime." I held out my bare wrists for inspection. "See, no handcuffs yet." I've had too much practice at deception to willingly hand Christina any more ammunition, so I asked coyly, "What have you heard?"

"All the latest buzz is about the missing painting."

I decided to go with that and held out hope she didn't know every detail about the face-off with Ekollon. Or that I'd been fired. At least not yet. I ventured in another, hopefully safer, direction. "Does that mean you've seen Mr. Hemcourt?"

"Yes, our paths have crossed. I had to go to Cambridge. Still answering questions about Roy. Now Curt's family's painting is missing from Nikkerbo." She pulled out a desk chair and sat down. "I'm getting tired."

"Come on, they can't possibly think Uncle Roy could have stolen that from the museum." I dared to hope that Ekollon hadn't shared his suspicions about my being responsible for the theft with anyone else, at least not yet.

"Thus far, they haven't ruled anything out. That's the official line I've gotten." Christina picked nervously at tiny specks of lint on her pants. The strain showed in her face.

"I would believe it of Ekollon before anyone else. He's got a devious, shifty look about him. He'd plan a museum heist." My attempt at humor wasn't gaining any traction, so I let my attention wander back to the artwork on the walls. "Uncle Roy shouldn't have given up on having a studio somewhere, downtown maybe. You know, like a real business. He could be in the Blacksmith Shop along with Gordon and the others, making a living instead of subsisting out here."

"He never got along with Gordon—oil and water. They had differing philosophies on everything. What is art? What is craft? How to make a living? Roy had the name, the family connection to Krans, but Gordon always considered himself the more accomplished talent, that and being a true Colony descendant. He never let Roy forget his family was a generation off the mark."

"Things never got better?"

"Not soon enough for Roy. Oh, I wish it had been different, but art or craft, whatever you call it, it's a hard business. Very few succeeded to any degree back when Roy tried to make a go of it. Bishop Hill has made a comeback since then. Hemcourt's money and his center have helped turn things around."

"So have you heard about Maskin and the stakeout?" I asked in the hope it might lighten Christina's mood. It certainly had done wonders for Talli.

"Now there's a story," Christina said, smiling. "There must have been a warm body behind every bush in the village last night."

I patiently listened to Christina's version of how Maskin, Gordon, and various bar buddies had chosen their hiding spots well before the deputies had a chance to set up their stake-out posts. As a result, the local guys got a drop on two of Henry County's finest. The deputies wanted to make a case against Maskin and company since weapons were involved, but Sheriff Henry said he'd handle it.

"How's he going to do that?"

"Well, first he has to come down to the village tavern ..." Christina couldn't make it any further. The thought of the serious, staid lawman in the often boisterous establishment set her to giggling. After wiping away a few tears, she gasped, "Oh, I so want to see that." I joined in, glad for the small respite.

After our mirth subsided, I strained to identify a noise. "Wait, I think I hear something. Someone's here?" My questioning look at Christina only brought a shrug and a small head-shake. We rose together, but I got to the door first in time to see Curt Hemcourt V confidently striding up the driveway toward the cabin. "Were you expecting him?"

"No. I saw Curt this morning but didn't have a chance to say much. He was too busy reporting the theft of his family's Krans painting. He was very vocal and quite distraught."

I evaluated the steady approach of the museum owner. "Looks okay now," I whispered. I also noted that he seemed pretty sure which cabin he needed to approach.

"Ladies, I hope I'm not disturbing you. I was on my way back to Nikkerbo and decided to stop by and see how you were faring." We all knew he had to drive out of his way to get here and it made for an awkward moment. "Is this the cabin I've heard so much about?"

"I guess so," Christina said. "This is Roy's cabin and studio." Hemcourt waited with a not-so-subtle air of expectation and the always polite Christina gave way and invited him in.

"Charmingly rural, I must say." He stepped closer to the walls and examined the various pieces displayed. "I'd hoped to see some examples of his work. We spoke of it the other night."

"That would have been Friday night," I said. I had an unsettled feeling in the pit of my stomach. This impromptu visit seemed out of place and out of character for the type of man who had people come to him for meetings.

"Of course. The Landers name is so closely tied with that of Olof Krans, I had to see for myself." He turned his gaze from the wall to me and proudly professed, "You see, young lady, I've done my homework, too."

"You were talking about Friday night," Christina reminded him.

"Ah, yes. Roy has been quite difficult to get a hold of. We've been missing each other for months. I finally tracked him down at the village tavern last Friday." He turned up his charm a notch. "We discussed the nature of primitive art in general, his current interests in Outsider Art, and the possibility of a commission." He continued his close scrutiny of a Red Oak landscape. "I could envision a mural such as this inside the main lobby of Nikkerbo, couldn't you?"

I turned to Christina as we exchanged looks of disbelief, with mine being far from inconspicuous. Thankfully, she came to the rescue. "I'm sure he'd love to, as soon as the unpleasant situation involving your painting is sorted out."

"Yes, of course. Speaking of unpleasant." He turned to me. "I had the strangest call from David a while ago. He was quite excited and a bit incoherent, but it seemed like he wanted to dismiss you and Lars. Taking liberties or some such thing? I was nowhere close to figuring out what he was talking about when he just hung up. While I can't condone any impropriety, I can personally assure you that I have no intention of asking anyone to leave. I trust I can count on you to show better judgment in the future for whatever he was referring to." He finished with a fluttering hand gesture and a serious downward stare at me.

"Oh, yes, sir," I said, and silently promised to move learning about video security systems to the top of my to-do list.

"Good." He held onto a tight smile. "Look, I'm keeping Nikkerbo closed until after Herb Anderson's funeral. Come in on Friday and we shall *all* have a fresh start." He took one last appreciative look around and offered his hand to Christina. "Thank you so much for putting up with this intrusion. I appreciate it." He turned for the door and left.

Christina regarded me with dubious eyes. "You took liberties?"

"It's not as bad as it sounds." I gave her a brief recap of why I had to take the prized Hemcourt family's Krans off the wall. I winced and wilted a little under Christina's disbelieving gaze. "At least I have my job back. I can't get over how generous and understanding he's been toward me. Maybe I have Uncle Roy to thank." I watched as he neared the BMW parked in front of the red brick house. "I showed up on time and presentable last Saturday, things seemed fine, and I got shown the door as soon as Mr. Hemcourt turned up with those lawyers, Mr. Patrick and the short pudgy one." Thinking about it now changed my opinion of what happened. "It was like he couldn't get rid of me fast enough." I looked at Christina with all seriousness and said, "I do believe Uncle Roy would call it the bum's rush."

"That sounds like Roy all right," Christina said as she stalked out and headed for the house. I followed.

Up ahead, Hemcourt's car eased out of the driveway, made the turn north, and disappeared over the rise. When I crossed over the spot where the parked car had sat, I noticed a clump of dried plant material. I didn't think anything of it. It was probably the same stuff I'd noted Saturday morning, finally shrunk down enough to fall from the bumper. But some vague inkling made me return and examine it closer. Nudging it with my foot dislodged a few reedy strands of cattail. Outside of the Edwards riverbank, there were only a few stands large enough and close enough to a road to get caught in a car's bumper. "Wait up a minute," I called to Christina.

"What's wrong now?" Christina turned back to see me staring at the ground and retraced her steps.

"Do you know what these are?" I pointed to the other assorted bits of vegetation.

With some effort, Christina knelt to take a closer look.

"Well, I see big bluestem, cattail, and teasel. Now give me a hand up. The knees don't work like they used to."

"Where would all three of these grow together?"

"Let me think. The bluestem and cattail grow in ditches in quite a few places, but that kind of teasel is harder to come by."

"Why's that?"

"The Colonists brought it with them. They used the dried seed pods in processing their woolen textiles before they got better tools. Other varieties of teasel grow around the county, but this one is quite a bit larger and spikier. It's very distinctive."

"So where would I find some?"

Christina gave it a serious thought before she said, "The closest would be the next road over, near Gunnar Olson's place. You would have passed right by it on the way to Red Oak grove."

I followed Christina into the house, lost in troubling thoughts.

╬ PEARL ╬

Summer 1915

Pearl Essie thought about running after Momma, *Mormor*, and Auntie Sophia, but the stricken expression on Olof Krans's face as he surveyed the damage to his wonderful painting kept her rooted in place.

It seemed forever before he spoke again. With a sad, subdued voice, he said, "In the old country, I witnessed the Prophet give a nighttime sermon. I came with my family and stayed in the back. I was so young, and sitting still for such a long time proved a chore. More difficult than cleaning out the barn." He shook his head slowly.

"I know," she said, and she did know a lot about barns. Matters about the Prophet were best left to the adults. She wanted to provide some measure of comfort to the old man and pulled over a chair and guided him into the seat.

Through this simple act she felt like a grownup for the first time and savored the sense of importance.

After sitting, Krans continued to speak softly. "I was less than eight when he was called away to the new land. Twelve the year my family made the crossing from Sweden. Not much older than you are now, my *liten Pärla*." He smiled at her with a world-weary expression. "*Ja*, we arrived in Bishop Hill in November, months after the death of the Prophet. He died in March. The Colony still mourned. I never had the chance to see him alive again.

"I have to fix this." He stared at the damaged painting in front of him. "What else can I do?"

"I can help," she said.

She'd seen him do it before and knew just what to do. He'd need to fashion patches for the wicked-looking tears. She went to his pile of scrap canvas and sorted through it, picking out two narrow strips.

He took them in hand and rose to begin the repair. He spoke as he worked. "There must be no telling of this demented act of a poor, troubled old woman."

Pearl Essie didn't understand why, but she had to swear on her own immortal soul never to breathe a word. She crossed her heart and nodded. He could trust her. She promised.

The work went well and the canvas grew whole again. Redeemed to its former glory. Stepping back from the painting, he released a heavy sigh and said, "Perhaps they are not ready for this one."

Pearl Essie may not have fully understood, but she instinctively knew he was right. She watched as he positioned the wet canvas to face a wall where it could dry unseen.

CHAPTER 25

Wednesday, June 4, 2008

I positioned myself well back from Herb's family at the funeral in Bishop Hill's other, more modern church. I wanted no attention and longed to be insignificant for their sake. I also hoped to stay out of Gordon Anderson's line of sight.

Not minding the hard wooden pew, I sat and marveled at how the morning sunlight streamed through the tall stained glass windows, enhancing their radiance. I closed my eyes and replayed the luminous colors in my mind as I listened to the sounds of scripture in English as well as Swedish. Later, the impassioned eulogies brought tissue-muffled grief to many around me. I tried to be stoic, but in the end, my own tears joined those of the others. Testament from the living to Herb's memory.

After the service, I appreciated those who stopped to offer their sincere sympathy with a hug. The simple gesture became a real comfort. I dodged the questions from those who only wanted more tidbits of information. The stares and whispers of the others made me yearn for the opportunity to slip away at the first prudent moment. Christina decided to stay and offer assistance to the workers setting up for the family gathering in the church basement and gave me the okay to head for home. I might have made it if I hadn't decided to detour past The Lutfisk. I spotted the Lowell's car parked out front and stopped in to get an update on Lars. I'd missed him in the crowded church and wanted to talk to him again.

I entered The Lutfisk to Talli's cheerful, "Good morning." As I poured a cup of coffee, Talli sidled over and gave me a warm hug, then whispered, "I'm so glad you came in today. You've got to show folks the stuff you're made of. Head up high and go on." I could only guess at the volume of gossip that would prompt Talli to give out such encouragement. I shuddered at the thought, but set my cup and shoulder bag down into the same spot I had held briefly yesterday. If Talli wanted nerve, I'd do it right.

The Lowells sat close by, and I walked over. "Good morning. I wanted to know if Lars was okay. I didn't see him at the service this morning."

"He's fine," Mrs. Lowell explained. "He got a call late last night and left early for Chicago. I think he's having family problems. His parents might be a little upset with him."

"But he didn't do anything," I said with exasperation. I wanted to say it was all Ekollon's fault. He was the one who'd made a baseless accusation. He was the one causing trouble. I had a great deal I wanted to say, but settled for, "I found the photo I wanted to show Lars."

"Give it some time to blow over and I'm sure he'll be back," Mr. Lowell said.

I returned to my table and tried to hide my disappointment by staring out the window. Again, I had the perfect perch to watch the comings and goings of people I'd known my whole life. I'd gotten polite acknowledgments from nearly everyone so far as the Café filled up. One farmer walked straight past without any sign of noticing me, but that was Gunnar Olson, our neighbor the next road over from us. When he had something to complain about, nothing sidetracked him. From the sound of things, the reputation of his daughter, Ulla, was getting ruined by a Wethersfield boy. I remembered her as a good student and one of the quiet kids on the school bus.

A minivan pulled into the driveway and came right up to the wide front porch. Someone was getting VIP treatment. It bugged me because somehow it looked so familiar. I should know it.

It became obvious just as it stopped and Pearl's white top-knot bun came into view. Today, the minivan wasn't coming straight at me and running me off the road. Amy came around to the passenger side and prepared to help

Pearl out. Talli emerged from behind the counter and went to offer her help as well. Together they got Pearl out of the car seat and outfitted with her walker. They formed a slow-moving procession by protectively flanking either side as the old woman made her way up to the porch. I hurried over and prepared to hold the door for them. I waited patiently for the right moment to swing it open.

Once we were all inside, I offered to give up my seat, only to be motioned to sit back down. Pearl's face had lit up when she'd seen me. With a look of relief, Amy asked me to stay. I would act as the designated guardian while Amy moved the minivan and went to the post office. A win-win situation for all.

"I'm happy to see you," I said to Pearl.

"I'm happy to see anyone," Pearl quipped in a raspy voice, and then leaned in to say, "Isn't it a sad state of affairs when a funeral becomes a social event for an old woman like me?" As Pearl turned to check out the other tables, Talli placed a hot cup of coffee in front of her and asked if she wanted the special for lunch. Pearl agreed to a half order, and with Talli a safe distance away she whispered to me in a conspiratorial tone, "Have you made any progress on finding the painting?"

I admired her directness and wondered how much of it had come from getting past the 100-year mile marker. "Since we spoke on Sunday, I've done a lot of research."

"But have you done any actual searching?"

"Well, I've had some problems."

Pearl huffed ever so slightly as she fumbled with a

cream packet for her coffee. I resisted the urge to help her, figuring it would only irritate her more. "I have some more questions."

"Of course you do." The packet finally gave way and Pearl stirred the powder around in slow circles as it dissolved into her coffee, lightening the color as it lifted her mood. "I had the dream again this morning," she chuckled softly. "This time I didn't steal a car."

"That's probably a good deal," I agreed.

"I thought about something you mentioned the other day," Pearl said when she resumed her matronly composure.

"What was that?" I couldn't imagine what she might be referring to. I had tried to listen more than talk. It was my most valuable interview technique.

"You mentioned photographs. Old pictures. It took a while, but it came to me. Krans had one."

"Krans showed you a photo?" I wanted to make sure I'd heard that correctly and leaned forward in an effort to keep our voices low. Everyone else was engrossed in their own conversations and ignoring us, but that could change at any moment.

"Oh my, yes. He had me write on the back."

I felt the air grow stale in my chest as it tightened. I waited for Pearl to say something more. She didn't. Instead she rummaged around in her shiny black purse. Finally pulling out a piece of paper, she said, "Here, I wrote down Krans's words."

"Can I keep this?" I inquired as calmly as possible.

"Yes, dear, it's for you."

I looked at it and frowned. "My Swedish isn't good enough to translate this." What I really meant was that I didn't trust myself to be accurate.

Pearl motioned for the paper to come back. She took out a pen and filled in the space underneath the Swedish words. "The Swedish words were his. Krans asked me to copy his words into English," she said as she wrote and handed it back when she finished. "That's what I wrote."

"Okay," I said. I exhaled slowly, trying to figure out what I was seeing. "This is what made Auntie Sophia so upset?"

"Upset? She stabbed the painting!" Pearl exclaimed. The look of shock on my face must have registered. She leaned toward me to whisper, "With scissors."

"Scissors? You didn't mention scissors before," I whispered back. A quick look around revealed no sign of Talli. She must be further back in the kitchen tending the oven.

"Oh, she scratched at it first while she screamed at the man in the painting. Then she used her quilting scissors on it." She clenched a fist and made stabbing motions for dramatic effect.

I put my hand on Pearl's to bring it back down to the table. "So she was angry with the man in the painting? Did she say why?"

"Auntie Sophia blamed the man for her sister leaving."

"Did she say where the sister went? What happened to her? Did she mention a name?"

"She cried so hard as she ran away," Pearl offered. "She couldn't say more."

"Okay. Where did she stab it, the painting, exactly?"

Pearl pulled her hand away and patted the center of her chest to indicate the heart.

"Wow," I said and sat back in my chair for a minute.

"She ripped it. A cross-shaped tear. He had a time fixing it."

"I bet he did." And, I thought, it gave me a way to identify the painting.

"You have to find it."

"I know. I'll do my best. Do you know what happened to the photo?"

"No. Never saw it again."

Amy came in and joined us with an overly cheerful, "How are we doing?"

A relaxed Pearl answered, "We're doing just fine. I was saying how important it was for young people to make plans and have goals."

"Yes, ma'am," I said. "I'll do my best."

CHAPTER 26

When I got back from The Lutfisk, I went out to the barn for a little kitten relaxation therapy and to ponder just what I could realistically do for Pearl and her mission. Her remembering about the photo and how she had transcribed Olof Krans's words offered only limited help. This new information didn't fit neatly into my budding theory about the man in the painting. I had wanted Pearl's memory of the name Hencourt to become Hemcourt. I didn't know enough yet to connect the dots back to the Colony.

Auntie Sophia's long-lost sister might be important, be a motive, but for what? I still had to trust that Pearl wasn't locked up in a far-fetched dream.

I came out of the barn brushing off bits of straw when I heard water running in the campground's shower building. That had to be Uncle Roy, back from the wilderness at last. I decided to wait for him in the Hemlock suite. He'd find me sitting at his table when he walked into the cabin. I hoped it would defuse some tension. He would have started fuming as soon as he saw how much cleaning had been done in his absence. I sat there stewing over the worry he had caused us over the past week. I debated what I'd say to him. Running over the dialogue in my mind was very satisfying. He could be such an inconsiderate jerk sometimes. I didn't think I could say anything without some profanity. When he finally came in, all squeaky clean and dressed in his usual jeans and t-shirt, instead of speaking my mind I went over and gave him a big bear hug. It was so good to have him home.

"I've been so worried about you," I whispered into his ear. "Christina kept your visits a secret as long as she could, but you guys didn't fool me." I wiped my eyes and tried to look stern.

"I'm so sorry, sweetie. I was angry. I needed some time to think of a way out of the fix I was in."

"Did Hemcourt threaten you?"

"Not in so many words. But he made it very plain that he didn't want any trouble from me. I had to be quiet or else."

"That would be about his family's painting, the Krans portrait that's really a Landers—your work."

He said nothing. He hung up his towel and sat down on the bed, giving me the good chair.

"You don't have to say anything," I said as I settled into

the chair. "I got a good look at it on Monday afternoon. Everything about it is right. You even added the initials and the Roman numerals to the back of the frame."

"I never did that. I refused. Hemcourt must've done it himself."

"What you also didn't do was leave Krans's technique unchanged. The original portrait, created in 1897, would have been done in his early style. The one on display is a better match to his mature period, therefore at odds with all known facts."

"That young man, the Swede, said you were close to figuring it out."

"You've seen Lars Trollenberg? How?"

"He found me up by the dairy cave. He had a map, one of those old brochures for the Oxpojke Trail. I thought they were all gone."

"Well, I picked one up, too. I would've found you first if it hadn't been for Marcella running off the road."

"That's who it was. Didn't hear the crash. Must've been out looking for food. Uh, speaking of Teeny, she around?"

"No. She stayed on after the funeral to help out. She should be back soon," I said, then stared at him with a long look of bewilderment. "How did all this happen?"

Uncle Roy rubbed his hands nervously back and forth on his jeans before beginning. "I guess it goes back to when every Swede in Bishop Hill and the country was making a fuss over the anniversary of the New Sweden Colony. 1988. I had a space in the Blacksmith Shop back then."

"You and Gordon," I said. "Christina told me you two didn't get along very well."

"Yeah, she's right about that. We were both painting up a storm and hoping to corner the market for Krans-like folk art. Y'know, primitive stuff."

"Surely there was room for both of you. Two people working with the same scene would produce two completely different paintings. I've seen it in my studio classes."

"You had to know Gordon back then. He always felt unappreciated, always in the shadow of his cousin, Herb." He paused for a moment as he remembered his friend. "When Mr. Curt Hemcourt V came looking for a painter, we darn near got into a fistfight over who'd land the job."

"Hemcourt was looking for a forger?"

"No, he was coy about what he wanted. He showed us an insurance photo. Never asked for anything improper, at first. He was just a guy who wanted a replacement picture for sentimental reasons. No mention of forgery or fake, just a new painting of an ancestor."

"Did he mention the fire?" I asked. "I wonder if his story would match up with the facts I found in online articles."

"He might've talked about it some. Don't remember. I was too bent on beating out Gordon, showing him up."

"So how'd you beat out Gordon?"

"I took my copy of the photo and did a mock-up, y'know, a rough sketch with my colors blocked out. Gordon did one, too. His was good, but I had my secret weapon. One of my great-grandfather's paintings was darn near a perfect match for what Hemcourt wanted. I used it for inspiration. My piece blew his socks off. I got the job and Gordon never forgave me. It was only later, after I had the portrait finished, that he insisted I find a way to age it and sign it with Krans's OK signature. We went round and round on that. Until—"

"Until what? What could make you do something you didn't want to do?"

"Nora, your mom," he said softly, obviously still hurt by the memory. "I could tell she was in big trouble. I thought money would be the answer. I told Hemcourt I'd do it and named a ridiculous price. Thought it was too far out there for him to even consider." He shrugged. "It wasn't. I took the money. After that, I was his."

"Oh, no," I said. I reached for his hand and gave it a reassuring squeeze. I waited a bit before asking, "Then what happened?"

"Nothing. He took the painting back to Chicago and all I had to do was keep quiet. To tell the truth, I forgot all about it. And then he shows back up here wanting to build that monstrosity to honor his family's ties to Bishop Hill."

"And your meeting Friday night at the bar was about you keeping quiet about the painting?"

"Right." He looked down as he rubbed his hands together. "But you know, I wouldn't have said anything anyway. I just wanted to forget I ever met the man. Hemcourt didn't have to say anything. He could've left well enough alone."

"Herb tried to talk to you that night. Any idea why?"

"No, the bartender gave me a note, but by the time I was tossed out the door, he was gone. I guess he couldn't wait."

"Did you contact him later?"

"No. I was so mad . . . at Hemcourt . . . at myself." He pushed a hand through his hair for a moment, then let his hand fall back into his lap. "I figured the best thing to do was disappear for a spell. Teeny filled me in later. Then that young fellow Lars found me." He stopped. I waited for him to clear the obvious lump in his throat. "I'm so sorry I wasn't there for you."

I found his hand again and gave it another squeeze. "Did she tell you about the break-ins here?"

"I can't figure that out. I never signed nothing. We had a verbal agreement and Hemcourt paid me in cash."

"You keep large amounts of cash in here?" I looked around. The cabin couldn't be a more insecure place to hide money.

"What can I say? I saved some by making small deposits, but most of it just plain got wasted."

"So you can't think of any reason why someone would be so interested in you or this place to break in here not once, but twice?"

"Nothing," he said.

But I could tell he wasn't absolutely sure and was struggling to remember.

"A letter, maybe? Sure, there was the one letter that had the insurance photo in it. I suppose someone could've wanted it, but why? It wouldn't prove anything."

"You said my mom was in trouble. She needed money? No one's ever talked about that."

"Nora was trying to build a life with that no-good moron."

I cringed at the mention of my father.

"I'm sorry, sweetie, but he was getting into some really bad stuff and I didn't want her going down the tubes with him. I'd hoped to buy him off, so he'd take off and leave us all alone. He took the money and left. But it was too late. Your mom fell apart. She wouldn't talk to me or Teeny."

I was holding my own considering these new revelations about my parents. Uncle Roy seemed impressed with my strength and curiosity. I followed up with more questions. Now was the time to keep him talking.

"According to Lars, Mom knew his uncle. He made it sound like they were close. Close enough to write letters to each other," I said.

"I don't know about that." He suddenly started massaging his back. I bet it tightened in response to the lie, but I had to keep still. "I knew his uncle while he worked here. He was nice enough, a down-to-earth sort. We talked about art, history, and the prospects of making a living here. He had some good ideas."

"What kind of work did he do here? Lars hinted that his uncle knew a lot about the restoration of the Krans paintings from the church."

"The paintings went to Sweden for cleaning. Not

everyone was happy about that, but the Swedes paid for it all. When the paintings came back, a bunch of experts accompanied them. Trollenberg came with that lot and hung around after they left."

I noticed he couldn't suppress the hint of a grin. He and Lars must be up to something. Keeping each other's secrets. Uncle Roy might even be responsible for coming up with that silly last name for Lars and his uncle, Trollenberg.

"Look, sweetie, why don't you go up to the house. I need some more time to get myself into one piece. I'll be up as soon as I can."

"Sure, meet up with you later." I gave him another hug and a kiss on the cheek. "I'm glad you're back and all right. Don't go and do that again. You hear?"

"Yes, ma'am," he said, and shooed me out the door.

I saw him reach around to rub his aching back. It served him right for not coming clean about the letters: Mom's old ones, the latest ones that belonged to me, and everything else he chose to keep secret.

CHAPTER 27

When Christina got back, I met her at the door with the good news about Uncle Roy's return.

"The weather's due to change. I figured that would make him show up. He just came in a little early." Christina went to the refrigerator, removed a large package, and took it over to place it in the sink. "I've been saving this broiler for a homecoming meal. Seems fitting. He's no spring chicken, you know." She pointed to the bird in the sink and gave me a devious smile. "Chicken. Get it? Chicken."

I groaned. "Is it any wonder I get into so much trouble? You're such a bad influence. Should I go get Uncle Roy?"

"No, not yet. The aroma will entice him in when the time comes. Give him some room. I imagine he was really peeved to find the place cleaned up."

"Well, he did seem a little cross at first. It's not like you had any choice. Things were really messed up after the first time." The first time, but not the second. The two incidents were very different.

I helped around the kitchen. We both wanted this meal to be special. By the time the chicken was starting to smell good in the oven and the side dishes were nearly finished, we noticed Uncle Roy hadn't come into the house. I volunteered to go check on him.

Outside, the gathering clouds had obscured the fading daylight enough for the yard light to flicker on. No rain yet, but it was on its way. I saw flashes of lightning in the distance. The storm front was still too far away for the thunder to register.

"That's odd," I muttered. There should be some lights on in the Hemlock suite. I walked up to the door and knocked this time. When there was no answer, I knocked again, louder, and called his name. When I got nothing but the sounds of local wildlife settling in for the night, I started to get steamed. I tried the doorknob and found it locked. That was the last straw. I went back to the house with my own storm clouds circling over my head. *How could he?*

I stomped into the kitchen. "You won't believe it," I started to say.

Christina saw the anger and disappointment on my face and supplied the ending. "Roy's gone again. So much for our happy homecoming. Well, I'll show him," she said and went to the stove to turn everything off. "We'll see how he likes that."

I wanted to say something snarky about not wasting good food. While I was searching for an appropriate cliché the back door opened, and I failed to recognize the person entering the kitchen. My angry mood instantly transformed into heart-stopping panic. A tall man in a dark hoodie, obviously not Uncle Roy, stood still for a long, menacing moment before reaching up to slide the hood back.

"Okay, I'm here," Curt Hemcourt V said.

Like deer caught in the high beam of an oncoming car, we just stared at him, wide-eyed and transfixed. We said nothing. We did nothing.

He stood there like an angel of doom until he spoke again, and his whiny voice broke the spell. "Look, I got a call. I came. It's going to start raining out there any minute now. There'll be mud and muck all over. Can we get on with this?"

I looked at Christina and she wasn't moving. I realized that one of us had to say something. "On with what exactly?" came my jerky reply.

"A guy called and said to meet him here with the cash."

"What guy? What cash?" I asked, and wondered if this was Uncle Roy's doing in spite of his apparent lack of interest in money.

Hemcourt's initial composure morphed from petulance into irritation. "The man said he had valuable information pertaining to the Krans portrait of my great-great-grandfather. And if I wanted it, I'd have to pay with cash."

"Information about the portrait you have," I queried,

"or you did have." The implication dawned on me and I shouted, "You think it's here." I told him flat out, "I did *not* steal your portrait. I have witnesses." I briefly thought about having proof that his family's precious Krans was a forgery. That had to wait.

"No, not that one, the other one. The one Krans painted in 1915, the year before he died."

"What?" I uttered with a hoarse whisper, and used every ounce of willpower to stifle what I wanted to ask. How could he possibly know about a *second* authentic Krans painting of his ancestor? I hoped I hadn't given myself away before I could learn more.

"I told you. I've done my research. Krans was known to paint the same subject more than once. And rumors about Bishop Hill do reach as far as Chicago. Even back then."

"What kind of rumors?" I ventured.

"That one painting in particular caused a stir among some descendants. Seen only once and then hidden away, perhaps lost."

"So you've been looking for this painting?" Now it made sense to me. "You're the one breaking into places, searching for this other Krans?"

"No, of course not," he said, regaining his usual tone of superiority.

"Okay, I was grasping at straws, or cattails, or whatever."

"What are you talking about?"

"Nothing. Let's see if I have this straight." I desperately tried to think as I searched for words. "You don't think I stole your family's painting from Nikkerbo."

"No."

"And you believe there's a second painting—another *original* Krans. Supposedly created in 1915."

"Of my great-great-grandfather. Yes, I'm certain."

"And someone called you to come here to deliver money."

"Is that a question?"

"I don't know." I looked at the silent, stricken Christina and had to ask, "Why would anyone think this lost Krans would be here?" I got nothing from her and faced Hemcourt again. "Look around. The only thing that comes close to an unverified Krans is an unsigned painting of a large stag in a forest."

"Let me see it," he said. The sense of entitlement hung heavily in the air.

CHAPTER 28

The three of us walked from the warm kitchen into the formal living room with its worn leather furniture and softly glowing floor lamps. Christina and I nervously stood aside as Hemcourt examined all the paintings on the walls, starting with a classic stag-standing-in-the-forest scene that especially enamored Krans. He revisited the theme many times and quite often without affixing his OK signature. It made authentication difficult.

After a couple of minutes of silent scrutiny in front of the stag, he turned his attention to two portraits on another wall. "I can see the resemblance here," he said, directing his comment to Christina, "but not so much here."

Christina had recovered enough to respond. "You're right. The first one is me and the other is Roy's sister, Nora, Shelley's mother." She stared at them with a sad, wistful smile. "Roy painted them a long time ago. Another age entirely."

The next two works, a rendering of the red brick farmhouse layered with myriad shades of Midwestern-green foliage and a farmyard scene populated with colorful livestock, failed to hold his attention for long. He concluded his inspection at a smaller, somewhat primitive-looking portrait. "Who's this? Don't tell me Roy did this one, too."

"That is Roy Landers, Sr., Krans's last apprentice, as painted by his son. The son, Roy Jr., became our Roy's grandfather." Christina must have assumed this would be clear enough to someone with personal experience of having multiple family members sharing a common name.

He reached out and took the painting off the wall and studied it closely. "That's why it's not a close likeness. Yet it feels familiar," he said.

"You're probably thinking of Roy senior's self-portrait," I said. "That one gets reproduced every now and then. His son painted this one as a teenager still learning his craft. He wasn't given the best materials to work with. Notice the poor surface quality of the canvas." I pointed to several uneven areas where heavily applied pigments had failed to correct the underlying imperfections. "Most likely, he had odd scraps of old canvas to work with, cast-offs from the studio that he had to paint over. I always thought it might have been the reason he never stayed with it, I mean, being an artist like his father or Olof Krans."

Hemcourt turned the painting around and examined the back. I held my breath—I hadn't thought of looking for

Pearl's painting so close to home. I relaxed when it became obvious that no hidden portrait had been concealed behind it.

He flipped the canvas around and studied it for another moment. "Frankly, he just didn't have the talent of his father," Hemcourt snorted. "I hope he was a better farmer."

"Really," Christina said, with an indignant snort of her own. She stepped forward to retrieve the painting and returned it to its place. "And you would know a lot about farming? Or how difficult life was for us back then? Even with our communal legacy we had a hard time keeping bodies and souls together and families on the land." She stood with arms across her chest, giving Hemcourt a hardy scowl.

"You're absolutely right. That was callous of me. Please accept my apology."

Christina nodded curtly, not ready to cool off just yet.

"I know a lot about the Landers family," Hemcourt said as he tapped the frame in front of him. "I uncovered a great deal of information when I researched Olof Krans. I paid particular attention to his assistants and apprentices. I looked for the kinds of connections that would help me." His voice began to waver as his emotions threatened to take control. "To help me replace the painting . . . I . . . destroyed."

To my mind, this confirmed Uncle Roy's portion of the story I'd heard earlier. I caught myself donning a smug expression and quickly dropped it out of serious concern for Hemcourt's frame of mind. "Really," I said, hoping I sounded sufficiently caring.

Christina looked at him in confusion. "What did you do?"

"Everything wrong," he said, and then nodded to me. "I figured you'd be the most pressing challenge for me to deceive. You're developing quite a reputation."

I tried to deflect the offhanded compliment with a polite "Not me," but Hemcourt brushed it aside.

"When I graduated from high school in 1979, I had the house to myself for a couple of days. I took the opportunity to throw a going away party for my best buddy. His appointment to the Air Force academy came through and it would be his last weekend home for a while." Hemcourt shook his head and reached into his pocket for his fire-charred memento. "My great party got out of control. Way out of control. I never lived it down with my father."

I noted his real sense of shame, but I had to find out what happened. "So, somehow you and your friend started the fire and the house was heavily damaged. And the Krans? The original 1897 portrait of the first Curt Hemcourt?"

"It was destroyed in the fire. The painting wasn't supposed to be there. It led to problems with the insurance. The loss never got officially reported. My father grew reclusive around then. Distant. He withdrew from everyone, from *me*." Hemcourt returned the coin to his pocket.

The father never forgiving the son. It explained so much. "When did you get the idea of creating a forgery, a fake?"

Hemcourt flinched at the words.

"I'm sorry," I said. "I meant to say," and struggled for something less offensive, "the re-creation."

"The publicity for the 1988 New Sweden celebration started me thinking about my heritage and my family's connection to Bishop Hill. I read everything I could find before my wife and I drove down for a weekend to check the place out. We toured. We ate. We shopped. My wife loved the crafts in the Blacksmith building; I focused on the paintings. I'd hoped to see something by Roy, your Roy, but another man's work caught my attention, too. I swear I never thought of forgery. I just wanted a painting. Something to fill the void. Later, I approached each of them and asked for a preliminary sketch or sample based on a photo from the insurance company. I wanted to see who could deliver the closest thing to our lost Krans. There was no contest. Roy's work was just tremendous, inspired, such a close likeness. I gave him the commission and bought a smaller piece from the other guy."

"When did it turn into more than a replacement?" I asked the question before I realized the answer wouldn't matter. I had to ask the more important question. "Why do you think there's another Krans portrait of your ancestor?"

"You've seen it." He paused. "The modern portrait, Roy's, up close. It's good. Amazingly good. Roy did everything right. It even passed Swedish inspection." I began a gentle protest, but he waved me off again. "Don't you see? To make a painting good enough to fool the experts, *all* the experts, he had to have access to an original Krans. It had to be sitting right next to him while he worked. The rumors about Krans's lost portrait were true and it had to be a *second* painting of my great-great-grandfather. It may still be here—somewhere. It *has* to be."

"So, three paintings?" Christina wondered aloud. "All at one time?"

CHAPTER 29

"Yes, three portraits: 1897 and 1915 by Olof Krans, and 1988 by Uncle Roy," I said to Christina, "but never all at once. Only two at any one time. Am I right?" I looked to Hemcourt and he nodded confirmation. I turned back to Christina. "All of our paintings are down here, right? I don't know where else to look. Do you have any other ideas?"

Christina gave a slow but determined shake of her head. "Nothing's coming to me."

"Damn. That's too bad," Gordon Anderson, Herb's cousin, said with a harsh laugh.

The oncoming rush of rain and the first peals of thunder had masked the sounds of his entrance. Now he stood framed in the doorway between the kitchen and the living room, with his hand in a pocket that bulged as if he held a gun.

"I have to agree with Hemcourt, that lost painting exists, and it has to be here. The only difference is now you're going to find it for me."

"I remember you. You're that other painter," said a surprised Hemcourt. He slowly lifted his hands. "Now take it easy. You must be the one who left the note. Threatening me with blackmail if I didn't pay up. You called this morning with instructions."

"Should I be flattered you finally got around to remembering me?" Gordon sneered. "Sure, I called, but Ekollon left the note. I needed money and tried working a deal with him first. I don't know what game he's up to. I can't find him, so it's just you and me now." Gordon glared at Hemcourt. "Hand over your gun." Hemcourt didn't react. "I know you have one. You people always have something expensive. Place it on the end table and push it toward me. Slow like."

Hemcourt seethed, but said nothing as he produced a shiny revolver from his pocket and did as told.

"Since you've already gone through here," Gordon indicated the living room, "we'll just head on out to the barn."

Christina started to protest. "There's nothing out there but animals and hay."

"Save it. I know Roy has some of his old stuff stored out there. He told me so. We're all going to do some exploring." Stepping aside as he picked up the gun, he waved his hand for everyone to go in front of him. "Let's go. And don't try anything stupid," he cautioned.

"It's raining," I said. The complaint was aimed more at my miserable luck than anything else.

"Nobody's going to melt." Gordon pointed toward the door. "Get moving."

I watched the rain cascade down in thin filmy sheets, bringing a premature grayness to the fading light. Off in the distance, the rolling sounds of advancing thunder foretold a turn toward yet more severe weather. Lifting my collar and hunching my shoulders together, I launched myself out the door.

When we reached the side door of the barn, I went through first and switched on the single overhead light. The horses nickered hopefully for extra attention. The calves followed me with dark, moist eyes that indicated they expected more food. The bare bulb offered minimal illumination, but not much was needed. Gordon knew the way to the small tack room where Uncle Roy stored the things he deemed non-essential.

"You go in and bring out those boxes." Gordon motioned to Hemcourt. Pointing to me, he said, "Bring the paintings." He told Christina, "You stay here where I can see you."

I entered the tack room first and flipped on its light. Hemcourt followed and soon brought out box after box, arranging them in a semicircle in front of Gordon. I did the same with the canvases. Since Uncle Roy often painted on anything he could find, I made sure to include any flat panel big enough to be of interest to Gordon.

After he finished placing the boxes, Hemcourt offered a

hopeful, "The money is in my car. It's up the road just past that big tree."

"We'll get to that later," Gordon said.

"You don't have to do this, Gordon. We know who painted Hemcourt's Krans. The one on display at Nikkerbo." Christina tried to manage a soothing tone. "Curt explained how he got Roy to do it years ago."

"It doesn't make any difference who painted what. There's another reason to find the lost Krans. This is a game-changer for everything." Gordon pulled a sepia-toned photo from his shirt pocket. I saw a head shot of a well-groomed early 1900s gentleman in his best suit. "This makes both paintings more valuable. This makes history."

I couldn't see much difference between that one and any number of other photographic portraits of that time period. I have some in my own collection. I needed to get a closer look. Maybe see the back. Check it for some words written in Swedish and for Pearl's childish handwriting.

Gordon saw me straining for a better view. "Nothin' doing," he said, pulling it closer to his chest.

His protective hand motion gave me an idea. Far-fetched, but the size of the photo and the crushed-in corners made it seem possible. "Was that in the other, smaller box?"

Gordon sighed. "Now, it's too bad you had to remember that box, Miss Shelley."

"You killed Herb, your own cousin, for that photo?"

Gordon's threatening expression hardened into anger as he gazed at the photo. "Herb didn't give me a choice."

He slipped the photo back into his pocket. "I bought that box at a sale. The *rosemaling* reminded me of Krans's decorative work. I wanted Herb to see it. He helped me find the photo hidden under a false bottom. I knew what it meant as well as he did. But he had to get all excited and started making phone calls. Acting like I didn't matter. 'A great discovery,' he said. 'It belongs to the people.' I'd had it with his high-minded, condescending attitude toward me. I've had to put up with that kind of crap all my life."

Pacing within the confined space in front of the Uncle Roy's possessions, Gordon's free hand slashed the air to accentuate his building outrage. All the while, the other hand retained a firm grip on the gun. "He never once treated me with the respect I deserved. Nobody has. No one has really seen *me*. I'm as much a Krans expert as Ekollon or Roy. I've put in my time with nothing coming back to me when I needed it. Well, I need it now." Fissures began to show in his tough façade. "Don't you see, I deserve this. It's *mine*."

Realizing he may have given too much of himself away, Gordon fought to regain control and resumed a weaker tirade against Herb. "He made me so mad. When I tried to take the photo back, he fought me. I only meant to push him off me. He fell against the lathe stand. One of the chisels must have . . ." He couldn't finish as he thought back to Friday night. Taking a deep breath to steady himself, he continued. "When he turned around, there was blood. But he didn't seem hurt all that bad. He ordered me out." He paused to slow his quavering voice. "It was an accident. I'm sorry I left. I'm sorry." He patted his chest pocket and forced out a weak, "Mine. This photo is mine."

Gordon blinked and struggled to refocus his attention on the boxes and paintings in front of him. "So, open them already," he commanded.

CHAPTER 30

Christina and I stood a little way off from Gordon's right side after I'd held up every painting for his examination. Nothing came close to satisfying his vague notion of what he was looking for. He had Hemcourt open the boxes. With every box opened and searched, Gordon could barely contain his frustration. He ran his left hand over his bald head as he ransacked his brain for his next move. The gun in his right hand wavered a bit before he swung it toward the door and Uncle Roy's chest.

"Good evening, Mr. Hemcourt. Ladies. Gordon," said a rain-soaked Uncle Roy. He stepped into the thin circle of light and held up his empty hands in a slow, non-threatening motion. He took a couple of steps toward the disorganized pile of artwork and boxes and away from the door. "Gordon, you'd better have a good reason for trashing my stuff."

"Roy!" Gordon trembled and backed up as he visibly fought to pull himself together. "You're here."

"It would appear so." He kept his tone firm, even, and friendly as his gaze held steady with Gordon's. "In case you hadn't noticed, it's raining out there." As he motioned back toward the open door and the rain falling beyond, he took another step away from it. "After roughing it for the last few days, I've got some catching up to do." He smiled, patted his stomach, and took another step away from the door.

Gordon seemed to wake up a little. "Of course I know it's raining. I came here for the Krans painting. The *real* one. The one you used to cheat me out of that Hemcourt commission back in '88. I figured it out, you know. It has to be here."

"Come on," Uncle Roy said. "Look at me. Am I the kinda guy who's got rare, expensive artwork just sitting around?"

My initial surprise and shock turned into puzzled concern. I watched him take another step toward Gordon. What was he doing?

He continued to speak in an assuring manner. "Come on, you *know* me, Gordon. Lose the gun, man. Let's go get us a couple of drinks and something to eat."

Christina still stood closest to Gordon. Uncle Roy glanced over to her and she responded by moving slightly away. Gordon noticed and grabbed for her, his left hand encircling her neck.

I shouted out a frantic, "*Mom!*"

I moved reflexively in a swift fluid motion that combined a lunge for the weapon and a knife hand strike to the inside of his elbow. It forced the gun to point up to the rafters when it went off with a deafening blast. The air filled with bits of wood, dirt, and hay sprinkling down from the overhead loft. The pungent smell of fireworks hung in the smoky cloud that centered on Gordon and me.

The horses and calves panicked in their stalls. The noisy cacophony of animal sounds and reverberations from the gunshot added to the confusion and gave Uncle Roy the chance to fly at a disoriented Gordon for a full-body tackle. Since I still held Gordon's gun hand, we all hit the ground hard.

I had the breath knocked out of me, but managed to roll out of the way. My ears were ringing, so I could only watch as Hemcourt stood off to the side. He studied the struggle in the dirt, doing nothing to help. His eyes stayed focused on the shiny weapon and followed it alone. Uncle Roy found Gordon's gun hand and slammed it against the ground repeatedly. When the pistol finally dislodged from Gordon's grasp, Hemcourt darted in for the retrieval.

Through the still-open door, a sopping wet dog came charging in, followed by an equally soggy sheriff's deputy, her weapon drawn. Gordon saw the hopelessness of his situation and went limp.

While keeping Gordon in her sights, Deputy Dana Johnson called, "Is everyone all right?"

I scrambled to my feet and rushed to Christina's side as Uncle Roy disentangled himself from a now-compliant

Gordon.

Two other men came charging in. One was Michael with his gun drawn. I didn't know the younger man behind him. The two of them stood at the ready until they were certain that the deputy had everything under control. Only then did Michael click the safety on and tuck his weapon out of sight.

Hemcourt surreptitiously slipped his pistol back into his pocket. He pointed to Gordon and ordered, "Search him for a gun."

Even if I couldn't hear everything, I doubted if Deputy Dana missed any of it. Her first job was to secure her prisoner. She handcuffed Gordon's hands behind his back. With that done, she performed a thorough search and found no other weapons. She called in the status of the situation to Cambridge headquarters.

"I was sure he had a gun," Hemcourt said.

"No," I called out a little too loudly, "he tricked you out of yours." The ringing in my ears seemed a little better, but my hearing was still off.

Hemcourt's face registered flustered disbelief at finding out he'd been conned out of his weapon by a mere bulging pocket. About that time he caught his first whiff of wet dog and in an obvious attempt to divert his embarrassment he uttered a disdainful, "Does that dog have to be in here?"

Sadie cocked her head, sniffed the air, and then shifted her attention away from the prone, cuffed Gordon to take up an aggressive stance in front of Hemcourt. His expression changed from callous contempt to one of fear when faced with the growling dog.

"Call off this animal," Hemcourt yelled as he cowered, seeming to shrink in size.

I realized the now-clear implications of Sadie's actions. "You lied to me. It *was* you last Friday night." My rage was building right along with my volume. "You were in the cabin—searching through Uncle Roy's things. You—"

Sadie and I lunged for him at the same time.

Michael had a dilemma on his hands, which female to yank back first. I guess he trusted his dog more, because he reached for me.

CHAPTER 31

Thursday, June 5, 2008 — Early morning

Sometime after midnight, the Henry County sheriff's deputies left the driveway of the red brick house and formed a caravan of flashing red and blue lights as they transported the hapless Gordon Anderson and the indignant Curt Hemcourt V to the jail in Cambridge. An apologetic Uncle Roy didn't have to make a return trip. Deputy Dana Johnson vouched for the crucial help he provided in apprehending Gordon without any more gunfire than the one ineffectual shot.

The unknown young man who came charging in with Michael turned out to be Ulla Olson's Wethersfield boyfriend, Nate. She and her dad came by to collect him. The elder Olson managed a somewhat begrudging but positive acknowledgment of the young man's role in the whole matter. Ulla was happy for the truce and obviously proud of both her guys for making an effort to get along.

They offered Michael a ride back to the tow truck, but he said he wasn't ready to go yet.

"Why didn't you take them up on a ride?" I asked.

"Are you kidding?" he said as he petted Sadie. "I've heard about Gunnar Olson's temper. That car was crowded enough without Sadie and me dripping all over his upholstery."

"Then let me give you a ride. You shouldn't have to hike through wet woods twice in one night."

Before Michael could respond, Christina in her Carl Larson-style apron came over. "No one else leaves without eating something first. Everything I started cooking earlier is finished. Now, come on in. And that means Sadie, too." The dog's ears went up at the mention of her name.

Christina led the way to the back door. By the time Michael and I ditched our muddy shoes, she held out a stack of towels. "Come in and get started with these."

I kept one and handed the rest over to man and dog.

Michael worked a towel through his hair and around his neck. He took a dry towel and went to the back door to let in a waiting Sadie. He caught her and gave her a good rubbing. I thought he missed a few spots, so I went over to add another dry towel to the cause. Sadie happily ate up the attention. As soon as we stopped, she did the universal wet dog shake. We tried to shield ourselves, but we couldn't avoid the residual spray.

"So much for getting dry," I said and started laughing.

Michael laughed, too. "Yeah. Glad to see you relax a bit."

"I can hear again. My hands have stopped shaking." I started to show him a hand for proof but took it back. No need to press my luck. "It's good to be alive. How are you doing?"

He nodded. "I'm good," and smiled like he meant it.

The oval kitchen table held a platter of oven-fried chicken surrounded by side dishes that smelled heavenly. I didn't think I'd ever felt this hungry before. Before we could squeeze ourselves around the crowded table, Christina intervened. "This is something of an occasion, so I decided we needed more space. You two go on into the dining room."

She shooed us over to the larger table set with the best dishes. Uncle Roy had a seat at the head. Christina came in with a plate made up with a helping of everything for Sadie and showed it to Michael. It met with his approval and the dog got a head start on everyone else.

When I'd eaten enough so I could slow down and remember my manners, I said to Michael, "Thanks for the rescue. Both times. Or maybe it's more than that. I've lost count."

He couldn't answer; his mouth too full to do more than grin. I had to carry on without him. "And Hemcourt. I don't like being pushed around and hate when people lie to me. He was just so . . ."

A chorus of opinions came in from around the table. "Smug. Brazen. Pompous."

"All those and more," I said.

"Michael," Uncle Roy asked, "please tell us how you got here. I only caught a bit of the story outside."

"I want to hear it, too," Christina said.

After sipping some water to clear his throat, Michael started. "It all began when Shelley pointed out the purple graffiti on the road signs. I was heading back to Galva after Monday's fiasco in the park—" He stopped to glare at me—"when I noticed a dark SUV leave the Varnishtree parking lot. I got a glimpse of squiggly purple spray-painted designs on the driver's side door as it pulled out in front of me. I lost track of it when it turned onto 34. When I spotted it again tonight, I followed it to Gunnar Olson's place. It just hit me, the U in the 'I Heart U' graffiti didn't mean 'you,' it meant Ulla, Ulla Olson. It got me thinking. What if those kids were out painting signs on Friday night? They might have seen something. It was worth a shot to ask. And it led me to the pickup truck parked nearby, partially hidden by some trees and brush."

"I bet I know the spot. I passed it when I was walking that way Monday morning, before I found Marcella." I gave Uncle Roy a finger jab and a squinty-eyed stare. "And I would have found you, too, if given the chance."

"I know. Guess I have to get a new hideout."

"Don't you dare," Christina said while brandishing her fork at him. "No more running away. And no more pulling stupid stunts with armed maniacs."

"Yes, Teeny," Uncle Roy responded, smartly saluting her with his knife.

"I wonder if it was Nate's SUV that passed by the house real slow on Monday night. It creeped me out." I shuddered at the sinister memory. "But it also made me want to fight back."

"It was him all right," Michael said. "Now, getting back to *my* story. When I saw it was Gordon's truck so close to the campground, I knew I had to get over here fast."

"How did you find out who it belonged to?" I asked. Michael suddenly looked sheepish and I knew exactly why. I beamed him an evil look. "You worked the lock. You wouldn't do it for me the other day. Your principles got in the way. You dog!"

Sadie looked up expectantly and begged for more attention.

"Sorry, honey, false alarm," I said. I gave her a good scratch behind the ears.

"Well, I'll never complain about your timing," Christina said. "It was darn good to see you guys. Did you happen to see what Shelley did?"

"No, everyone was down on the ground by the time I came through the door." Michael clucked his tongue sarcastically. "Such a lady."

I wrinkled my nose at him. "Like, this lady pulled the most awesome self-defense move *ever*."

"I have to agree. All those Tae Kwon Do lessons in Kewanee paid for themselves tonight. Or last night. Whatever." Christina turned to glower and point her fork at me, "Don't you ever do that again. I nearly had a heart attack."

I pulled myself up straight. "Hey, no one messes with my Teeny Mom."

I could tell my using her childhood nickname left her with a rare moment of speechlessness.

I drove Michael and Sadie over to the tow truck and came back to find Uncle Roy in the kitchen with all the pots, pans, and dishes cleared away and the leftovers stored in the fridge.

"Someone's been busy," I said.

"Not all my work. I did help a bit. Teeny finally wore out and went to bed," he said.

"Good, now that we're alone I want to ask you about Lars."

"What about him?"

"Like, why did he go looking for you? Who is he really? Who's this uncle of his and why are they suddenly interested in Nora?"

"There's nothing more to tell than what I've already told you. Nora, your mother, met this Swedish guy when he was over here working on a farm. They were just friends as far as I know."

"Friends enough to write letters. Friends enough to worry when the letters stopped. Friends enough to send an emissary to collect information." I harrumphed. "I certainly don't have friends like that." I didn't let on that I had those letters in my shoulder bag. I needed time to go over them again, to fully understand what they meant.

He shrugged. "That's all I know."

"That's all you're willing to tell," I countered.

"Come on, it's my first night back. Uh, I mean day. Truce?"

"Sure thing," I said, not at all placated. So I switched gears to the other thing bothering me. "It just bugs me to death. I figured out the Hemcourt family's portrait at Nikkerbo wasn't a Krans at all and you painted it. But I can't figure out the other Krans painting. The 'lost' one of Pearl's dream. It was probably his last portrait."

"I don't think you should put too much stock in what Gordon and Hemcourt were raving about," he said.

"Except I've talked to Pearl. She saw Krans create the thing. Even remembered a name. Well, she remembered the name Hencourt, which sure sounds a lot like Hemcourt."

"Okay, she saw something, but what? Come on. We're talking, like, over 90 years here. Who knows what she saw."

"What about your great-grandfather's painting? You said it won you the Hemcourt commission from Gordon. You said it was a perfect match. How could that be? Didn't you ever wonder?"

"I said it *looked* enough like Hemcourt's insurance photo to be useful. I didn't care about anything else. I used it to improve my sketch and to select the colors for my palette. Hemcourt loved it. I never thought it was anything more than dumb luck. And at the time, I needed some luck."

"I've never seen anything like it in your collection of old canvases. What happened to it?"

"I think I gave it away."

"You think," I exclaimed. "Why don't you *know*?" I added in exasperation.

"After Hemcourt was done with me, I couldn't stand myself. I drank practically every night. Teeny tried to help. Pretty soon, I had very little left that I was proud of. That painting was it for me, the last of my heritage and the last of my self-respect. I remember I wanted to keep it safe— from *me* most of all."

"So you gave it to Teeny Mom, Christina, to protect. Right?" I hoped he would say yes. I also hoped he'd take a pass on any comments about the name change. I couldn't call her Christina anymore, not after the close call we had in the barn. Reverting to my childhood pet name for her seemed comforting and natural.

Dejected and spent, Uncle Roy stared at his folded hands. "I don't really know. I was having blackouts by then and I lost track of it." He gave me a helpless shrug. "I just don't remember what happened to it."

If Teeny Mom had it or knew its location, she certainly put up a good show of ignorance last night. I decided that after 93 years the mystery could wait a little longer. We were both exhausted.

CHAPTER 32

Thursday, June 5, 2008 — Afternoon

Sunlight reflected off small pools of rainwater still trapped in the deeply rutted driveway and farmyard, testimony to last night's turmoil. I paced from room to room, stewing, too keyed up to settle anywhere for long.

I replayed scenes from last night's confrontation with Herb's cousin, Gordon, and my employer, Mr. Curt Hemcourt V. They built within me a mountain of frustration that I couldn't let go of and couldn't get over. I didn't know if I could believe Gordon's story of Herb's accidental injury on the lathe. And if Herb had really sent him away, what did that make him: a murderer, a coward, or an idiot? Gordon was still responsible for fighting with Herb in the first place. Who could tell where Hemcourt's lies began? He had broken into and searched Uncle Roy's cabin. How many other places had he searched? And why had he taken such risks when he had paid minions to carry out his bidding?

I had finally cleared out my car. Now, I had better find something else to do before Teeny Mom spotted my pacing and assigned some inane chore. Work was her answer to all problems. I craved diversion, escape, and decided a trip back to Galesburg and Knox would provide the ticket out of her radar range. I'd check in on the senior art show. I couldn't be absolutely sure I'd have a job to go to on Friday, and it made sense to be prepared anyway by picking up my pieces from the show today.

As I drove, I watched the remaining storm clouds dissipate on the horizon and allow the early afternoon sun to shine through. The lightning had worked its magic and everything growing along the roadside and in the fields had an electrically intensified, after-the-storm shade of green.

The campus also looked freshened from the storm and still soggy in the low spots. It seemed quieter; quite a few students had gone home. In the art building I found someone to give me permission to retrieve my photo display early. Getting most of the pieces down wouldn't be a problem. Only the large collage in the center would require something to stand on. The stash of old towels and sheets I used for moving everything was still safety tucked away in the studio. All was good to go.

I looked at each piece as I lifted it off the wall. They were all portraits of a sort. Some, like Krans, were posed and serious with no attempt to hide personal flaws. Others were close-ups of important landmarks, but skewed off-center to offer a different perspective. That was my homage to Uncle Roy and his intuitive Outsider Art.

I smiled at the picture of Stanley, the itinerant cat, sitting in front of a gift shop. The newly christened beggar waited for his handout surrounded by festive holiday decorations. I thought this photo had turned out well enough to merit the extra cost of a digital fine art gallery-wrapped canvas print. I felt compelled to include it in the show as a salute of one orphan to another. The effort hadn't won any points from my instructor. He wasn't a cat person.

With the smaller items down and lined up in an orderly fashion, I stood on a stepladder in front of the collage. I'd designed the piece to reveal what I knew about Nora, my birth mother, and how much remained unknown, unknowable. I thought about Lars; he had to see this. It might help explain the complexity of my feelings toward her.

As I reached up for it, I thought back to the time I'd found the dusty blank canvas in the barn and had appropriated it for the central part of this piece. I'd taken it without actually asking permission. I reasoned that if Uncle Roy hadn't gotten around to using it before then, it was fair game. Besides, I liked the connection between the siblings it provided. I had left the rough blotchy surface untreated and sketched a crude likeness of Nora, my first mom. Leaving it rough and uneven symbolized the unfinished life. I constructed a framework around the canvas to support my selection of photos and found objects. I pieced everything together to depict two lives: the one that was, and the one that might have been. The back had been covered over with heavy burlap. I'd left that intact as well and used the space to stencil a personal message.

It occurred to me now that this canvas by all rights should have turned up in last night's search. If this one had been missed, there must be others scattered around and overlooked. It made me weary to think there might never be an end to this missing painting business. Herb was dead. Gordon had been arrested. Hemcourt and Ekollon had both been pushed to extremes. How many other people out there, desperate to find treasure, would end up on Uncle Roy's doorstep? As I studied the canvas, a plan began to take shape.

I shuttled everything down to my car. After all the time it had taken for me to get it cleared out, I now had the back seat packed full again. I carefully placed one wrapped piece on the front passenger seat, trying not to draw attention, knowing full well that it wouldn't seem natural at all.

The drive north on Seminary Street took me past my favorite coffee shop, what used to be the meeting place for Marsha Ellen and our little group, christened Pippi's Posse. We were mainly a bunch of art students who felt recklessly creative and dangerously underappreciated. We consumed caffeine and plotted how to gain recognition and fame and power. Fun times for sure.

There was a tantalizing open parking place in front. I made a snap decision to swoop into it, telling myself I probably wouldn't run into anyone I knew. It was a just reward for surviving thus far. I sat inside sipping a cappuccino and watching the passing traffic. Today, it didn't bother me that I was on my way home again. Last week those thoughts would have vexed and annoyed; now, I had things to take care of, loose ends to tie up.

I thought again about Gordon's account of Herb's death. Only an accident, he'd said. That didn't jive with how I remembered the shop or Herb. After all, Pearl held a bloody hammer when I found her. If Hemcourt lied about breaking into Uncle Roy's cabin and searching it, I shouldn't discount the possibility that Gordon might have lied about Herb's "accident" as well.

I retrieved the slip of paper Pearl had given me and read it again.

Är detta Hemson's ansikte?
Is this Hemson's face?

I thought about Ekollon's meltdown over finding the computer printouts. That was mere speculation about what a Hemson portrait might look like using composite images of Hemson's three closest relatives. What would he do over something like this coming from Pearl? Would it turn him into the maniac that Lars described?

I was certain that Hemcourt had searched Uncle Roy's cabin on Friday night; Sadie's reaction made that fact enough even if he never admitted it. What if Ekollon had been the second intruder? The photos had been handled carefully. Certainly a knowledgeable expert such as he could be that considerate.

Hemcourt had a pretty good argument for thinking the second 1915 Krans portrait existed. Perhaps another guilt-ridden attempt to atone to a father he had disappointed. But that didn't go far enough to explain why he might need to slip into Uncle Roy's cabin a second time.

Ekollon had to have his own reasons for searching for the Krans. Scholarly reasons? Maybe. But to what end? What had he said in front of The Lutfisk—it was "sacrilege" and "blasphemy"? I wouldn't get away with besmirching the Prophet's memory. Ekollon had a different quest. His needs were also personal, but to save the painting? I had a chilling dread to think of what might happen if he found the painting first. Would he be capable of making it disappear forever? Destroy an irreplaceable artifact? Such a high price tag on saving the Prophet's honor. What did he know about this particular Krans painting? How much did Hemcourt really know?

While ruminating over puzzling fragments of information and savoring my foamy coffee, I spotted a corner-mounted security camera trained on the front door. They must be having some problems in this neighborhood. Looking around, I saw another camera. Feeling surrounded, I snapped the lid on my cup and prepared to leave. When the ever-practical and efficient Teeny Mom had learned of the Galesburg trip, she'd given me a grocery list to fill. There was no way I'd be able to do that now. I couldn't leave the car alone that long. I'd have to pull off the "I forgot" excuse.

Leaving the coffee shop and walking straight to the car, I purposely avoided looking at the figure standing in the shadow of the building across the street.

CHAPTER 33

I almost made a clean getaway. While fumbling with the key to my door, a car pulled up alongside and stopped. The passenger side window lowered. The car was unfamiliar and I leaned down to peer inside. I was quite surprised to see Michael.

"No Sadie. No tow truck," I said. "I didn't recognize you." I offered him a polite smile, but he wouldn't reciprocate. It seemed like a bit much for him, but after last night, who could blame him for being serious.

"Can we talk? I've heard things you might find interesting," he called out, pointing to the coffee shop and waiting for me to respond. I nodded. He aimed for an open parking spot nearby while I retrieved my coffee cup and made a show of locking my doors.

"Nice to see you again," I said as he caught up with me on the sidewalk. "I didn't expect to run into a friendly face

261

today." He made an attempt to smile, but it didn't come out in the effortless way I took for his kind of normal. "Something wrong? You look like something's wrong."

"I talked to Dana a while ago and thought you'd like to get filled in," he said. "I was told you'd be near campus, so I drove around trying to spot your car. Hope that was okay."

"Yeah, sure. I'm cool with Deputy Dana." Not much I could do about it. He was here already. I led the way back into the coffee shop and reclaimed the window seat while he went up to place his order.

When he came back, he caught me staring at my car and asked, "Something wrong with your car?"

"Oh, it's fine," I said. "I picked up my stuff from the senior art show and I'm anxious to get it all back home. I've already got the wall space set aside in my room to hang everything up."

"How'd it go?" he ventured.

"What?"

"Your show."

His look betrayed concern, perhaps some doubt, about the condition of my mind. I hurried to add a pleasant, "Fine. It's all fine. I'm glad it's over with. Mr. Hemcourt said he'd reopen the museum tomorrow and everyone would have a fresh start. I'd rather have a complete do-over, but I could settle for a clean start." I swallowed a sip of coffee. Then I thought to ask, "He *did* get released, didn't he?"

"That's what Dana said. He had to come up with his

FOID card to make everyone happy."

"What's that?"

"Firearm Owners Identification card. Every gun owner in the state has to have one."

"Oh," I said. "What about Gordon? Did Dana say anything about him?" Calling the deputy by only her first name felt a little strange, but I went with it anyway.

"They're still holding him. The autopsy results aren't in yet. It might confirm his story of an accident. But still, he started the fight that seriously injured Herb. He has to pay."

"That's too bad. But he hasn't exactly made things easy for himself, threatening us like he did at the Varnishtree last Monday."

"Speaking of trouble and threats and all, that's kind of why I tracked you down."

"Oh?" I said.

"Dana and I were talking and we both think you're still in danger."

I sputtered, almost choking on the next sip of coffee. "Me? Why me?"

"This business about the Krans painting. Two people, Gordon and Hemcourt, have already gone to desperate lengths to get it. And, well, I think there may be another." He stirred his coffee and related how Ulla and Nate had seen two different cars before Gordon showed up in his pickup truck.

I gathered my composure while dabbing at my chin with a napkin. I thought about stuffing some extra ones in my shoulder bag to keep on hand as my new go-to accessory. "You know, I've been sort of thinking along those lines, too. That the break-ins were the work of two different people. Hemcourt did the first one, but the second one didn't have the same look or feel. Someone else had another mission. Gordon sounded like he just wanted a big payout to bolster his self-respect. He wouldn't take the time to go through Uncle Roy's files. Plus, he had his own photos—the insurance shot he'd gotten from Hemcourt years ago and the old-fashioned one he had in his pocket at the barn. He didn't have to go looking for any more."

"Any ideas about who the second intruder was?" he asked.

"Oh, yes. Ekollon has my vote." I filled him in on my run-ins with my boss at the museum's opening night party and later in front of The Lutfisk.

"That was a pretty good stunt with the cell phone," he said.

"Just lucky," I said and looked down at the table. I couldn't believe I was acting embarrassed in front of him. "Did you see the photo Gordon had in his possession?"

"No, I didn't see it last night. Dana didn't mention anything about a photo or if they'd been tracking Herb's phone. She's been instructed to be extra careful not to give out any specific info on an ongoing investigation."

I pulled up my shoulder bag and started poking through it while I gave him a description. "It looked like an old-style sepia-toned photo of a man. Darkish hair.

Moustache. Nice suit and tie. Fairly ordinary for the early 1900s. The really interesting part would be to find out if anything was written on the back." I finally produced a small sheet of paper and handed it to him. "Read this."

He let out a short huff. "Great, more Hemson weirdness. Where did this come from?"

"Pearl handed it to me after the funeral. I guess this part of her dream came back to her sometime after Sunday."

"This isn't ever going to end," he said. He fished a folded piece of paper out of his pocket and handed it to me. "Here, you probably want this back."

I unfolded the computer printout, smoothed the ridges so it would lie flat, and spent too much time studying it.

"Now what's wrong?" he asked.

"It's all starting to fit together. Pearl's story. Hemcourt's story. Uncle Roy's, too, for the most part, but his has gaps. Too many blackouts." After I pressured him into a promise for secrecy, I explained how Hemcourt had come to Bishop Hill for a painting and ended up with a forgery painted by Uncle Roy.

"If you're suggesting that your uncle had that second original Krans, the one Great Auntie Pearl saw in 1915, then where is it? They searched his cabin, the house, and the barn. Nothing. Nada."

He followed my gaze out the window to my car. "It's in your car?" he hissed through clenched teeth, and stared in utter amazement.

"Keep your voice down," I shot back in as near to a whisper as I could manage.

"Unbelievable."

I could tell his mind was crowded with a million questions, but he sat back, stunned into speechlessness. It made me smile to think my little ruse had already begun its work.

"Look, I know it's too much to ask, but I need your help. Alan and James, too. Please, help me."

"I thought you looked on edge. Are you worried someone is watching you?"

"Actually, I'm counting on it."

CHAPTER 34

Friday, June 6, 2008

I didn't feel angry as I drove to Nikkerbo; I was confident I could face Hemcourt without overt hostility. I had too much at stake to let myself go down that path. However, I wasn't prepared when I began to experience flashbacks from last Friday. They didn't unfold in an unbroken panorama like a movie, but jolted me with sudden bursts of vivid images: Pearl driving me off the road, Pearl by Herb's body holding a bloody hammer, sirens and flashing lights, Hemcourt and Ekollon showing up and precipitating the urge to flee. I felt a chill go down my spine and my grip on the steering wheel steadily tightened, until I forced myself to recall Sadie's warm brown eyes and soft blue-speckled fur.

Relax and breathe. I followed my orders by taking in air

through my nose and holding it briefly before exhaling slowly through pursed lips. It helped hone the sharp edges off the memories.

Still nervous and tense by the time I arrived at the museum, I parked exactly where I had last Saturday. One week had passed and so much had happened. I didn't feel like the same person at all. My goal had been to work the summer, do my time so to speak, then get out and move on. Now, I forced myself to focus only on today. Tomorrow would take care of itself.

As I walked to the back door, I passed the reserved parking spaces and saw only Hemcourt's BMW. Ekollon's spot was vacant, no Mercedes, just a dried-up clump of prairie grasses. I paused to tap it with my foot. It sure looked like the same combination of stuff that had fallen off Hemcourt's vehicle when he parked at the red brick house. Just a little more proof he had been parked over by Gunnar Olson's house. I was on the right track.

Inside I found employees with coffee cups in hand, sitting around the conference room table and speculating about how they could keep the museum open with the Hemcourt family's portrait still missing. Some reasoned that it was immaterial if they had the painting or not. The best option would be to take advantage of all the publicity.

The faces were familiar and I greeted everyone politely without adding anything to the conversation. That changed when someone tapped my shoulder, causing me to jump. I spun around, ready to let loose a burst of crude expletives, when I saw Lars standing there with a goofy grin. Without thinking, I gave him a quick hug.

Then the self-consciousness set in and I stepped back to adopt a more professional demeanor. "I'm sorry. You shouldn't sneak up on me like that."

"I'm not that sorry." A warm smile spread across his handsome face. No one would ever think of him as any kind of shy. "I got back early today and came straight over," he said.

"The Lowells said you went back to Chicago to check in with your family. I hope you're not in too much trouble."

"All is fine with them. I'm not so sure about here. Have you heard anything?"

I shrugged my shoulders and glanced over to the others gathered around the table. "We're waiting to find out. By the smell of it, the coffee is still fresh," I said with a sly smile.

Almost on cue, the doors opened and Hemcourt strode in with his lawyerly suits on either hand. The sound level around the table dropped to zero. This time I caught both names and titles as he introduced Les Patrick, the familiar figure of our family attorney from Galva, and Thomas T. Gubben, the new face and CFO from Chicago. I shook hands with both and noted the contrast in personalities. Patrick's handshake was firm, sure, and friendly. Gubben's limp grip conveyed the coolness and detachment of a man who wanted to be somewhere else. He barely looked at me before moving on to the next outstretched hand. The encounter, although brief, was enough for me to recall his reddish-gray hair from last week's introductions and to place it across the street from the Galesburg coffee shop yesterday.

"Ladies and gentlemen," Hemcourt said. "Thank you for being here this morning. Please be seated. We have our work cut out for us."

Hemcourt began by stating the obvious: his family's portrait was still missing. Authorities were doing their best to recover it, but there were few viable leads. He listed Ekollon's status as unavailable due to taking an extended emergency leave of absence. Surprise registered on almost everyone's face. Lars and I exchanged knowing looks. Hemcourt added more surprise by announcing the immediate need for an interim director to keep the museum open and the staff organized. Most of the people seated around the table were locals who had worked their way up the employment ranks without having any formal education or certification in museum studies. Everyone looked around wondering how he could find anyone qualified and able to step in on such short notice. He turned to me and asked, "Ms. Anderson, could I persuade you to fill in at that capacity until this situation with Mr. Ekollon is resolved?"

After letting my temper get the best of me in the barn the other night, I halfway expected to be either ignored or harassed into quitting. This turn of events caught me totally off guard. I nodded shyly and uttered a weak, barely audible, "I guess so." I cleared my throat and slid my hands under the edge of the table, trying to bury their shakiness in my lap, and let out a stronger, "Yes, sir."

I quickly calculated the odds of successfully filling this position, even for a limited time, and came up with a disappointing near zero. Lars was the only person I looked at. I imagine the others stared at me with various looks of disbelief, shock, and maybe outright jealousy. I was the summer help, the newest hire, but, as Hemcourt well knew, the only one with a diploma that would allow me to sign off on some of the official forms that would pass through the office in the immediate future. He needed me, and I could think of a few ways I could use him.

As Hemcourt and the lawyers left, Les Patrick flashed a smile in my direction. I wouldn't be surprised if Teeny Mom knew all about this little event within minutes, if not already. Gubben's icy stare wasn't much of a surprise either.

I needed to buy some time until I could get myself up to speed, so I told everyone to stick with their last scheduled day. Lars hung back as the others drifted away. "I'm glad Mr. Hemcourt gave you this opportunity," he said.

"Let me guess, you turned him down."

"Why would you say that?" He drew his face into a quizzical mask of mock pain.

"I've learned to be cautiously skeptical when it comes to you, Mr. Diplomatic Immunity," I said as I shook a finger at him. "You had to be Hemcourt's top choice. No matter, I need your help. First, though, use your keys to go open the front door."

"*Ja*, right away, madam director." He performed a stiff salute and left.

I would deal with him later. Now, I had to inspect Ekollon's lair, his private office, the inner sanctum that few people ever saw.

I only had one close encounter of the office kind last year. I knocked on the door and got no more than a couple of paces into the room before he was on his feet and ushering me out to the employee break room. My fleeting impression was of a neat, tidy extension of his personal appearance: everything carefully coordinated, pressed into shape, and controlled. Now, stepping inside, I wasn't prepared for the feeling that overcame me—I was the interloper. Having to poke around in here left me with a growing sense of uneasiness, like he'd just stepped out and would be back at any moment to catch me in this act of intrusion.

On the surface, the room appeared orderly enough. The bookshelves overflowed with scholarly information on Colony history. They ranged from the prolific volumes of George Swank, Galva's revered chronicler of Colony history, to various Swedish books and periodicals, some translated into English, some not.

Interspersed between the crowded bookcases were framed maps, diagrams, and illustrations, all of which were Colony related. A few reproductions of well-known Krans paintings were carefully placed here and there. His framed diploma and an assortment of awards and plaques filled the remaining wall space.

The wall directly across from Ekollon's desk held two

sets of framed pages from Karl Hemson's catechisms. I remembered the fundraising project that had auctioned them off. Long ago, the pages had been printed on both sides in preparation for publishing, but were never bound into book form. Herb had been commissioned to construct a hardwood frame for each set of pages and designed his frames in such a way as to leave the pages readable from both sides. He was quite proud of the result. I stroked the closest one lightly and marveled at the smooth finish of the wood. It conveyed an almost unnatural softness, like the solid surface melted away under the gentle pressure of my fingertips. Ekollon had paid dearly to possess these treasures from the past. In stark contrast, a modern flat screen TV set was mounted on the wall between Herb's frames and was centered above a narrow accent table.

I sat down at Ekollon's desk. I'd have to search for the time and scheduling sheets. I was grateful at last for all the extra work he had given me last summer. It did indeed leave me with some practical management skills. First things first, everyone needed to know when to work and that they'd get paid on time. I wouldn't mind coming across the personnel files. Although I didn't expect to find anything pertinent relating to Lars, I wanted a quick peek anyway.

There was no sign of Ekollon's personal laptop computer, but a monitor and keyboard occupied the desktop. A computer tower sat on the floor nearby and I switched it on. While I waited for it to boot up, I went back to pulling open drawers. No sign of a handy password list.

I closed my eyes, counted to ten, and then opened them slowly, trying to note what caught my attention among books, paper, and lots of Bishop Hill stuff. Too much to be useful. Something needed to stand out. I expelled a sigh of frustration before noticing the license plate, a commemorative knickknack leftover from the Colony's sesquicentennial celebration. Embossed in big block letters was BHC ONE. Of course he would choose a plate that listed him as Bishop Hill Colony descendant number one. I typed the letters in and smiled when the computer took my second combination as the password.

I searched the main menu and found a screen that displayed an auxiliary feed from all the security cameras. I ran through the settings and committed the images to memory. I'd want to spot the exact locations of the cameras when I made my way around the building. However, what I wanted most was the special camera that focused on the Hemcourt portrait section and operated independently of the main system. Ekollon had used it to spy on me last Monday. It had to be here somewhere, but I couldn't find an icon for it on the screen. Puzzled, I sat back in the upholstered office chair and discovered it staring right at me. The flat screen on the wall opposite the desk had come to life and revealed its sole purpose—to focus on the Hemcourt family's "Krans" painting. The one that I now knew was painted by my Uncle Roy in 1988.

The painted immigrant trunk was in place. But with the painting missing, a large blank space filled the middle of the TV screen. There was no doubt about the intent.

Ekollon spent his office time watching that face. I stared at the screen and thought about how two things were missing: the portrait and the director. Probably not a coincidence.

I cycled through all the employees watching their posts while each went on a break. To pass the idle time between visitors, I brought up a computer translation program intending to have a little fun. I already knew what would come up if I typed in Lars' last name, but I entered it anyway. Sure enough, *trollenberg* came back as Troll Mountain. On a whim, I typed in the name of Hemcourt's CFO, Thomas T. Gubben. Nothing. As an experiment, I started entering variations on his name. *Tom te gubben* became "empty tea man." Entering *Gubben* alone got "old man." For some reason, *Gubbe* came back with "strawberry." Strawberry Man kind of worked for me. He had that topmost streak of reddish hair. It seemed humorously appropriate for the little man who always looked out of place.

Back when I had been searching Ekollon's desk, I couldn't shake the vague feeling that someone else had gone through it before me. If it had been searched, it hadn't been done in a crude, haphazard manner. The drawers just hadn't been pushed back into perfect alignment. Many items were just a bit off, not quite as centered as I was sure Ekollon would have left things. Now I wondered what Gubben, Mr. Strawberry Man, might be asked to do for his boss. Or how far he would go on his own.

By design, Lars came up last on the break schedule and it gave us a chance to talk.

"How's it going for you?" Lars asked.

"Not bad. I've managed to calm down quite a bit. Look, my hands aren't shaking." I held out my hands and concentrated on holding them still. They stayed steady for a bit. I withdrew them when a telltale tremor started. "Who knew all those boring afternoons I spent at the portrait museum doing Ekollon's busy work actually left me with some useful skills. I thought he was just keeping me out of his hair. Oh, wait, he doesn't have any hair."

Lars refused to take the bait. "You said you needed my help. What can I do for you?"

"Okay, late this afternoon I need you to act as an escort. I'm expecting a delivery and it needs to go directly to the archive room."

"*Ja*, fine with me. But escort? Is that really necessary?"

"Yes, very."

CHAPTER 35

Saturday, June 7, 2008

I walked into The Lutfisk Café to the hearty aroma of fresh eggs and bacon sizzling on the grill and a round of cheerful "Hellos" and "Good mornings." I wasn't comfortable with this much attention and couldn't wait for it to fade away. However, one greeting was most welcome and I responded with an enthusiastic "Marcella! You're back."

"Yes, ma'am. I'm back among the living. Thanks to y'all." Marcella with her new quad cane sat at the head of the farmer table and held complete command of all she surveyed. "I'm not too mobile yet, so come on over here and give me a big ol' hug."

I gave her a generous squeeze and sat down next to her. Talli appeared with coffee and asked if I wanted anything to eat. It was Saturday and I had a full breakfast menu to choose from. Since I was headed to the museum, I ordered enough to keep me going all morning.

"So, Missy, I hear Knox got another big name speaker for commencement this year. I hope it doesn't make the place too crowded."

"Actually, I had planned to go hear Madeleine Albright, but with Ekollon still a no-show we have our hands full out at Nikkerbo. I won't be able to make it."

"That's a shame and darn inconsiderate of the nut," Marcella said. "Y'know, I've had folks swear they saw him buying gas in Woodhull. Another guy spotted him in the hardware store in Kewanee. Someone else said Galva. The man has had more sightings than Elvis." It gave me the warm fuzzies to note her laugh sounded as strong as ever.

Talli came to the table with Marcella's order and inserted her opinion. "Well, I for one wouldn't mind if he truly was gone." She smiled at me and added, "I'll get you fixed up in a jiffy."

"So, how are things in the important museum world?" Marcella asked. She dressed up the thin pancakes rolled around a lingonberry center with several pats of butter and drizzled syrup over all. "Y'all getting by without the big man's painting?"

"The trunk's back in the main display. We have to remain hopeful about the family's portrait being recovered. You know how they say any publicity is good publicity. I won't be surprised at all if we have a really big day today." I smiled more to myself than Marcella as I sipped coffee and waited for my breakfast feast.

I didn't rush my eating. I let Marcella and plenty of others leave the Café as I lingered over my plate and pretended to look through some folders. It hadn't escaped my attention that Michael sat with Deputy Dana at a small table in the back of the room. If Michael noticed me, he didn't let on; he was too engrossed in their conversation. I secretly hoped that by letting the room clear out some, I might catch a few words. As I covertly listened, I began to make out a hushed tirade of frustration over the familiar topic of Bishop Hill behavior. Polite or not, I tuned in for more.

"Come on, Michael, admit it. There's something in the water here, isn't there?" Deputy Dana pointed a finger at him. "How else can you explain this insane streak of stubbornness? This sense that they can get away with doing anything they please, thank you very much. All anyone ever says is, 'it's Bishop Hill.'"

My good mood tanked. Their conversation sounded like it was about me and the plan I cooked up. As I looked over to the Bunn coffeemaker, then back to my cup like I was trying to decide if I wanted to get my own refill or not, I heard Michael utter a consoling "There, there."

Out of the corner of my eye, I saw how he reached over to pat her hand and let it settle there.

"My initial reaction ran that way, too," he continued, "but I've had a day to get used to it. Plus, Alan and James are on board and they ran the technical aspects past me last night. As much as I was able to understand, it looks like a workable scheme. If you're still smarting over the incident in the park, you've got to let it go." He seemed to become conscious of the deputy's uniform and withdrew his hand to a respectable distance.

"Thanks for reminding me how the Bishop Hill boys got the drop on my partner and me before the Monday night stakeout even began. I'm still getting flak and hearing snarky remarks about that."

I didn't like finding out about the trouble she was in. It took a little of the shine off what I remembered of being in the park that night and the stories I'd been hearing ever since. And I wasn't sure how I felt about the hand holding. It was none of my business and I made myself refocus on my spying.

". . . and I'm getting grief about my mileage, too."

"But didn't you get any points for showing up first at the barn the other night? Gordon Anderson *was* your arrest," Michael said.

"That went down alright," Deputy Dana had to admit.

"And didn't I tell you about Herb's cell phone being in Ekollon's pocket?" Michael said.

"That's true." She seemed to calm down further and lowered her voice a notch. "But to be fair to the department's techies, they were close to pinpointing the GPS signal."

"And you said yourself that no one was likely to leave Roy and his family alone until this deal with the lost Krans painting is sorted out."

Deputy Dana didn't express any enthusiasm over being

reminded of her own logic. She stared at him and said, "I know it makes sense on the surface. But if this goes sideways it's my ass on the line, professionally speaking of course, and you do know there's a high probability of that happening." She started to jab her finger at him again. "It is, after all, Bishop Hill."

I hated hearing my situation assessed with such unsympathetic coldness. I guess I'd hoped for confirmation and approval. Her apparent lack of faith in my plan made me wonder if I should have spent more time on it. Made more preparations. But I was so sure of myself. In such a hurry to set things in motion. I could have waited. But for what?

Before I could overhear more and have my doubts grow to unmanageable proportions, I decided to forget about getting the coffee refill. I had to be *right* about this.

As I picked up my shoulder bag and swept the pile of folders together, I noticed Talli wiping off a nearby table. Great, I wasn't the only one listening in. I wondered how much she knew. I couldn't delay. Everything was in place. *Now* had to be the best time.

CHAPTER 36

After turning into Nikkerbo's parking lot, I debated the merit of taking one of the two closest spots marked "Reserved for Director." I might have been entitled to one given the upgrade in my status, but no matter how you spelled it, interim director still meant temporary. I did not want to be seen as putting on airs. I bypassed the opportunity and parked in my usual spot. The morning's stop at The Lutfisk hadn't cost too much time. My car was all alone.

Tapping in the security code, I entered the vestibule and proceeded to the control panel for the main corridor lights. I figured on having an hour to myself. Plenty of time. Most of the prep work had been done yesterday and last night. I got out my cell phone and sent text messages to Alan and James. I hoped they were paying attention and not engrossed in some stupid video game or, worse yet, still sleeping. My part this morning was to get the package into the painted trunk before anyone else showed up; after that, everything would be remotely recorded by the guys. It would be safe. It would be easy. It would surely catch Ekollon or anyone else monitoring our security system. I congratulated myself on dreaming up such a clever trap and persuading the guys to make it work. It had been a hard sell. I couldn't back out now.

As I walked, I listened to the sound of my footsteps echoing in the empty hallway. Even though I didn't have to, I self-consciously tried to step lightly.

I opened the door to the archive room, flipped on the overhead lights, and deposited the folders and my shoulder bag on the central worktable. When I turned toward the storage area, I caught a glimpse of an area in the back corner that looked wrong: too dark, too lumpy, too not right. As I watched, the darkness shifted and stepped forward.

"Good morning, Ms. Anderson," a haggard Ekollon said as he pointed a gun at me. "I see you've been a busy girl."

The only sound I could force out of my dry, pinched throat was a weak "Um."

"As articulate as ever," he sneered. "Didn't expect anyone to get here ahead of you, did you?"

"How? The alarm was still set and there was no sign of your car."

"I had no trouble hiding my car and the security company made sure I knew how to handle all aspects of the system. Even how to set things up for remote-control access." He patted the bag he now placed on his side of the worktable.

I could see the outline of a laptop computer in the bag. A string of swear words bounced around in my head. No, I hadn't counted on losing the advantage of a head start. *Stall.* I had to stall for time so the guys could get things going. But would they find me in here? This wasn't part of the plan.

"So where is it?"

"What?" I answered, trying to muster an innocent smile and channel enough calmness to keep from betraying a rising tide of panic and fear. How far could I trust him to hold steady? Not do anything stupid?

"The bait for your little trap."

"I don't know what you're—"

"Oh, save it. I've been watching you since Thursday. If those idiots searched the cabin, the house, and the barn without finding the painting, that only left your pitiful little art show offering as a viable hiding place."

Okay, he had watched me pack the car. At least that part of the plan worked.

"It's over there behind the poster board." I pointed across the room to a set of vertical bins specially constructed to hold large flat items such as framed prints, posters, and large sheets of paper.

"I knew waiting for you would save time," he said with satisfaction. "Now go get it."

I had to keep him talking. "Why did you break into

Uncle Roy's cabin? What were you looking for?"

He appeared surprised by my question and hesitated before uttering a scornful "Well, if you must know, I was looking for a photograph."

"I figured as much. But why think Uncle Roy would have anything you'd want?"

His voice wavered and betrayed reluctance to talk. "Herb's message to me last Friday talked about a photograph that surely held a close likeness to Karl Hemson. He mentioned something about Roy and a painting. It didn't make sense to me at the time. I had to check out Roy's place."

"You said looking for images of the Prophet was blasphemy."

"Yes, I said that." His face flushed. "I meant that people shouldn't poke around and ask questions. They might not like the answers."

I couldn't let it go. "Don't you mean *you* might not like the answers? You seem to have set yourself up as Hemson's number one protector." I glared at him. "You're trying to be a spin doctor for someone who's been dead for over 150 years."

He bit back his anger and ordered me, "Go on. Get it now."

I did as commanded, moving as slowly as I could while frantically thinking about the best way to handle it. Fingerprints were admissible evidence. Besides making a video recording, the goal had been to gather fingerprint impressions from whomever handled the package. *Edges.* I had to limit myself to the edges without looking too awkward about it. And again, do it as slowly as possible.

I had to make myself think of something to say, a plausible distraction, to buy some time. "Thank you," I said.

"For what?"

"I figured out why you gave me all the extra work last summer. It gave me some practical management experience. So, thank you."

"I was busy and you weren't."

"But it really helped—"

"Save it." His upper lip curled in a menacing way. I was out of time.

While I knelt and wedged myself into position to retrieve the package from behind the cabinet, the door opened and with dismay I heard Curt Hemcourt V's voice as he entered. I wondered if he had his gun back. Michael had implied it could be possible. But would he have it with him now? I waited as long as I dared, then rose to find my foreboding had not only been justified but multiplied by two. Gubben, the frumpy-looking excuse for a CFO, also stood across from Ekollon. Each held a gun on the director, who slowly surrendered his weapon, placing it on the work table. I sank back against the wall. Great. If Lars came in next, I'd have a full house of trouble. *Some plan.*

I took a breath, gathered myself, and rose. Hemcourt noticed I came up empty-handed. "If you don't mind, Ms. Anderson, please retrieve the parcel. We don't need to spend a lot of time on this."

"How do you know about it?" I asked. "I was careful."

"Mr. Gubben here saw you and Lars bring it in yesterday. You may have tried to be careful, but in the end you simply made too much of a fuss over it," Hemcourt said.

"I didn't see Mr. Gubben," I protested weakly, because now I knew I had seen him across the street from the coffee shop.

Hemcourt flicked the muzzle of his gun to indicate the video camera high up in the corner of the room. "It has a clear view of everything." He had no idea how much I hoped it did.

Ekollon snorted. "And you thought she could replace me? Really. You should have kept to our deal."

"What deal?" Hemcourt said with contemptuous exasperation. "Gordon Anderson said you were the one who left that note. The one demanding money to keep quiet about my portrait. Then nothing. Just Gordon showing up in Christina's kitchen and taking over that futile search. I know you've been on the run since Tuesday. *None* of that constitutes any kind of a deal."

"If that really is the 1915 Krans she has in that package, then yes, you do still need me."

Hemcourt tried to mount a protest.

Ekollon cut him off by reciting the facts: how Herb left an overly-excited message about a sepia-toned photograph, how he'd heard about Pearl's mission to find a lost Krans, how it had to have been painted in 1915 when she was a ten-year-old child, and the strange reaction it got from a Colonist. He turned to me and said, "There are very few real secrets around here. It wasn't difficult to put it all together. Given the reception it got in Krans's studio, that painting had to have held a likeness to Karl Hemson. It was the most likely reason why Krans would have hidden the painting away. It was easy to surmise that Pearl passed the task of finding it on to you, Ms. Anderson."

And I thought no one was paying attention to me last Friday. Was I ever wrong.

"I'm the only one to authenticate it," Ekollon boasted.

"You can't do squat anymore," Hemcourt said. "Your reputation is . . . is as dead as Herb Anderson."

Ekollon became stiff and livid. He hissed, "You can't be serious. You know who I am. My position. My credentials." He seethed with anger and made a defiant stab at me with his finger. "This is your fault."

"Really? Really! It's my fault?" It was my turn to jab a finger and shout back at the red-faced Ekollon. "You can't get away with *murder*."

"I didn't," Ekollon protested. His face began to lose color as he stammered another incredulous denial. "I didn't."

"Why did you have to go and kill Herb anyway?" Hemcourt demanded. "That just blew the whole thing up into a gigantic mess."

Ekollon's face grew paler as he again denied that he had killed Herb. "He was already on the floor by the time I got there. I took his cell phone because it had his message to me on it. I didn't do anything else. One of you two must have done the evil deed." Ekollon's stare darted between Hemcourt and Gubben.

"I was still up at the bar trying to persuade Roy Landers to keep his mouth shut about how he had painted my 'Krans' in '88," Hemcourt said, his face beginning to flush crimson as the volume of his voice began to rise.

I stood there watching the two of them go at each other as their shouting match escalated with no sign of abating. Then I noticed how Gubben, positioned well back from the two combatants, stared at me with gray, flinty eyes. I returned the withering gaze of the stone-faced little man. "It was *you*. You killed Herb. Why?"

Gubben responded by swinging his gun to point at Hemcourt, who took a few beats to realize the turn of events. "I'm sorry, sir. You too must place your weapon on the table."

Clearly caught off guard, Hemcourt hesitated before uttering an incredulous "You can't be serious."

"I most assuredly am, sir. Now, if you please." Gubben indicated that Hemcourt should lay his gun down.

"You? Why would you kill Herb?" Hemcourt said as he reluctantly did as instructed.

Gubben leveled his gaze at me and said emphatically, "No, I did not kill that man."

"I don't understand," Hemcourt stuttered. "You're here to protect me."

"No, not you specifically," Gubben corrected. "I was sworn to the family and its legacy." I thought I detected the faintest flicker of a thaw in those icy gray eyes.

"Right, your firm has worked with our family for years, generations even," Hemcourt said.

"As far back as Sweden?" I asked, hoping for a favorable reaction and maybe a side trip into a nostalgic memory.

"That's what I was always told. Britta Nelson was the American name of my great-great-grandfather's Swedish-born mother, our connection to Bishop Hill. Britta and her family followed the Pietist preacher Karl Hemson while in Sweden. It led them here," Hemcourt stated. "Obviously, that's not been long enough," he added weakly, as he continued to stare down the barrel of Gubben's gun.

In an attempt to keep Hemcourt talking and Gubben listening, I asked, "What happened to her?"

It almost worked.

"We don't have time for this," Gubben said.

We most certainly *do*, I thought, and noted the cold hardness that had been in his voice had almost disappeared. But the look on Gubben's face told me it would be pointless to try stalling any longer with talk of ancestors and ancient history.

"I suppose you want the package now," I said and prepared to fish it out from its hiding spot, hoping even a small delay might improve the situation.

"Yes, miss," Gubben said.

"How did you know it existed? That I had it?"

"Simply a process of elimination," Gubben said. "Last week, I followed the trunk. I figured Ekollon here had to have a good reason to send it out like that. Those two bumpkins had quite a time Friday night. First, they found a false bottom in your trunk." He nodded to Hemcourt. "That got them to look closer at that bentwood box. They found that photograph with the writing on the back. You should have seen them go at it." Gubben produced a dry cackle. "I merely waited for them to leave and go their separate ways. Then I let myself in to search. The one man, your Herb, came back too soon. It wasn't hard to keep him under control; he'd lost a lot of blood. He tried to threaten me with a hammer." Gubben sniffed. "I had no need to worry. He didn't have the strength left to use that hammer or anything else. He collapsed all on his own."

"Anything in that trunk belongs to my family," Hemcourt said.

"The trunk was empty," Gubben said.

"I don't believe you," Hemcourt said firmly.

Gubben sighed. "There's no way to tell if anything of value had ever been there." He regarded me with a softening gaze. "If you please, miss."

"It can't belong to the likes of you," Ekollon said to Hemcourt. "You're not worthy of such a treasure." His voice dripped with contempt.

"And what were your plans for this *treasure*?" Gubben asked Ekollon. "Were you going to do the noble thing and share it with the world? Let everyone in on its secret?" Ekollon stood motionless and silent. "I didn't think so."

Gubben confirmed what I had suspected. Ekollon was capable of destroying an irreplaceable work of art out of some misguided sense of honor.

Ekollon stared daggers at Gubben and whispered, "Since you know what it is, then you know why it can't be found."

"I'm not interested in false pride or the reputation of the long dead," Gubben said to Ekollon before turning to Hemcourt. "The price I'll get for a Krans painting in Sweden will ensure that I have a very comfortable retirement."

"I don't understand," Hemcourt stammered.

"Of course you don't. You've been such a fool," Gubben said.

"I know I had trouble getting the blackmail money together. But I thought it was just a clerical thing with the bank."

"And no one bothered to explain the precarious state of your finances."

"No," Hemcourt said. Judging by the contortions playing across his face, he was resisting the notion that Gubben might be right and he was in deep financial trouble.

"They were probably trying to save themselves," Gubben said and shook his head.

I saw the weariness and warned, "You'll never get away with this."

"Oh, I think I will," Gubben said.

"Do you guys realize you might all be on a wild goose chase?" They each gazed at me in disbelief. "Think about it. This all started 93 years ago with a ten-year-old little girl. What if you're all wrong and there is no special portrait? No special meaning. Just another artifact. Come on," I shouted. "A *child* made that promise of secrecy. You are adults. You should know better."

Gubben merely shook his head again and looked forlornly at me. "You know, miss, this little trick of yours, getting all your suspects together, may work out quite well. Solve all my problems. I think we're going to have a tragic confrontation here between greedy rivals and you unfortunately got in the way. Such a pity. I arrived much too late to stop them." He aimed his gun at Hemcourt's chest, but hesitated as a last few conflicting emotions shifted across his face.

Hemcourt lifted his hands and staggered back as he began to form his mouth around a shouted "No!"

The plea barely passed his lips when the lights went out. The room plunged into total darkness for what seemed like an eternity before the emergency lights kicked in.

The door to the hallway opened and allowed in an additional flood of light. I only saw blurry, silhouetted forms. I learned later that Deputy Dana Johnson entered the room ahead of Michael, with her service revolver drawn. Gubben saw her and shot.

He missed.

She didn't.

"I have to know," Ekollon said before they led him off. "What did you have wrapped up in that package?"

"An adorable photo of Stanley the cat. A digital fine art

print on canvas. One of my best," I said. I watched the less-than-pompous Ekollon get stuffed into a squad car for the ride to Cambridge and a long-overdue meeting with the sheriff and his investigators. Hemcourt had a separate ride with his own pair of deputies. Gubben, Mr. Strawberry Man, waited for the ambulance under heavy guard. I couldn't look at him directly and only stole a glance to see if his wound had stopped bleeding. It hadn't. I found something else to study until my stomach settled. To add to my misery, I knew the shaking would start soon. This hadn't been in the plan.

Michael came over to lend moral support along with a long-sleeved flannel shirt. "I'm sorry, but this is all I've got with me. I make sure there's a blanket in the tow truck, but . . ."

"I know. No truck. No dog either," I said as I pulled it on. "Thanks, this helps."

"I'm glad this is over," he said.

"So am I," I said, and tugged the shirt's collar a little higher and tighter in an attempt to quell my shivering. "You'll see Alan and James before me, so tell them . . ." I let my thoughts trail off into a dark cloud of what-could-have-been scenarios.

He waited patiently before intruding with a prompt. "Tell them what?"

It brought me back far enough to pick up my train of thought where I'd left off. "Tell them . . . they did an awesome job. They hacked into the system before I asked them to. They used the camera feeds to find me. Turned the lights off. They saved me. They saved us all. A thank you is not enough." I told myself never to sell them short again. I used the corner of a sleeve to sop up a tear I couldn't control.

"Hey, that's what friends are for," he said. He smiled and gave my shoulder a light fist bump. "Give it some time and we'll celebrate properly."

I caught myself having the most absurd thought. What if J now stood for Just Right?

CHAPTER 37

Sunday, June 8, 2008

"Can you believe what they found when they searched David Ekollon's house? He had a shrine to Hemson in there. With Curt Hemcourt's stolen Krans right in the middle. The one that's really Roy's painting." What Teeny Mom told me about Ekollon's home hadn't come as any kind of surprise. I'd seen his office.

"He's done a lot of research, collected about as much material as anyone could on Hemson and the Colony," I said. "I can see how it might look that way with the painting and all, but I'd be skeptical about a real shrine." I couldn't fathom why I defended Ekollon. He was a long way from earning back any kind of respect or trust from me. After all, he had made a limp attempt to pin the theft of Hemcourt's "Krans" on me.

We had the kitchen to ourselves, and Teeny Mom practically bubbled over with newsy updates on the fallout from yesterday's incident at Nikkerbo. "I still say shrine. And Curt needs to be honest about who painted it. Are you sure you want to go to the Nikkerbo today? You still look a little pale."

"Yes. I can't seem to sit still for long, so I might as well go and try to do something useful," I said.

"Well, Curt's back. Probably out on bail or something. I'm sure he could use the help," she said. "David is facing charges for theft, tampering with evidence, and interfering with the investigation—more to come if Sheriff Henry has his way. That odd-looking little man is still in Kewanee hospital. He's doing well enough. I bet they charge him pretty soon. The nerve of him." She made a sour face to accentuate her distaste for the whole business.

"Where are you getting all this information?"

"You're not the only one who knows a deputy," she answered.

I tilted my head and gave her a skeptical look.

"Okay, I have a friend who has a friend whose cousin's daughter is married to—let's leave it as an unnamed source—and . . ."

My skeptical look hadn't gone away.

"Oh, all right." She caved completely. "It's from Marcella."

My look of surprise turned into a broad grin. "I'm so glad you two are speaking again. You guys were friends far too long to be on the outs forever."

It was her turn to look skeptical.

"What?" I countered.

"I hate to press the issue, but you and I certainly haven't been on good speaking terms lately. You've held a lot back. And that's not including this business about setting a trap at Nikkerbo."

"Will you look at the time? I should get ready for work." I made to get up from the table.

"No, you don't, young lady," she said with the stern, no-nonsense tone she reserved for the serious occasions that required full attention. In the past, it might have included some kind of punishment.

"Just kidding, Teeny Mom." I lifted my hands in mock surrender as I sat back down. "When you're right, you're right. I've piled up a huge backlog of stuff to discuss. Where do you want to start?"

"I'll leave it up to you," she said, and struck a patient pose.

"Well, you might have heard a little something about me in the park last Monday night when Winston Maskin had the run-in with the sheriff's deputies."

"Yes, I heard all about that," she said, and waited.

"I was totally innocent and minding my own business for that one." I waited for some kind of acknowledgment and got nothing, so I forged onward. "Ekollon tried to pin the disappearance of Hemcourt's 'Krans' painting on me."

"I gathered that something like that must have happened." She continued to wait.

"I really turned the tables on him, Ekollon, I mean. I

called Herb's cell phone. It started ringing in his pocket. You should have seen the look on his face." I wanted to chuckle, but managed to stifle the urge in time.

"Talli told me you did something with cell phones out in front of The Lutfisk." More waiting.

I grew solemn as I contemplated how to break the really bad news. I decided to take a breath and just put it out there. "Okay, I didn't get the financial aid package I applied for. I can't go to grad school without it. As bad as I want it, I won't go into the kind of massive debt I'm hearing about other kids doing." I couldn't judge her reaction at first. But then the stern façade faded.

"I kind of figured the news had to be bad when you made no mention of grad school again."

"Uncle Roy needn't have bothered pilfering my mail. There wasn't any reprieve to be had in the stuff he took." I wilted with the confession. "It just crushed the life out me and then everything else began to pile up. It was easier to hide it all. I'm sorry I didn't confide in you. Trust you. I'm so sorry."

"Look, if it's something you really want to do, then we can talk, work something out. Don't give up just yet."

"But the thing is . . . I'm not so sure I want to go anymore. Things have changed. I've changed. Bishop Hill doesn't feel like the dead-end prison I've made it out to be for all these years. I've got ideas. I think I can make a difference at Nikkerbo. If Mr. Hemcourt will give me the chance." I couldn't tell if I was getting across the shift in my feelings and the new vision of a future I'd begun to imagine.

"And if you give him a chance."

"What does that mean?" I asked.

"That you have to forgive him for his transgressions."

"But he broke into Uncle Roy's cabin. Then he lied about it. How can I forget about that?"

"Forgiving is not forgetting. Forgiving is taking the first step forward. Toward new possibilities. It helps if both parties do it at the same time, but you are ultimately responsible for yourself alone."

I probably looked like I was pouting, but I was weighing the possibility I'd be up to such a monumental task. "I'll think about it" was all I could promise.

She reached for my hand to give it a squeeze and asked, "Is that all?"

I winced as I replied, "Well, you might want to brace yourself for a visit from Lars."

"This would be the same Lars with the fake last name?"

"The very same."

"Why so serious?" She stared at me.

"He wants to ask questions about . . . Nora." I felt flustered because I stumbled over the name. The same age-old problem for me, having two mothers. I paused for clarification and made sure she knew my choice. "Nora, back when she would have known his uncle. High school, maybe, or just after."

That gave her pause. "Oh," she said, a simple word uttered in a way that hinted at things waiting to be explained. "All I can do is to tell him, tell both of you, what

I know. I promise I will. But let me get some things together first."

Before I could say anything else about her evasiveness, she changed the subject. "You know, when they thought Roy's old family painting was the real 1915 Krans everyone was looking for, I halfway expected to see it show up in the barn. When it didn't, I chalked it up to Roy doing something foolish. It's been such a long time since I've seen it." She shrugged. "I don't know what could have happened to it or where else to look."

"When did you last see it?" I asked.

"You kids were still babies. Just a couple of years old."

"Okay, so that would have been around 1988."

"Sounds right. I saw him with it a few times and then never again. I didn't think it was a big deal."

"You didn't think it was a big deal when he used it to beat Gordon Anderson out of a fat commission?" I was sure she'd remember.

"You know, I do remember that now. Roy was so happy. He was sure it would fix all his problems. Make the world right. But it didn't last long. Pretty soon his drinking was worse than ever. The only thing that saved him was you kids."

"How could we have saved him?"

"He had to pull himself together, quit drinking, so he could have custody after Nora . . ."

"After Nora disappeared."

"Yes," she said, without adding more.

She obviously couldn't go on, so I filled in. "I've been

wrestling with my feelings about how you and Uncle Roy handled our adoption. How you guys got married. How you had to have Nora declared legally dead." I waited for her to say something.

"I'm so sorry we waited too long to tell you kids. We—"

"I know. You did it for us. So we could all be together. I understand now how hard that must have been."

"Roy needed it so much. To have you two in his life."

Teeny Mom looked like she might start tearing up, so it was my turn to change the subject. "I asked him about that old family painting. He thinks he must have done something with it during one of his blackout periods. He has no clue what. I guess it's just gone. It's sad. Herb's favorite saying was, 'This too can be saved.' I guess some things can't."

She had a sad look on her face.

"Remember how calm Hemcourt looked when he showed up on our doorstep last Tuesday? He was only interested in scoping out Uncle Roy's work. The great family heirloom had gone missing and he chatted about unimportant stuff."

"So? What are you suggesting?" she asked.

"I'd bet anything that after he'd gotten the blackmail note, the first inkling that there would be real trouble maintaining the authentication of his painting as a genuine Krans, he stashed it somewhere and reported it missing."

"I never would have thought that possible of him."

"Well, I'm only speculating here. But if Ekollon had known about it or even found it by chance, he was presented with a golden opportunity to steal it for real."

"I don't envy the sheriff's job," she sighed. "This is a terrible tangle to sort out. Everyone claiming they're not murderers. Paintings are coming and going. Pearl thinking her dreams are real. And yet . . . Herb is still dead."

I was glad she didn't bring up the business of how the portrait might look like Karl Hemson, the Colony's Prophet. The whole thing had to be the work of Pearl's childhood imagination.

CHAPTER 38

I allowed myself a small touch of optimism. It felt good to get the air cleared with Teeny Mom, Christina, and be rid of some of the excess baggage that had weighed me down over the last week. Things were far from settled, but it seemed like a fresh start on a new path. Well, almost a new path. I was driving back to Nikkerbo. Before me lay the inevitable face-to-face meeting with Hemcourt that would surely test my skills in diplomacy.

Walking the quiet corridors of the museum gave me mixed feelings. I liked the feel of the building, but I felt anxious about talking with the not-so-honorable Curt Hemcourt V. Logically, I think I knew where he was coming from, and I had a handle on the anger I felt over being lied to and manipulated, but I couldn't be completely confident about what my reaction would be when I actually saw him again. I still needed this job to go well enough for a good referral. I had to straighten out the issue of trust. Maybe try a dose of Teeny Mom's forgiveness advice.

While rolling those thoughts around in my head, I forgot about trying to take smaller, softer steps to quell the echoes in the hallway. I gave into an impulse and got down with some dance moves I'd been meaning to try out. My impromptu efforts ricocheted off the walls as a discordant racket. I didn't care about the noise. Loved it in fact. I assumed I had the place to myself. Again, I was proven wrong.

A surprised Curt Hemcourt opened his office door. "What's going on out here?" he called out before he recognized me. "Ms. Anderson, are you all right?"

"I'm sorry, sir," I said, embarrassed, but not ready to give up on the lighthearted moment. "I thought I'd gotten here first. Second day in a row for that mistake."

He looked visibly relieved. "I walked over early. Since I wasn't sure who'd show up today, I thought I might try to be as prepared as I could manage. After yesterday, I reset the alarm when I got to my office. I figured I'd stay put for a while."

"Can we open up the building?"

"The sheriff's people said they didn't expect to be finished with the archive room until late tomorrow. They gave permission for access to everything else." Hemcourt brushed a hand in the direction of the phone console at the main lobby desk. "And judging by the lights on the phones here and in my office, there'll be a lot of interest in us today. I'm glad you came in. I'll need your help to handle this."

"Yes, sir," I replied with a pretty good dose of enthusiasm.

"We've got some time before our official opening and I've got fresh coffee in here. Can I interest you in a cup?"

"Executive coffee? Why, yes, sir," I replied.

"Don't get your hopes up. I made it myself."

I walked into the wood-paneled office and looked around. I didn't have to wonder where to sit. The space held a large desk positioned in front of an arched window with one chair behind, one in front, and little else. An assortment of framed artwork and photos leaned against the far wall, and the lone extra chair was filled with room design sketches and fabric swatches.

"This will give us a chance to talk about your plans for after the summer," Hemcourt said. He busied himself over a tray set on the corner of his desk and poured two cups of coffee from a carafe. "Cream? Sugar?"

"Just cream."

Hemcourt handed me a delicate porcelain cup and saucer and carried his set over to his place behind the desk. I settled in opposite him. "My wife's idea," he said, nodding at the delicate china. "I think she was trying to make me look a little more sophisticated than I actually am." He adjusted his position, trying hard not to squirm. The CEO handbook must forbid such behavior. "I'll get more furniture in here someday. There hasn't been enough time for the finer points of decorating."

"Things have been, well, unusually busy," I said. "This hasn't been the typical Bishop Hill experience by a long shot."

"I hope not. I've seen far too much of Sheriff Henry in his official capacity. I could use a break."

"Will Mr. Ekollon be coming back?"

"That remains to be seen. Ekollon could be facing a lot of charges. You're still interim director for the time being." Hemcourt sipped at his cup and creased his forehead in a frown. "I just can't get the hang of that espresso machine." He sat his cup down and regarded me. "So what are your plans?"

"Well, sir, my plans for entering a graduate program in the fall haven't turned out the way I'd hoped. I've been meaning to ask you if I could stay on after the summer. I need to look for another way to get my master's degree and, in the meantime, build up my savings."

He said, "Excellent," before catching himself. "I'm sorry. I didn't mean to make light of your situation." He paused to reflect. "I also know I have a lot of other things I have to apologize for as well. I am truly sorry for the liberties I've taken and the distress I've caused you and your family."

So, I thought, he's taken "liberties." That's as good a place as any to start a truce.

"Why search Uncle Roy's cabin in the first place?" I asked. "What were you looking for anyway?"

The important businessman, land developer, and card-carrying member of the elite looked embarrassed. "I wanted to find his copy of my letter and the insurance photo I'd sent him years ago."

"And did you find it?"

"Yes. I found Gordon Anderson's, too. But I wasted my time. I got blackmailed anyway."

He paused again as if trying to gauge my reaction before going on. "Still, I had hoped to find a way to persuade you to stay."

I was so pleased with my politeness, my correctness, my skill in holding my tight-lipped smile in check. I just wished I was more adept at balancing my cup and saucer on the knee of a crossed leg.

"I really think I can be a great asset for the museum, sir. I've been thinking of ways to make the most of what's happened. I know that sounds crass, but I don't think it should all be seen as negative. I believe your core mission here was to connect with your past, to fulfill a pledge to your father, your family, and your Colony ancestor. That's a great message. We can use that."

He looked uncomfortable. "Not everyone sees it that way. And that's not considering the whole story of Britta Nelson, my great-great-grandfather's Swedish-born mother. When she left the Colony she had little more than the clothes on her back and a basket on her arm."

I'd heard stories like that before, former Colonists leaving the communal society with only the barest of necessities. "You should try not to let that get to you. The past is past." I looked earnestly at Hemcourt in an effort to convey the depth of my meaning. "Hemson wasn't as perfect a leader as he could have been, as he might have wanted to be. After all this time, he doesn't need to be. He was who he was. We are all here because of him and we've done a pretty good job overall. Original Colony-era buildings are still standing and descendants still live here. We have our own uniquely American heritage. We have to find a way to live with the ghosts of our ancestors, forgive them their mistakes. Forgive our own mistakes." I could tell I was talking way too much and way too fast. I had to let my thoughts pour out. "Last week I was *so* eager to leave, to make a new start somewhere else. That's changed now. I've changed. I want to stay and help out. Herb's favorite saying was, 'This too can be saved.' I can do my part. Save our history *exactly* the way it is. How about you?"

"I hope we can save this," Hemcourt said as he looked around his incomplete office. "Gubben was right about my finances. They're in total disarray. I can't tell yet how much he's taken or where it went."

"I'm sorry." It felt lame, but I had to say something.

Hemcourt smiled patiently. "We have our work cut out for us. You're welcome to stay as long as possible. I'm going to need all the help I can get."

Thinking that things may work out yet, I took a sip of coffee and fought back the reaction to its bitterness by asking, "Any news about the photograph that Herb and Gordon found before they started fighting?"

"It's being held as evidence along with my painting. I'm afraid it will be quite some time before either one gets released. And they have to determine the rightful owner of the photograph, whoever that might be. It won't be an easy process once the lawyers get involved."

"As an artifact, it's quite fragile," I insisted. "You should make a request for special handling and offer our climate-controlled facilities for storage. We can make sure it's safe and secure. Perhaps even begin the process of getting it stabilized and restored. That would also help with the authentication process." I assumed he'd read the message on the back. We'd have to verify that the Swedish words came from the hand of Olof Krans.

"I think we may need the help of your friends, the young men with the computer skills, to guarantee the secure part. I'll talk to Mr. Patrick about the rest. His Galva law firm will be running point for me on this."

"And Gubben's law firm?"

"The investigation has already begun." Hemcourt gave a resigned sigh before sipping his coffee. He sucked in his lips and grimaced. "I have to ask, what in the world made you try to set a trap in the museum's archive room? What did you hope to gain?"

"I was tired of feeling helpless. I wanted to be in control for a change. I thought if I used Ekollon's private security system, I could get video and fingerprints without being in too much danger. It just didn't work out the way I'd planned. I never thought anyone would get hurt."

"Well, I hope you never have to try anything like that again," he said.

"Teeny Mom agrees with you," I said, and looked at my

cell phone for the time. The lights on Hemcourt's desk phone had flashed incessantly the whole while we sat attempting to sip the bitter liquid from the fancy cups. The outside world couldn't be put off any longer. I excused myself and left the office. In my honest opinion, Hemcourt definitely had to work on his coffee-brewing skills. Money or not, position or not, he wouldn't last long around here if he didn't.

CHAPTER 39

The attendance numbers for a Sunday afternoon were indeed impressive. Higher than I would have expected at any of the other museums in the village. Impressive enough that I seriously wondered how long I could keep the yellow crime scene tape up. A month maybe. Why not integrate some of it into a permanent display? I was on a roll with increasingly garish designs when Lars came by on his way to lock up the front door and interrupted my daydreaming.

"I see you smiling," he said. "Are you happy that so much has been—I'm sorry, but I can't think of the right word here, how best to describe what happened yesterday."

"That's okay. I'm having trouble with that, too. Settled might be a good word. I wouldn't spend too much time on it," I said. "Actually, I was smiling about today's visitation numbers."

"They were good?"

"Definitely. So good, I was indulging in thoughts about how to turn the crime scene tape into a permanent display, something along the lines of *Homage to Ancestor Worship*. What do you think?"

The sigh. The head roll to the side. The sad look of disagreement. The unmistakable sound of a Swedish tsk-tsk.

"Come on," I said, struggling to keep a straight face. "We Americans are crude and opportunistic, remember."

"You can't be serious," he said after a long moment.

I let him stew a little longer. "No, I wasn't serious. Just having some fun. This is the best I've felt in weeks."

After smiling with more relief than necessary, he cleared his throat. "I had a chance to talk to Michael Anderson before I came over this afternoon."

"By the way, thank you for that. I mean, for showing up today. Between you and the other people who came in on their own, I didn't have to make any phone calls. That was awesome."

"*Ja*, glad I could help," Lars said, and he appeared to slowly frame the rest of his thoughts. "Michael seemed to think that I was in on your plan." He paused as he looked at me, much too directly. "You let me help, but I didn't know of your plan to set a trap. Did you not trust me?"

I took a breath and admitted with my own sigh, "No, I can't say I did trust you enough to let you in on everything."

"But why? Have I not been honest with you?"

"Well, frankly, no, you haven't."

He looked stunned. Hurt, maybe. It was hard to tell what his gorgeous blue eyes tried to convey. I had to make myself remember how mistrustful I was of him. How annoyed. "You haven't been up front with me about why you're really here. Why you were interested in me or my birth mother. You haven't even been using your real name."

He raised his hand to stop me from going on. "I'm sorry. But I couldn't use my real name. It would have drawn too much attention to my uncle and me."

"Oh, right, Mr. I-have-diplomatic-immunity. You're on a secret mission." I crossed my arms and waited for what had to be a good story.

"My family is well known in Sweden and in some circles here. I had to be careful because I needed to investigate . . . see how well Mr. Hemcourt and his company were doing and report to some investors back in Stockholm."

I kept quiet. Not so much for Hemcourt's sake, but to draw out more information. This tactic always worked when Teeny Mom used it on me.

"These are sensitive matters that involve a great many Swedish *kronor*. I cannot say more."

I could almost see him sweat. Gubben must have been a very busy thief. I decided I might be able to wring a little more out of Lars, so I prodded him with, "And what about Nora?"

"My uncle *was* a friend of your mother's and he really does care to find out what happened to her."

"Thank you for that much," I said, and uncrossed my arms. "Teeny Mom, Christina, has agreed to talk to you about Nora. She told me she has to look up some stuff. I'll let you know when she's ready. In the meantime, I've found the group photo I mentioned to you. It's in my bag. I'll show it to you after you finish locking up."

I waited again to see what else he'd come up with. When he remained silent, I had no choice but to add, "Look, I found your uncle's letters to Nora. Some of them, anyway."

"This is good," he said.

"Not really. My Uncle Roy kept them from her. They were still sealed. She never had the chance to read them."

"And you? Have you read them?"

"Yes. A couple of times." I waited silently. I would not apologize for reading Nora's ancient mail.

"And no one else?"

"No. Your uncle is still safe," I said. "But you do have to tell me more about this Count Curt Von Stending and explain why someone born half a continent away in 1746 is so important."

He hesitated. "What do you want?" he asked with a suspicious look.

"Let's start with the truth."

Lars began to fill me in on the life and times of Count Curt. As a young man, Curt had a distinguished military career in service to the Swedish royal family. He was rewarded with a title and an estate. As was the custom at the time, the title and the estate were inherited by the eldest son. Other sons had to choose between careers in the military or the Lutheran Church of Sweden. All was fine until one rebellious great-grandson emigrated to America.

"A lot of Swedes emigrated beginning around 1850. That's hardly a big deal."

"Trust me, it was a big deal. He came *before* 1850 and brought a few hundred of his closest followers." He waited for it to sink in.

"Oh? Are you saying that he was somehow connected to Hemson's group? The ones who founded Bishop Hill's Colony?"

"I'm saying he *was* Karl Hemson."

That took a while longer to sink in. In the meantime Lars explained how his uncle looked up genealogical records and census data during his stay in Illinois. He was convinced of a family connection. What's more, as sure as he was that Karl Hemson was a long-lost relative, he was just as sure that Hemson didn't die in Bishop Hill in 1850 as was the common belief. That Hemson slipped away to Chicago and assumed a new name and a new life with his Colony bride.

"Do any of you people use your own names?"

Lars shrugged. "What can I say? The Lutheran Church of Sweden wanted to put him in jail and the family wanted him to sacrifice his Pietist principles. He couldn't win."

"So what name did he end up choosing for this new life in the big city?"

"It wasn't all that difficult to find. My uncle looked up likely dates and similar sounding names. He eventually found Karl Hemcourt. The same Karl Hemcourt who named his firstborn son Curt after his great-grandfather. You know about the rest."

"So that's why Ekollon was seeing Karl Hemson's likeness in Curt Hemcourt the first's portrait," I said.

"Exactly," he said. "I have to ask you again, what do you want?"

"No demands. But we have a lot more to talk about when we meet up with Teeny Mom."

CHAPTER 40

On my drive home, I thought back to Lars and how I definitely had to be there when he had his talk with Teeny Mom about Nora. I wanted to know what she and Uncle Roy had to say. What they knew and when. They might have thought silence was necessary when I was little, but I needed to know it all now.

I pulled into the driveway of the red brick house and sat for a few minutes watching the clouds. Pearl had seen an omen in the sky; maybe I should look for one. Jet contrails traced across the blue expanse on their way to points beyond the horizon. It didn't bother me that they were headed to exotic and exciting places. Someday, it would be my turn.

A dusty Teeny Mom came up from the barn.

"Let me guess, you've been cleaning up in there," I said as I got out of the car.

"Yes, you know me. Everything has to go back into its place. Did you have a good afternoon?"

I shared my news about coming to a truce with Hemcourt and having a job at Nikkerbo for as long as I needed. "I've got time to sit and think, look out the window, and appreciate where I came from. I know it sounds corny, and a week ago I never would have dreamed of saying anything like that." I paused long enough to take in the red brick house, the barn, the campground. "I guess I like the simple way Michael put it. Here is better for right now."

She seemed pleased to hear that, or maybe she was relieved. I couldn't tell the difference. She told me there was a new batch of chicken salad in the fridge and directed me to help myself. She had more to do in the tack room.

"No thanks, not just yet," I said. "I'm going up to my room and finish hanging my stuff from the art show. Minus Stanley the cat, of course. I might get his gallery-wrapped canvas print back tomorrow." I headed for the stairs without looking back.

I arranged and hung the smaller pieces so I could position the large collage in the center of my wall where I could see it from all angles. As I gave it a final nudge to make it hang straight, a photo loosened and popped off. I picked it up and as I prepared to reattach it, my fingers lightly touched the canvas. The surface felt uneven. Then I remembered how this spot had given me trouble with the preliminary drawing. I had opted to simply hide the defect. The roughness nagged at me. The more I stared at it, the more I noticed its position relative to the whole. I bent in closer and could make out where two narrow strips of canvas intersected and how cross-like it appeared. Pretty much just like the patch Pearl had described.

"It can't be," I whispered, and furtively glanced around to verify I was alone. I saw Teeny Mom in the doorway with a plate of chicken salad and chips.

I instinctively felt a rush of guilt and uttered an apologetic "I'm sorry."

She looked confused. "What have you got to be sorry for? You haven't had time to get into any more trouble."

My eyes went to the canvas. Her eyes followed. They didn't register any comprehension.

"I worked with this canvas for weeks. Chose it precisely because the back had been covered. I briefly considered using both sides as part of a mobile before settling on creating a multi-layered wall piece. I used the back for a poem to . . . Nora."

"So?" Her quizzical look slowly turned to alarm as the pieces in front of her started to add up. She sat the plate down and tilted her head to study me. "Then that came from the barn."

"Yes," I said. "I'm so sorry," I repeated.

"Stop apologizing and let's have a look at it."

I gingerly lifted it off the wall and carried it over to my bed. I carefully turned the collage over before laying it down and loosening the four clamps that held the external frame in place. When the back was fully exposed, I pointed to the staples holding the burlap cover in place. "These are modern staples. Why would Uncle Roy bother to go to this much trouble if he had thought this was merely the work of one of his ancestors?"

"Roy may have had something special in mind. Some new kind of project. Maybe like you said—a mobile." I could tell by the way she said it that she thought it was a pretty weak argument.

After going through a couple of desk drawers, I found a stiff palette knife and pried enough staples loose to lift aside a sizable flap. Sure enough, perfect soulful eyes stared back at us.

"It's been a long time, but this sure looks like what I remember Roy showing me all those years ago," she said.

I held my hands in various ways as to block off different areas without touching the surface. "Judging from what I can recall—these eyes are doubles for what Uncle Roy did for Hemcourt's portrait. The nose, not quite so much. The mouth, also a little less so. Still, there's an amazingly close likeness between the two paintings." I couldn't shake the feeling that the overall effect was exactly as Pearl said, *mesmerizing*.

After pursing her lips, she gave me a nod. "Yeah, it's pretty much the same all right."

"I'm sure this has to be the portrait Pearl witnessed Krans painting. See down here?" I pointed to the cross-like tear in the canvas. "That's exactly how Pearl described it. The OK signature is probably down further." I waited for her to say something, but I only saw sadness.

She said at last, "Roy must have hid this away and

forgot about it?"

"I don't dare try to uncover any more of the painting without a more controlled environment and proper instruments. No sense taking any more risks. Time and poor storage conditions have done enough damage." I stood by the bed and considered the dilemma.

"Did I ever tell you what was written on the back of an old photograph Krans showed to Pearl . . . which may have been the same one Gordon had in his pocket?"

"No, of course not," Teeny Mom said, and started to give me her standard look of motherly disapproval.

"I'm sorry."

She responded with an exasperated sigh. "Stop already and just tell me."

I inhaled, held the air in, and wished my Swedish could be better than it was. No luck there. I had no choice but to get it out. "'*Är detta Hemson's ansikte?*' was written on the back. Pearl said Krans made her write it out in English. 'Is this Hemson's face?'"

"Oh, my," she whispered.

"A part of Uncle Roy must have known his family's painting might be, as Marcella would say, the real deal, or, at the very least, close enough to cause a stir among Colony descendants. Since these staples aren't too rusted, I bet having Hemcourt come back to the area made him leery enough to cover it up. Something sure did."

"Did Hemcourt ever talk about the name Curt? Or why the family's matriarch insisted on an unbroken line of sons named Curt?"

"He laughed it off as an old woman's quirky way to stay linked to the Colony and her past." She paused, and then added thoughtfully, "He did mention that genealogy mattered a great deal to his grandfather." She gave her head a slow shake. "But not to him. He meant to repay the debt he owed to his father by building Nikkerbo, but wouldn't promise to go further than that."

I stared at the painting on my bed and wondered aloud, "After all this time, could this really be the face of Karl Hemson, the Colony's Prophet?" My head spun with thoughts of possible scenarios. Great discovery: yes. Historic discovery: yes. Dangerous discovery: absolutely.

Krans had witnessed the old woman's violent attack on this painting in his studio. He had to fear there might be similar reactions when other Colonists saw it. He had good reason to roll the painting up and put it away. To wait for a safer time for it to be found.

Somehow it made its way into our family. An earlier one of our line of Roys must have found it, beginning a family tradition of preservation . . . and secrets.

"What are you going to do?" Teeny Mom asked. "You have it now. This is a piece of our history. You're the one who makes the point about personal biases not affecting the judgment of a curator."

"Herb's motto was always, 'This too can be saved.' I certainly can do that for Herb's sake. Will do that." I exhaled deeply. "But Krans had been right to slip it into hiding." With resignation, I ended the impromptu inspection by smoothing the canvas back down and started pushing the staples back into place. "After this past week . . . its time still hasn't come."

Teeny Mom watched as I prepared to hang the collage back on my wall and asked, "What are you going to tell Pearl?"

I stopped to think. "Michael probably wouldn't be all that curious. He doesn't like to believe in Bishop Hill legends, but I can count on Pearl asking. She deserves to have a rest from the recurring dreams of Krans sending her out on endless missions to find this painting. She needs to know the quest is over."

"What can you say that won't upset her?"

I shrugged. "Perhaps a simple truth. Unlike a wounded and suffering Herb, left alone and defenseless, Olof Krans's last portrait will be cared for. Safe at last.

"Like me, it is home."

Teeny Mom put her hand on my shoulder and told me to wait a minute. She gave me a firm, meaningful look and said, "We don't need any more secrets in this family. There has to be a way to display this painting, this work of art, which will let people make up their own minds about what it means. Think about it."

"Okay, I'll think about it. I promise."

╫ PEARL ╫

Summer 1916

Pearl hung back from the crowd of adults clustered around the hayrack that displayed the smaller items of Olof Krans's household goods. The auctioneer had already been through the larger pieces of furniture: the bed, tables, chairs, and bookcases. People began drifting over to the food tables to buy a slice of pie to go with the free coffee. The paintings and art supplies would go on the block last, almost an afterthought.

Pearl stood by the pile of rolled-up canvases and knew which one she wanted to bid on. But she only had a few pennies wrapped up in her *näsduk*, her handkerchief. An eleven-year-old girl didn't have many opportunities to earn cash, and it stung her pride. She vowed to earn her way in life. But a promise for the future wouldn't help her now.

An older boy stood nearby. He'd been examining the art supplies, picking up tubes of paint, fingering brushes, and making his way toward the canvases. When he got near, he offered Pearl a quiet "*Hej.*"

She recognized him. Last summer he too had hung around Krans's Altona studio. He was the son of Roy Landers, a trusted helper when Krans had his painting business in Galva. The polite hello was about the nicest thing the boy had ever said to her. Most of the time she was simply ignored, too much of a child to be noticed.

Pearl returned his politeness by inquiring, "What are you looking for?"

He cast his eyes downward as if embarrassed. "My pa sent me over here. He said I should buy the already used things to practice my painting." He gathered his pride. "I think I've found a few that will work fine for me." His gaze moved past Pearl to the pile of rolled-up canvases behind her.

"Do you like to paint?" Pearl asked, stepping aside.

"*Ja*, sure," he said. "I'm not as good as my pa. He says I must work harder." The first flush of crimson began to color his cheeks and he fell to brooding over which canvases to choose.

After he had separated several and placed them together over to one side, Pearl picked up another to add to his pile. "Here, you should have this one. It is a prize."

"*Nej*, that one has been torn. See where the tear has been patched?"

Pearl kept her promise to the old man, to Olof Krans. She didn't tell the boy what she knew about the painting on the damaged canvas. Why the paint should be spared and not stripped away or covered over by this young artist. She, to the best of her ability, impressed upon him the instructive benefit of this one last piece from the old master's hand. After he unrolled the canvas far enough to see the mesmerizing eyes, he agreed with her opinion and later bought it, along with the other things he'd chosen.

Roy Landers, Jr., left the auction happy.

Pearl Essie left happy, too.

Pearl Anderson awoke to the pale light of a new morning. Images of her dream slipped away, but she felt a warm calmness lingering. Perhaps now old man Krans would stop sending her off after ethereal crosses and her dreams could settle down. She missed revisiting the many faces of past generations of students and the more tranquil lessons she'd taught to them.

This new generation kept itself moving too fast and too busy with the unimportant. Life wasn't all that complicated. That's what she'd talk about this afternoon at Nikkerbo. She'd be the guest of honor and the one to pull the cord to unveil the new art exhibit, the one that featured a recently discovered painting by Olof Krans.

ACKNOWLEDGEMENTS

A great many people helped me along the way to getting this book written, published, and out into the world.

The first person to encourage my writing was Doug Boock, editor of the Galva News.

Jen Karsbaek has my thanks for getting me to change my protagonist's POV to first person in an early draft.

I received much-needed editorial feedback from Amy Parker, Jodie Toohey, Jane VanVoren Rodgers, Lyle Ernst, Lilly Setterdahl, Susan Carroll, and Misty Urban. I always paid attention to whatever they had to say.

The diehard members of the Writer's Studio never failed to offer insightful comments and suggestions whenever I read a few pages. Thanks to Steve Lackey, Mike Bayles, Lynn Bartek, and Jan Rittmer. Thanks also to the many others who came as often as they could.

I imposed early drafts of my novel on friends in

Illinois and Iowa. Thanks to Diana Whitney, Susan Strodbeck, Jo Donna Loetz, and Judy Benson.

I consider myself a product of the Midwest Writing Center. They were always there for me with workshops and information on whatever aspect of writing I needed most. Thanks to Susan Collins, Ryan Collins, and the many members of the board of directors and the special committees that participated in the process of getting this book published. I hope the end result is a worthy tribute to the MWC Press.

A sincere thank you goes to Lori Perkins and Ken Small. They were instrumental in cover design.

Thanks to Marsha & Steve Carleson, Beth Magnuson, and Suzy Dietsch for inspiring me to be a better "maker."

I reserve my most special thanks for my husband, Mark. He has always been the reader I relied on the most for constructive advice. He's been the loyal fan and the morale booster whenever I needed it. This book wouldn't exist without him and his support.

ABOUT THE AUTHOR

Mary Davidsaver was born in Cedar Rapids, Iowa, and graduated from the University of Iowa, Iowa City. She had no choice but to attend school in Iowa City because generations of family craftsmen helped build the county courthouse, the dormitories, and the student union.

That tradition of craftsmanship had her living in Bishop Hill, an Illinois state historic site and a national historic landmark, first as a silversmith and then as a writer, for twenty-four years. She and her husband have returned to Iowa.